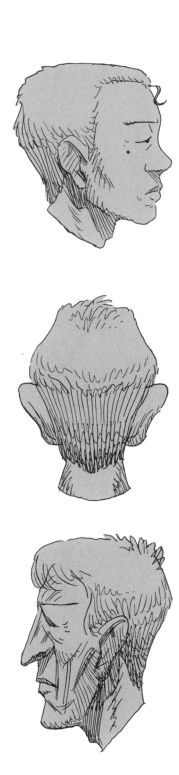

HERMAN
BY
TRADE

First published in 2017
by SelfMadeHero
139-141 Pancras Road
London NW1 1UN
www.selfmadehero.com

Text and images © 2016 Chris W. Kim

Publishing Director: Emma Hayley
Sales & Marketing Manager: Sam Humphrey
Editorial & Production Manager: Guillaume Rater
UK Publicist: Paul Smith
US Publicist: Maya Bradford
Designer: Txabi Jones
With thanks to: Dan Lockwood

A CIP record for this book is available from the British Library

ISBN: 978-1-910593-28-8

10 9 8 7 6 5 4 3 2 1

Printed and bound in Slovenia

HERMAN
BY
TRADE

CHRIS W. KIM

SELF MADE HERO

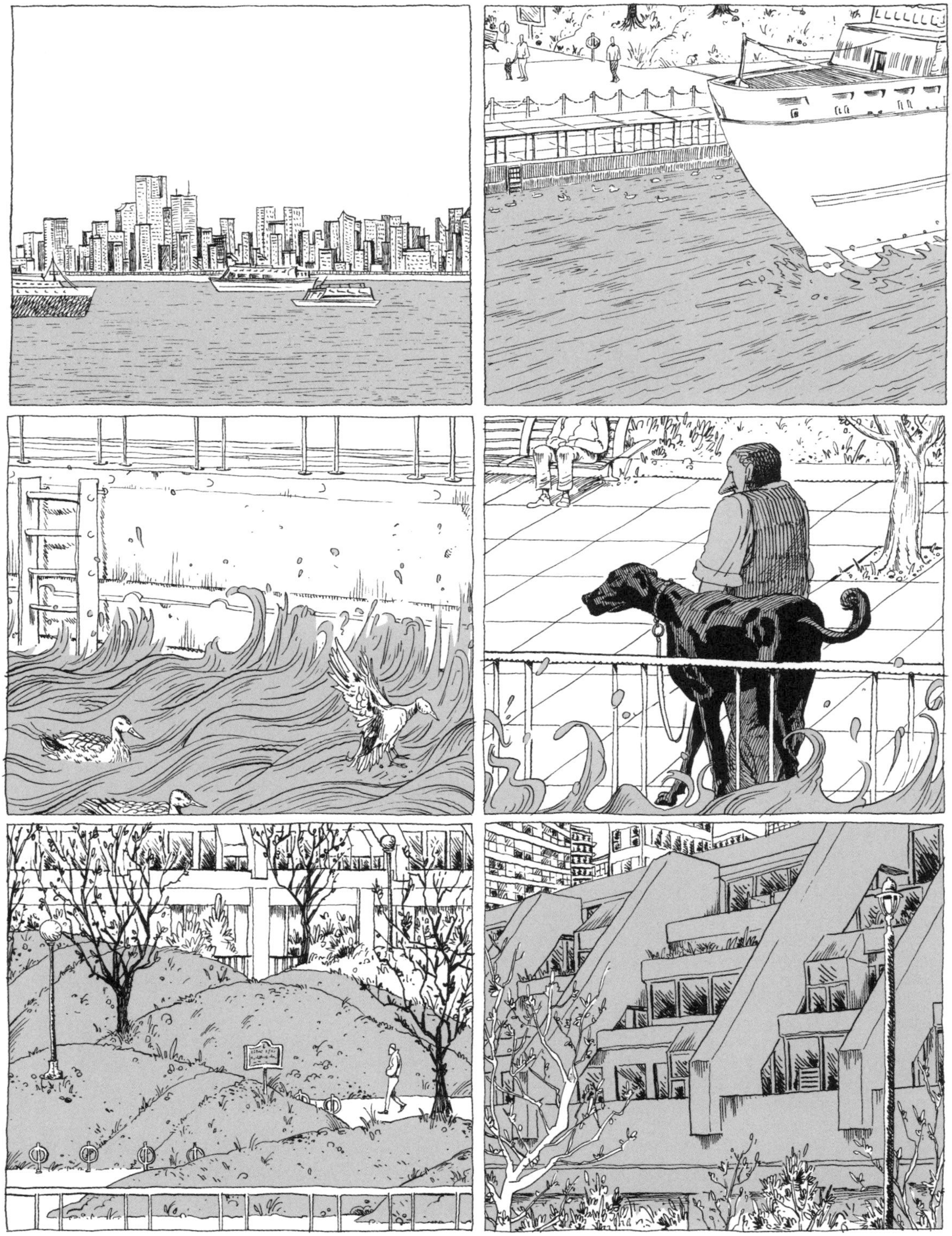

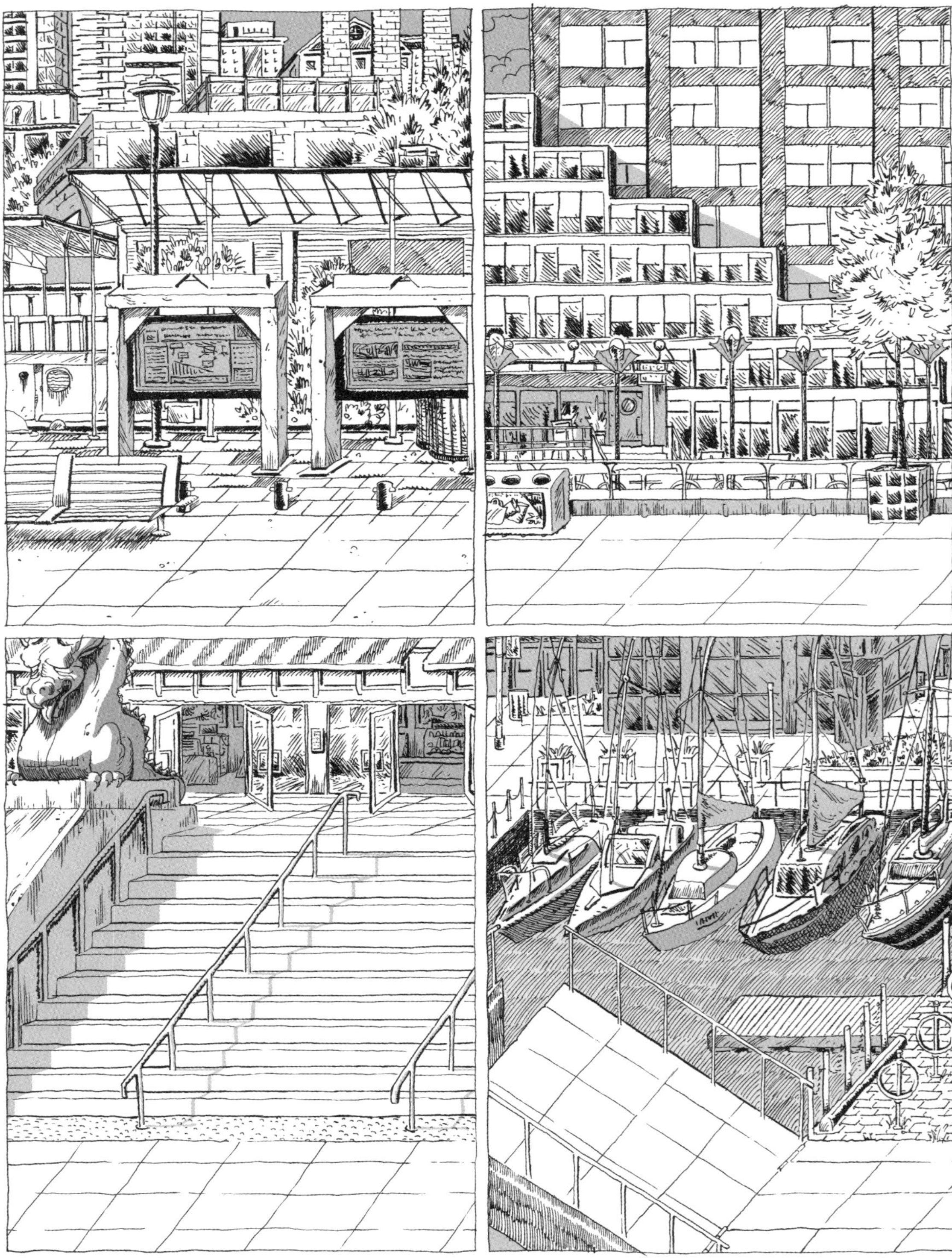

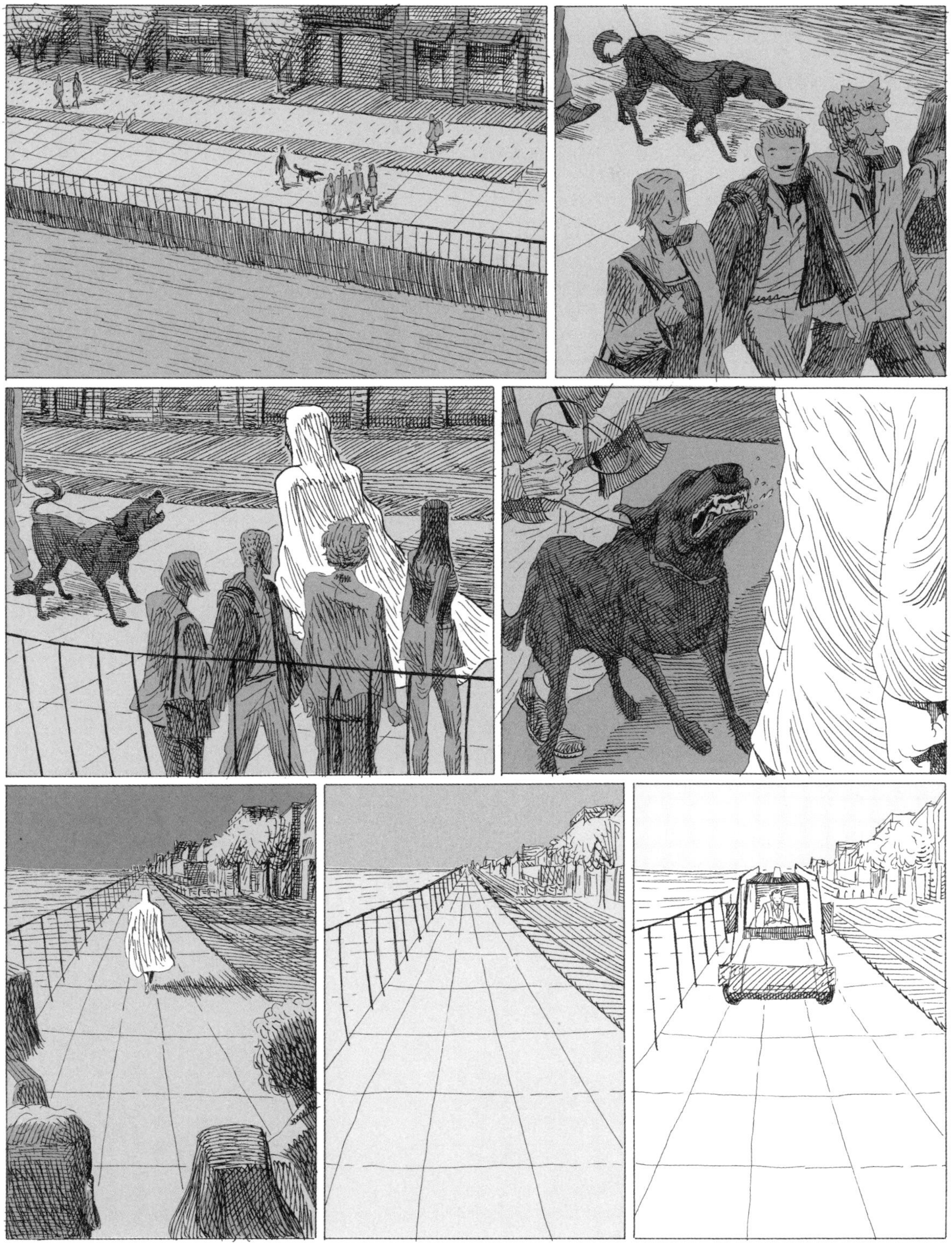

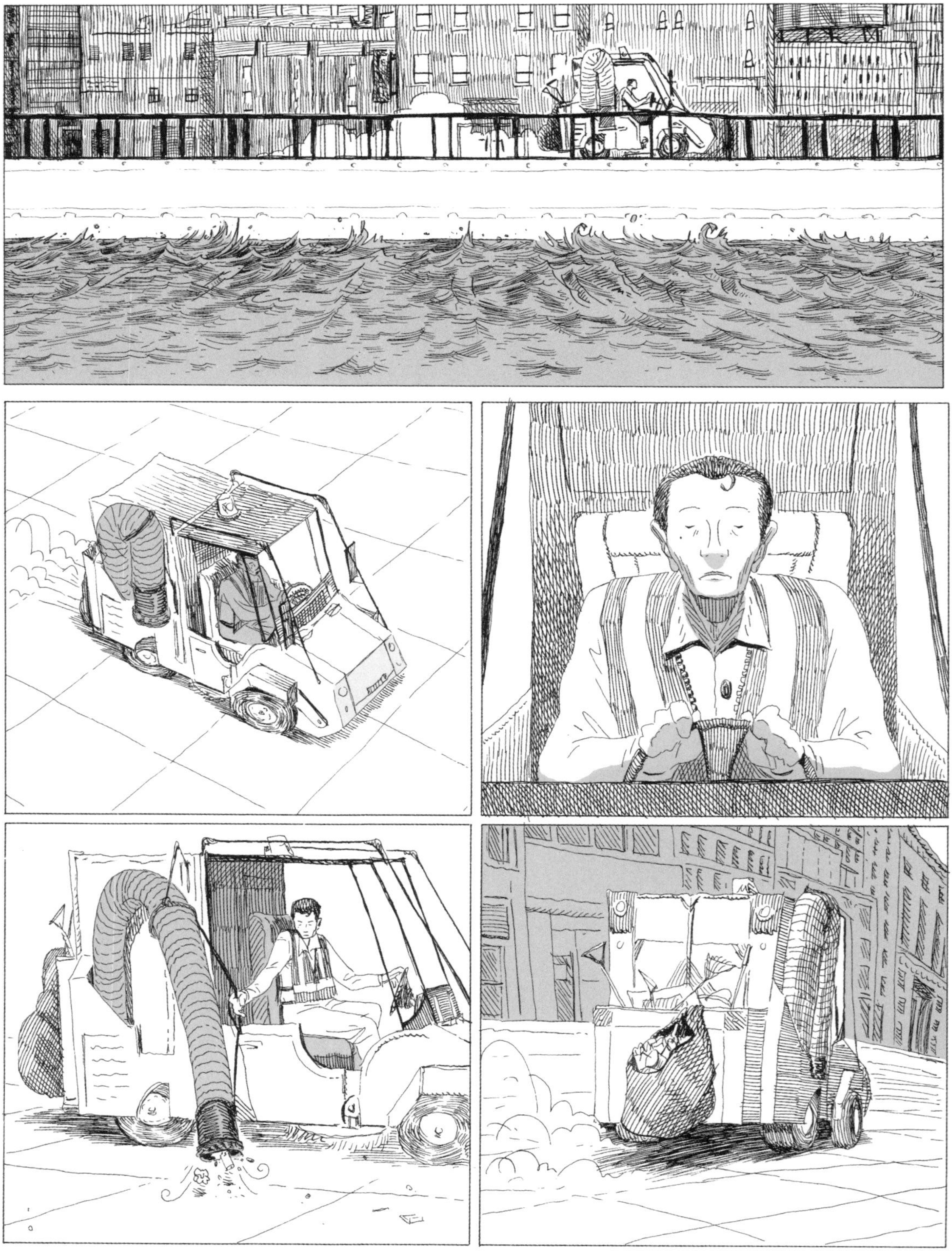

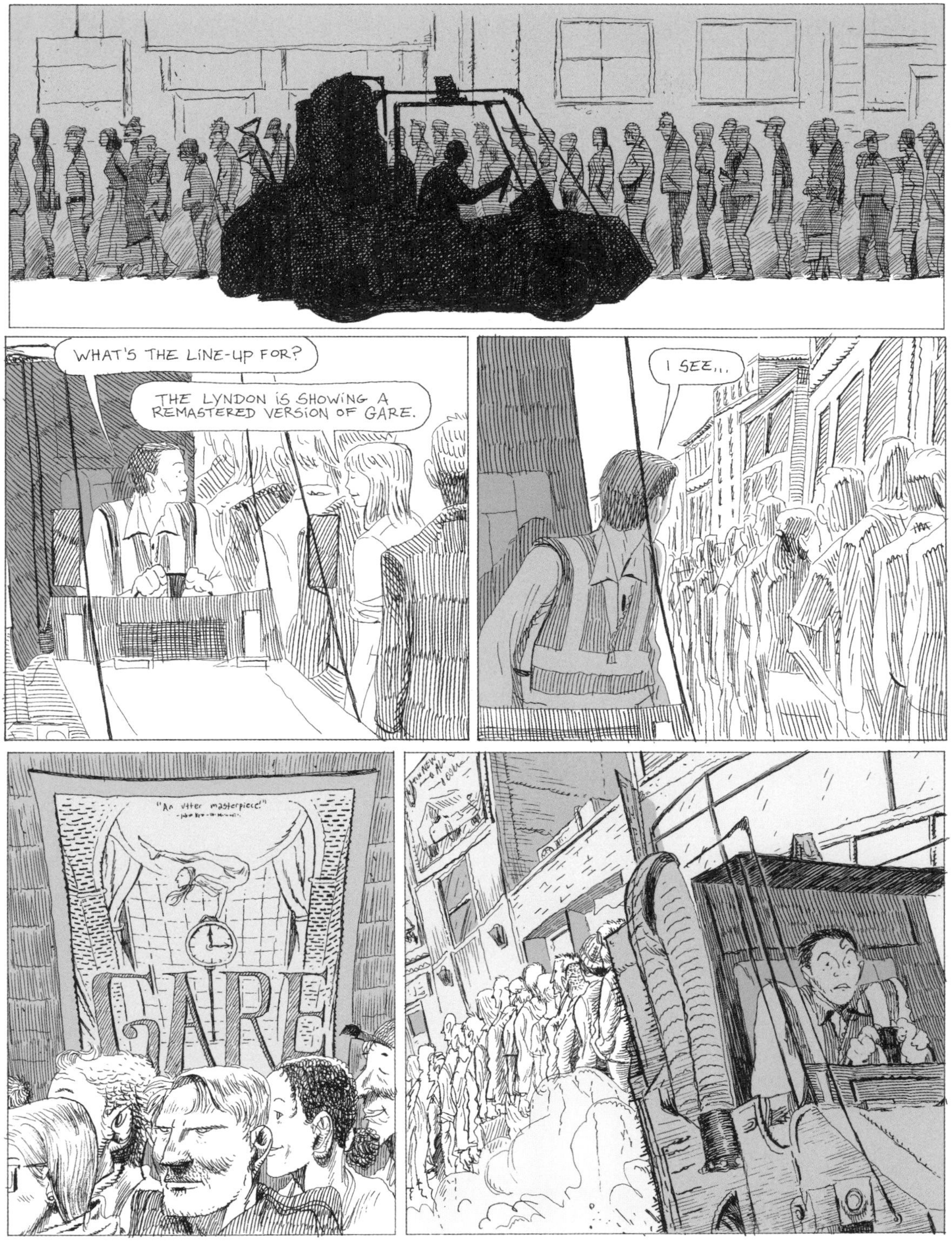
WHAT'S THE LINE-UP FOR?
THE LYNDON IS SHOWING A REMASTERED VERSION OF GARE.
I SEE...
"An utter masterpiece!"
GARE

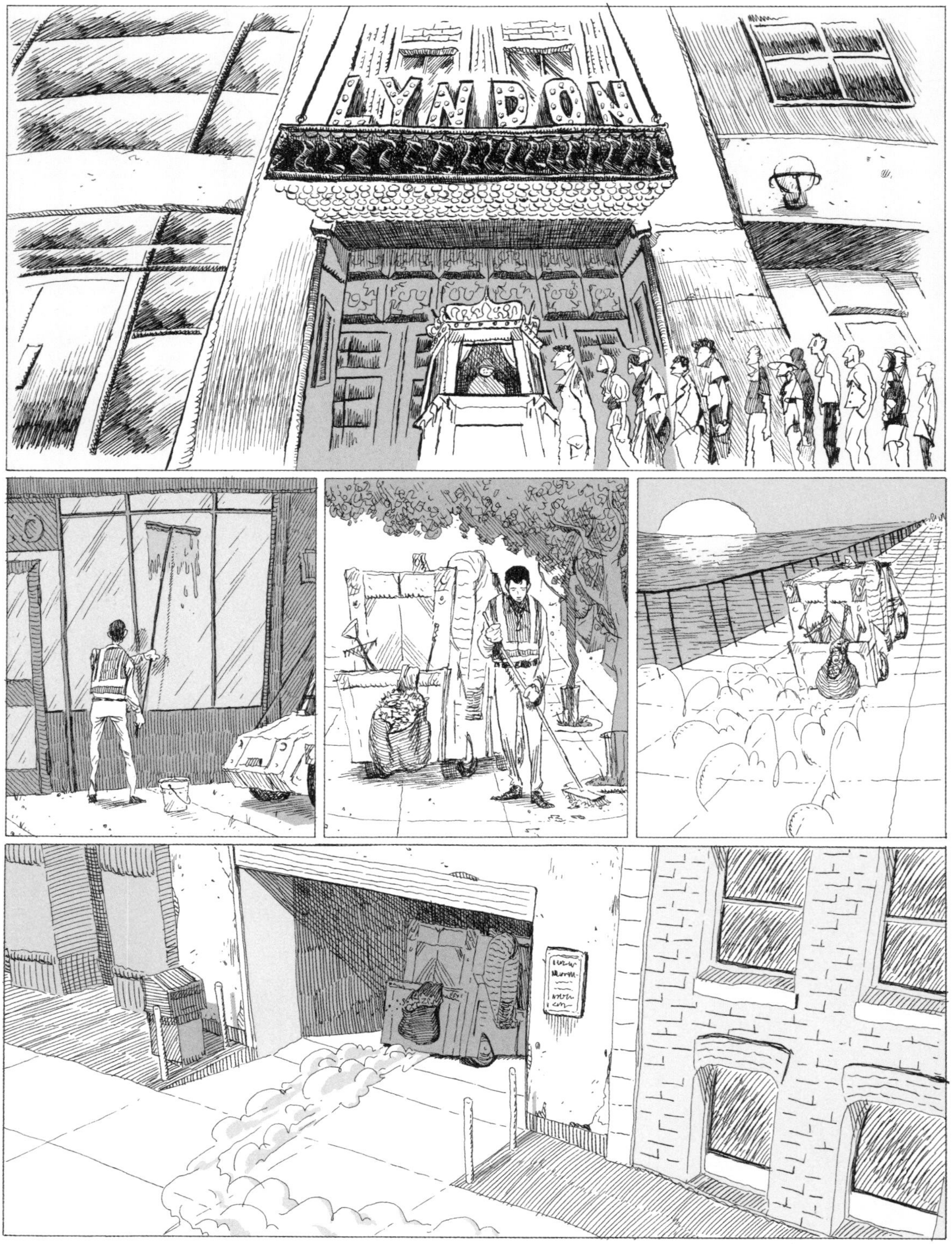
LYNDON

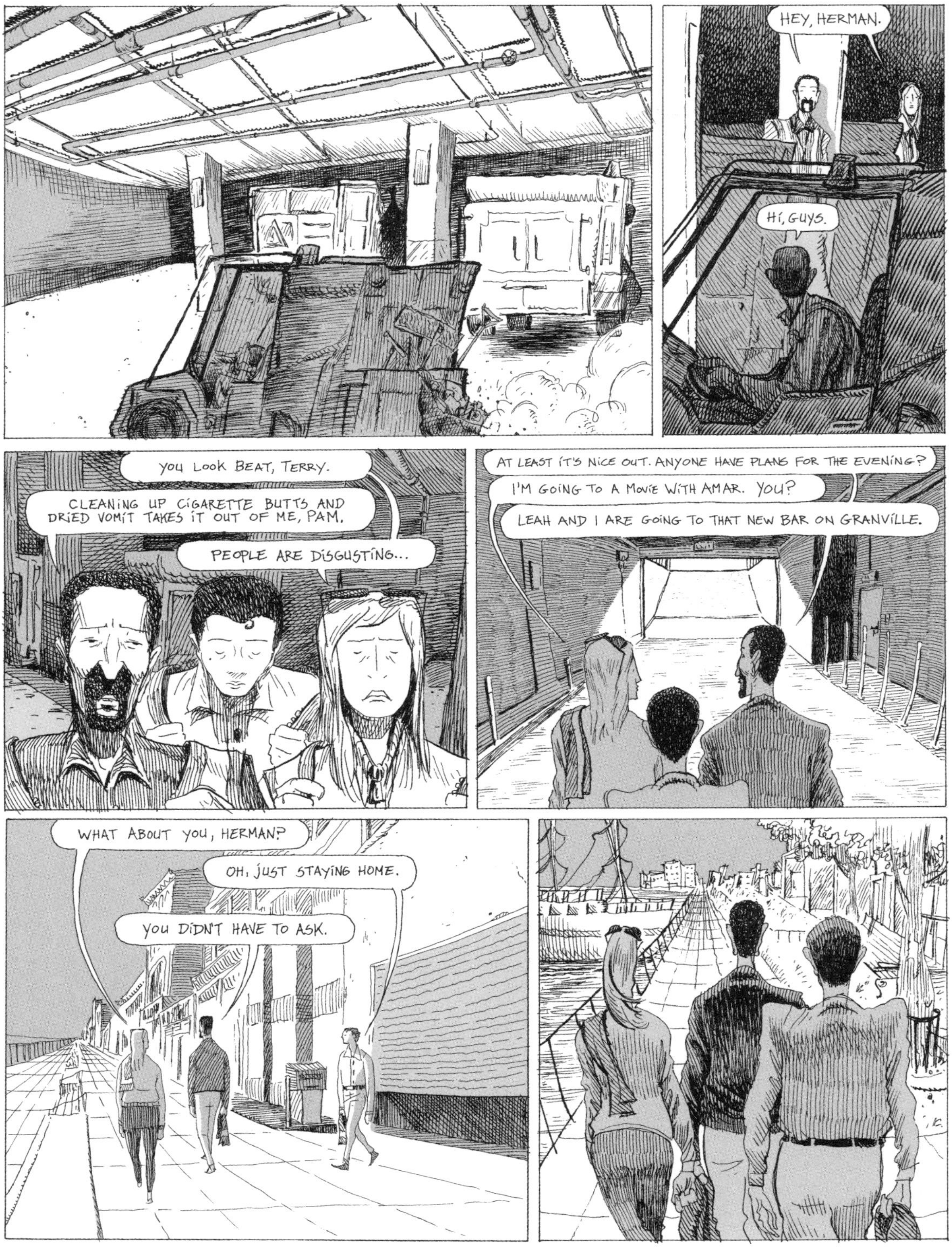
HEY, HERMAN.
Hi, GUYS.
YOU LOOK BEAT, TERRY.
CLEANING UP CIGARETTE BUTTS AND DRIED VOMIT TAKES IT OUT OF ME, PAM.
PEOPLE ARE DISGUSTING...
AT LEAST IT'S NICE OUT. ANYONE HAVE PLANS FOR THE EVENING?
I'M GOING TO A MOVIE WITH AMAR. YOU?
LEAH AND I ARE GOING TO THAT NEW BAR ON GRANVILLE.
WHAT ABOUT YOU, HERMAN?
OH, JUST STAYING HOME.
YOU DIDN'T HAVE TO ASK.

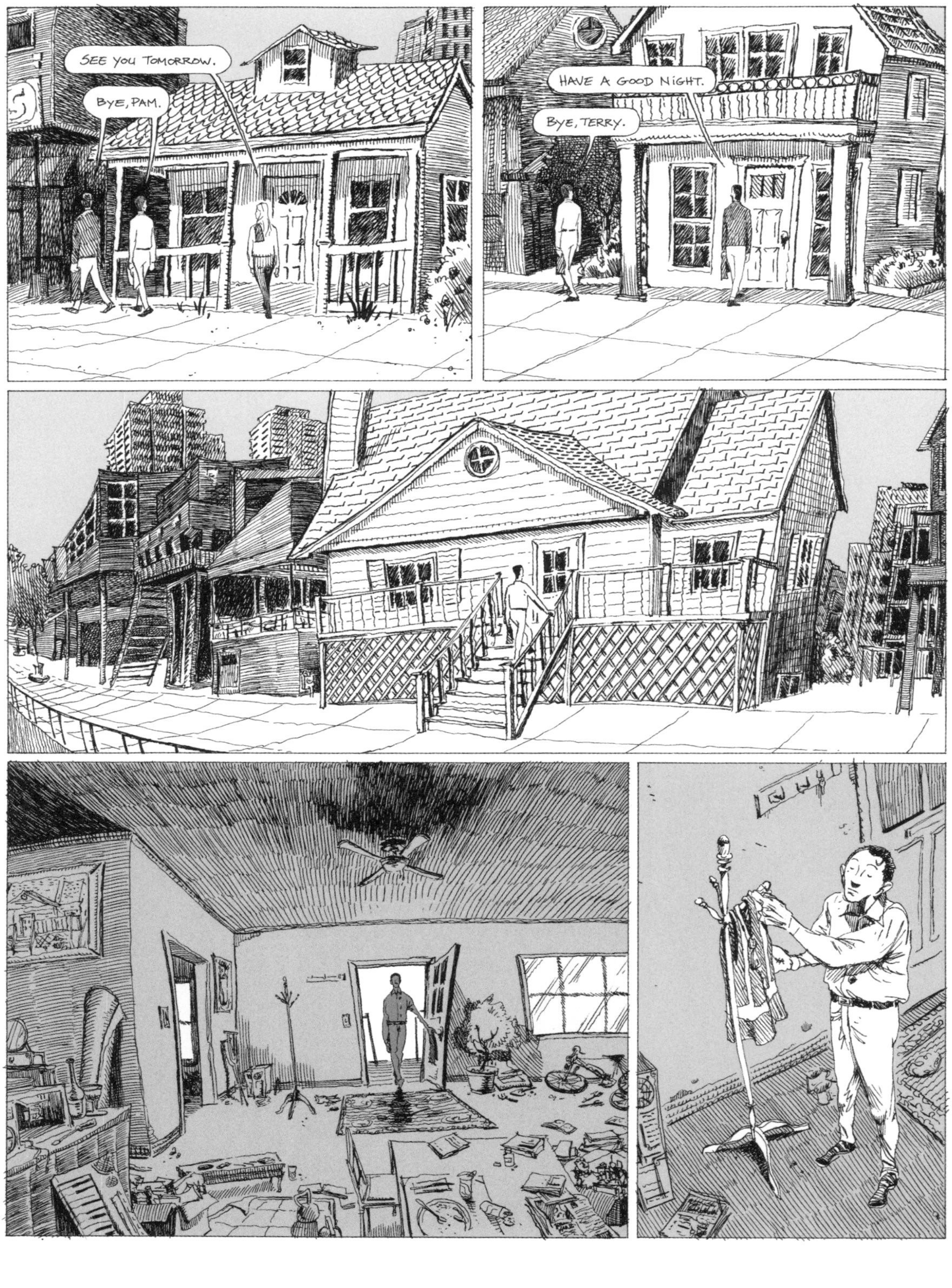
SEE YOU TOMORROW.
BYE, PAM.
HAVE A GOOD NIGHT.
BYE, TERRY.

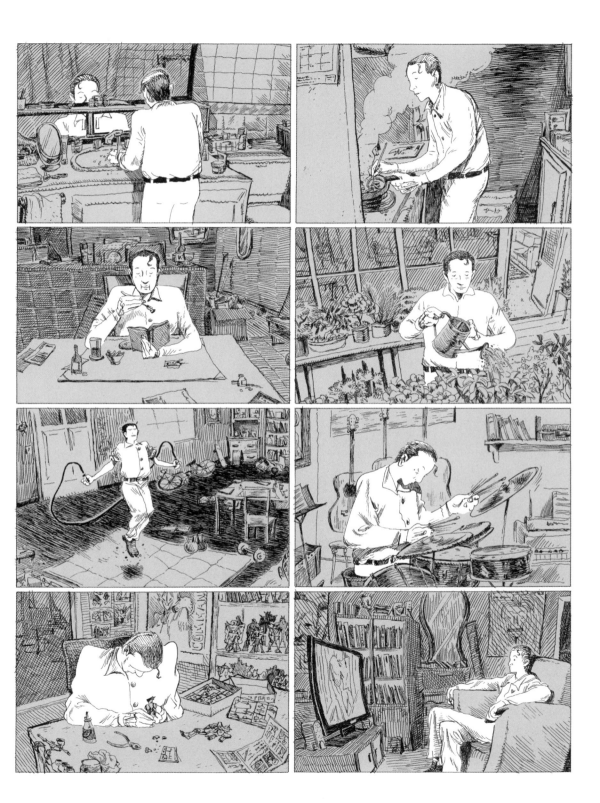

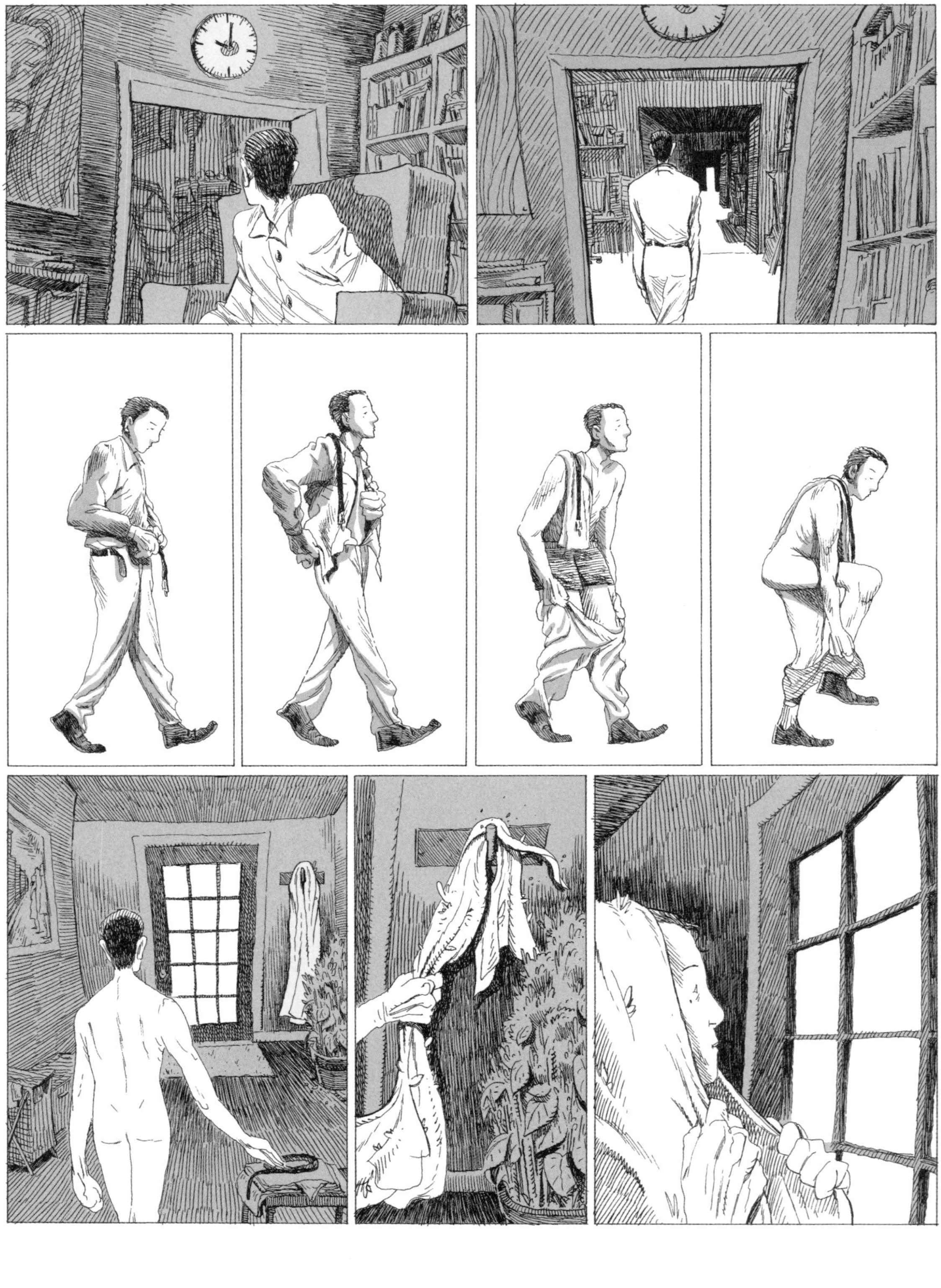

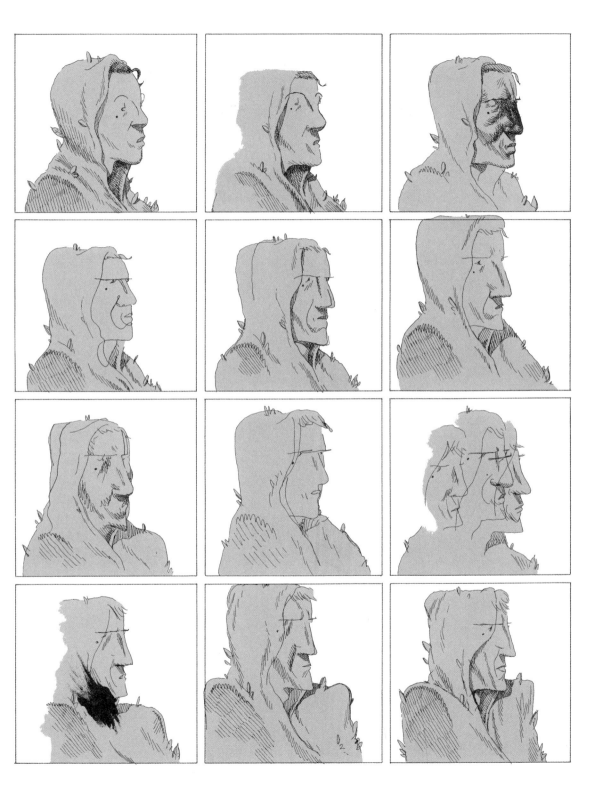

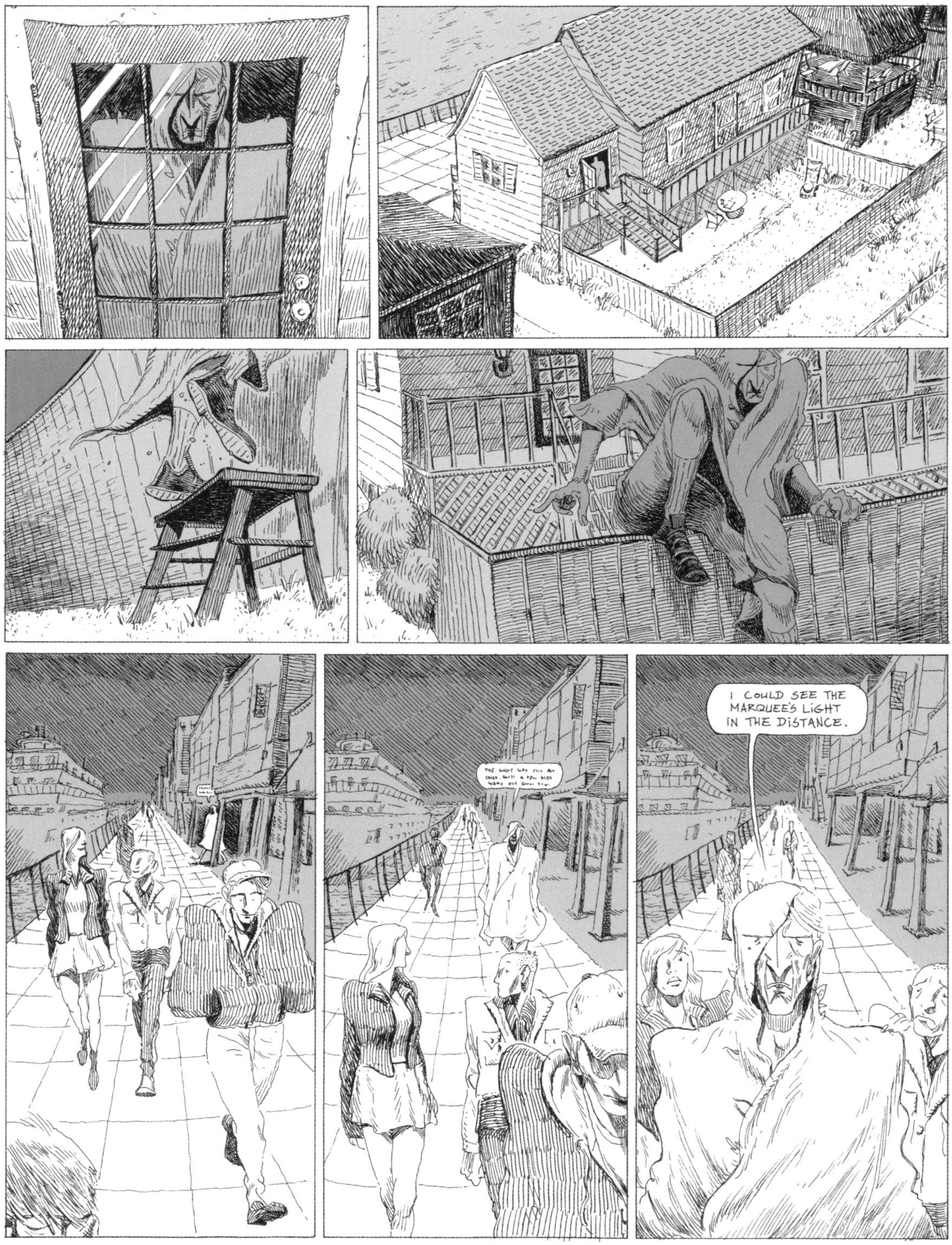

I COULD SEE THE MARQUEE'S LIGHT IN THE DISTANCE.

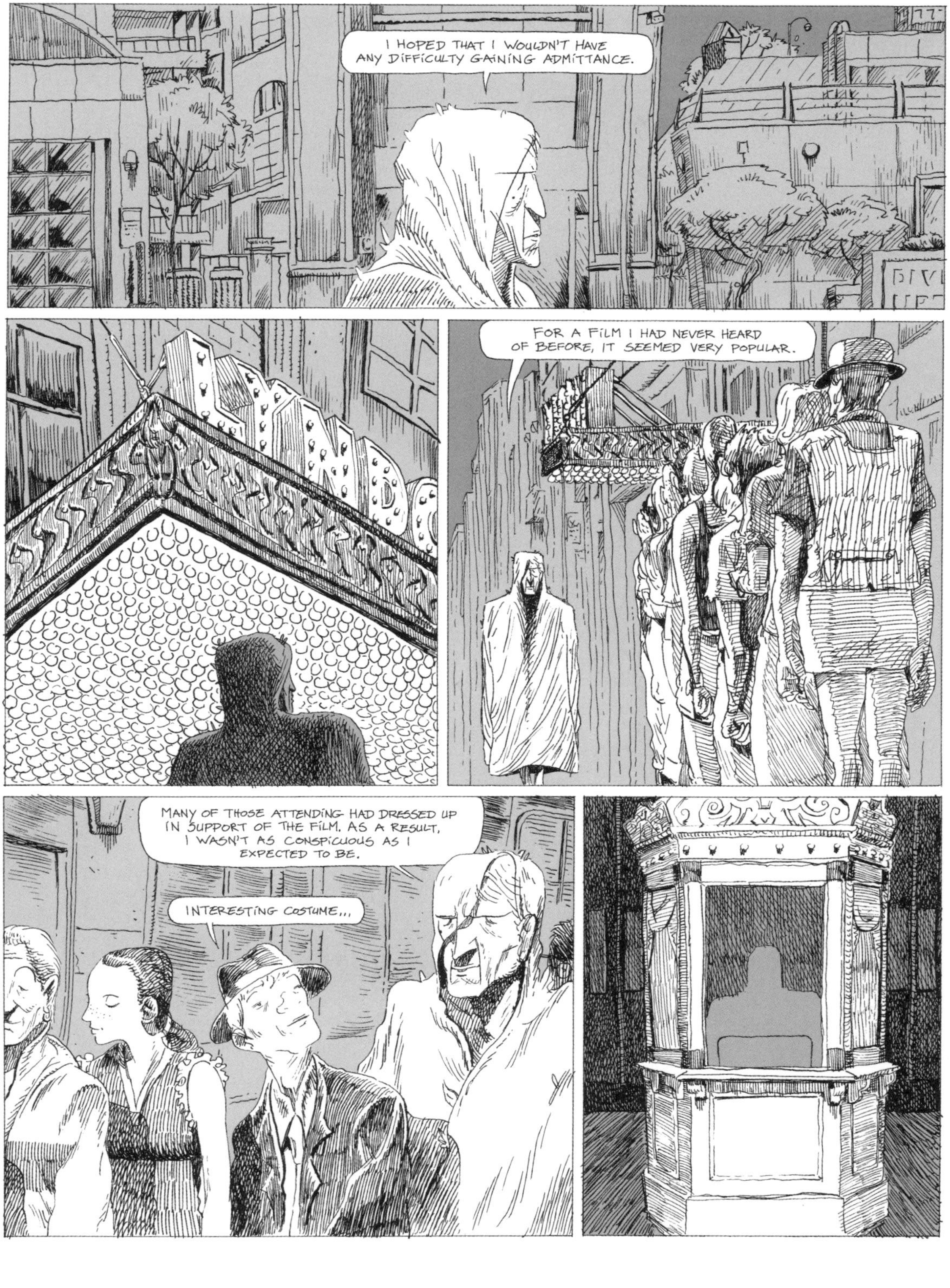
I HOPED THAT I WOULDN'T HAVE ANY DIFFICULTY GAINING ADMITTANCE.
FOR A FILM I HAD NEVER HEARD OF BEFORE, IT SEEMED VERY POPULAR.
MANY OF THOSE ATTENDING HAD DRESSED UP IN SUPPORT OF THE FILM. AS A RESULT, I WASN'T AS CONSPICUOUS AS I EXPECTED TO BE.
INTERESTING COSTUME...

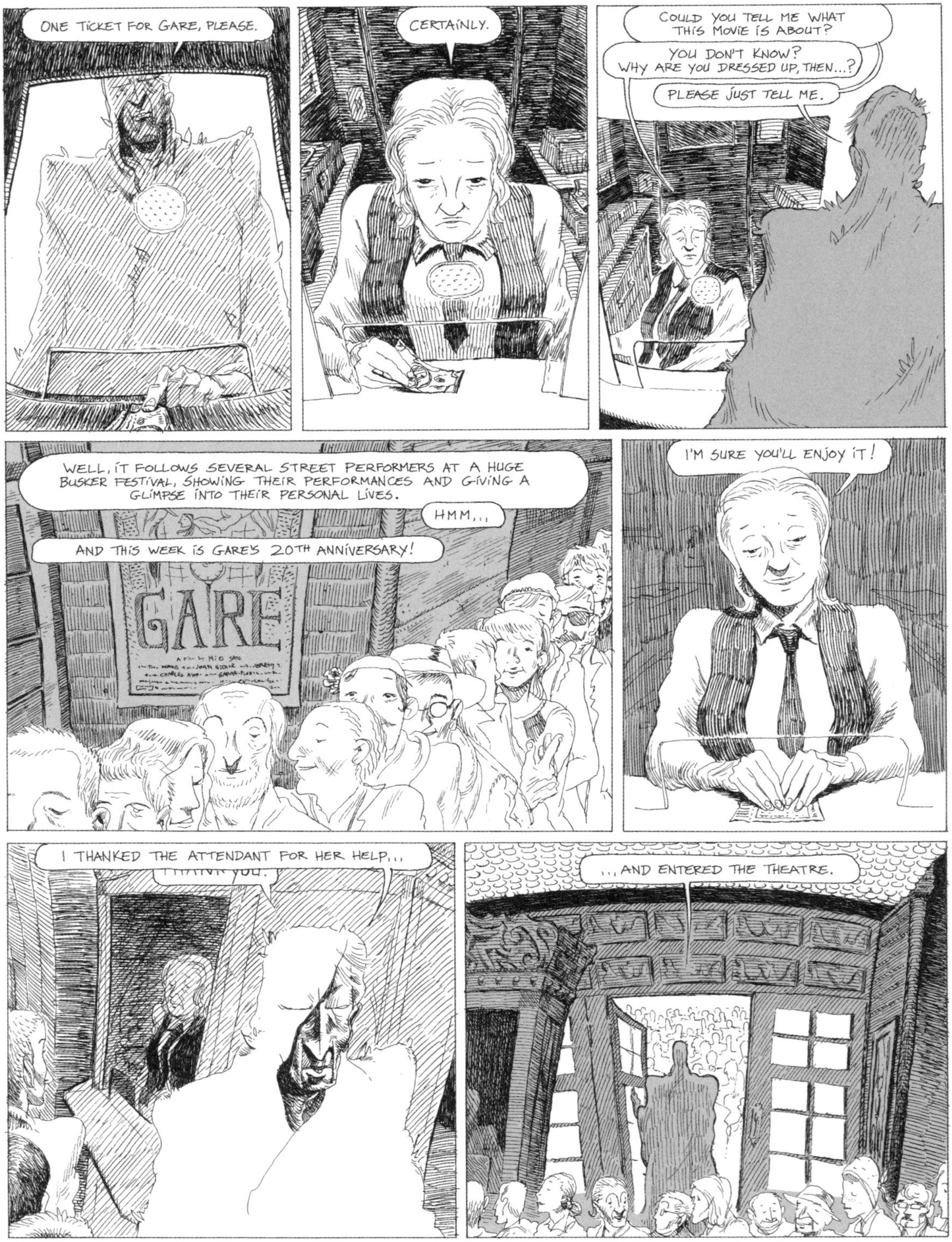
ONE TICKET FOR GARE, PLEASE.
CERTAINLY.
COULD YOU TELL ME WHAT THIS MOVIE IS ABOUT?
YOU DON'T KNOW? WHY ARE YOU DRESSED UP, THEN...?
PLEASE JUST TELL ME.
WELL, IT FOLLOWS SEVERAL STREET PERFORMERS AT A HUGE BUSKER FESTIVAL, SHOWING THEIR PERFORMANCES AND GIVING A GLIMPSE INTO THEIR PERSONAL LIVES.
HMM...
AND THIS WEEK IS GARE'S 20TH ANNIVERSARY!
GARE
I'M SURE YOU'LL ENJOY IT!
I THANKED THE ATTENDANT FOR HER HELP...
...AND ENTERED THE THEATRE.

AUDITORIUM SIX, AUDITORIUM SIX, PLEASE, FOLLOW THE CROWD TO AUDITORIUM SIX...

CH A CLASSIC!

ENTED.

HAVEN'T SEEN IT
I WAS TWE

T NOTHING LIKE
BEEN MADE SINCE.

I SAW IT WAY BEF

I'VE NEVER SE
ON A BIG SCR

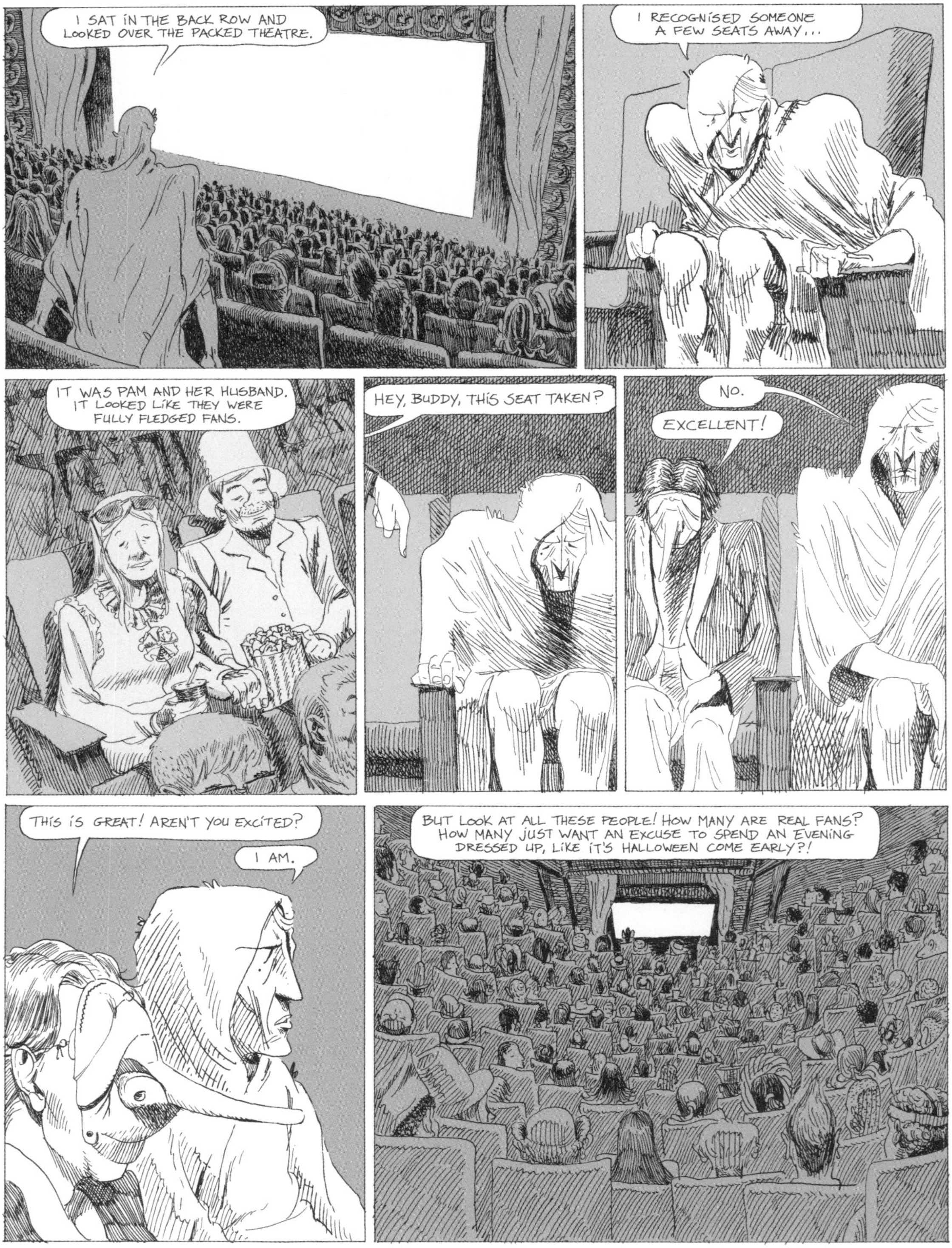
I SAT IN THE BACK ROW AND LOOKED OVER THE PACKED THEATRE.
I RECOGNISED SOMEONE A FEW SEATS AWAY...
IT WAS PAM AND HER HUSBAND. IT LOOKED LIKE THEY WERE FULLY FLEDGED FANS.
HEY, BUDDY, THIS SEAT TAKEN?
NO.
EXCELLENT!
THIS IS GREAT! AREN'T YOU EXCITED?
I AM.
BUT LOOK AT ALL THESE PEOPLE! HOW MANY ARE REAL FANS? HOW MANY JUST WANT AN EXCUSE TO SPEND AN EVENING DRESSED UP, LIKE IT'S HALLOWEEN COME EARLY?!

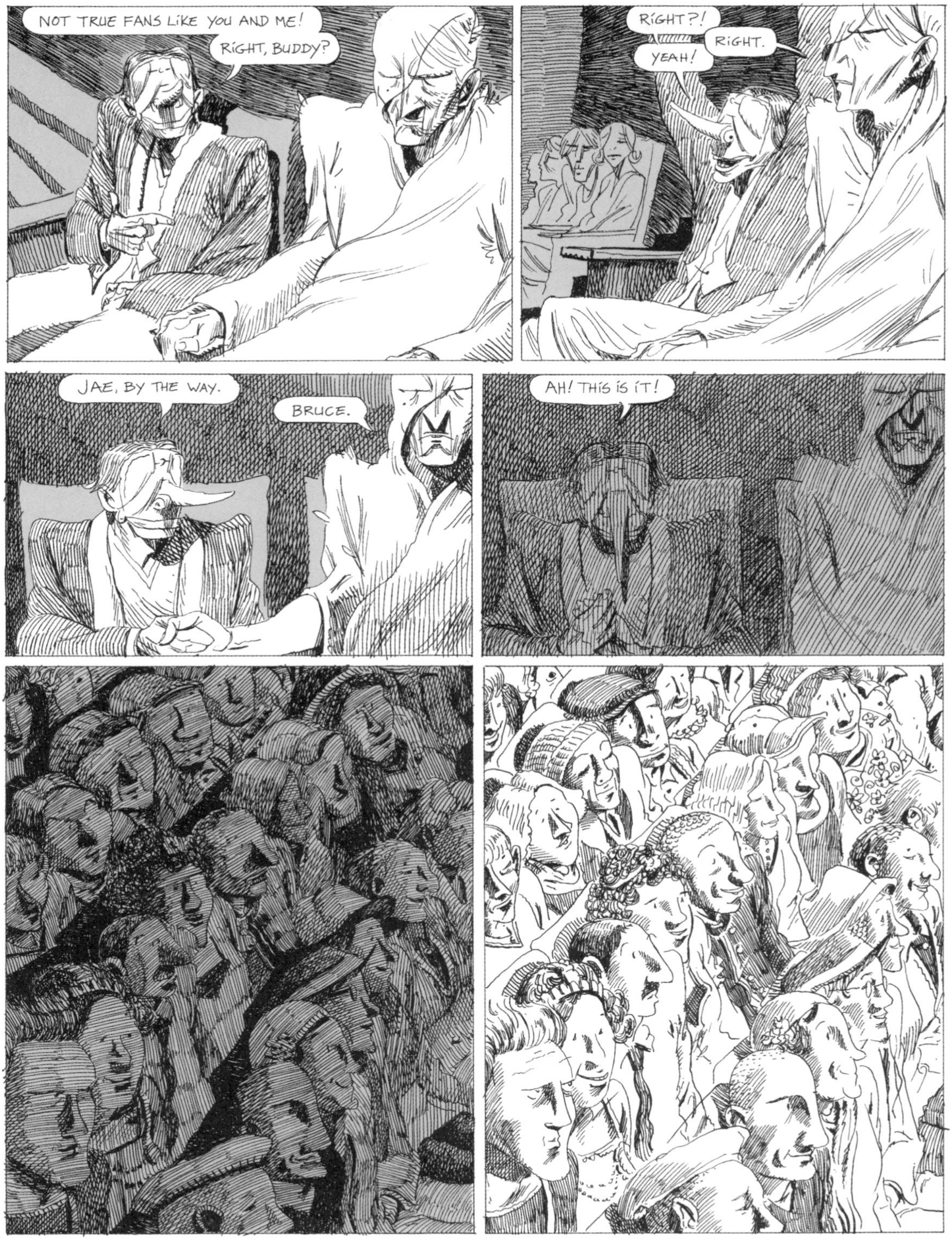
NOT TRUE FANS LIKE YOU AND ME!
RIGHT, BUDDY?
RIGHT?!
YEAH!
RIGHT.
JAE, BY THE WAY.
BRUCE.
AH! THIS IS IT!

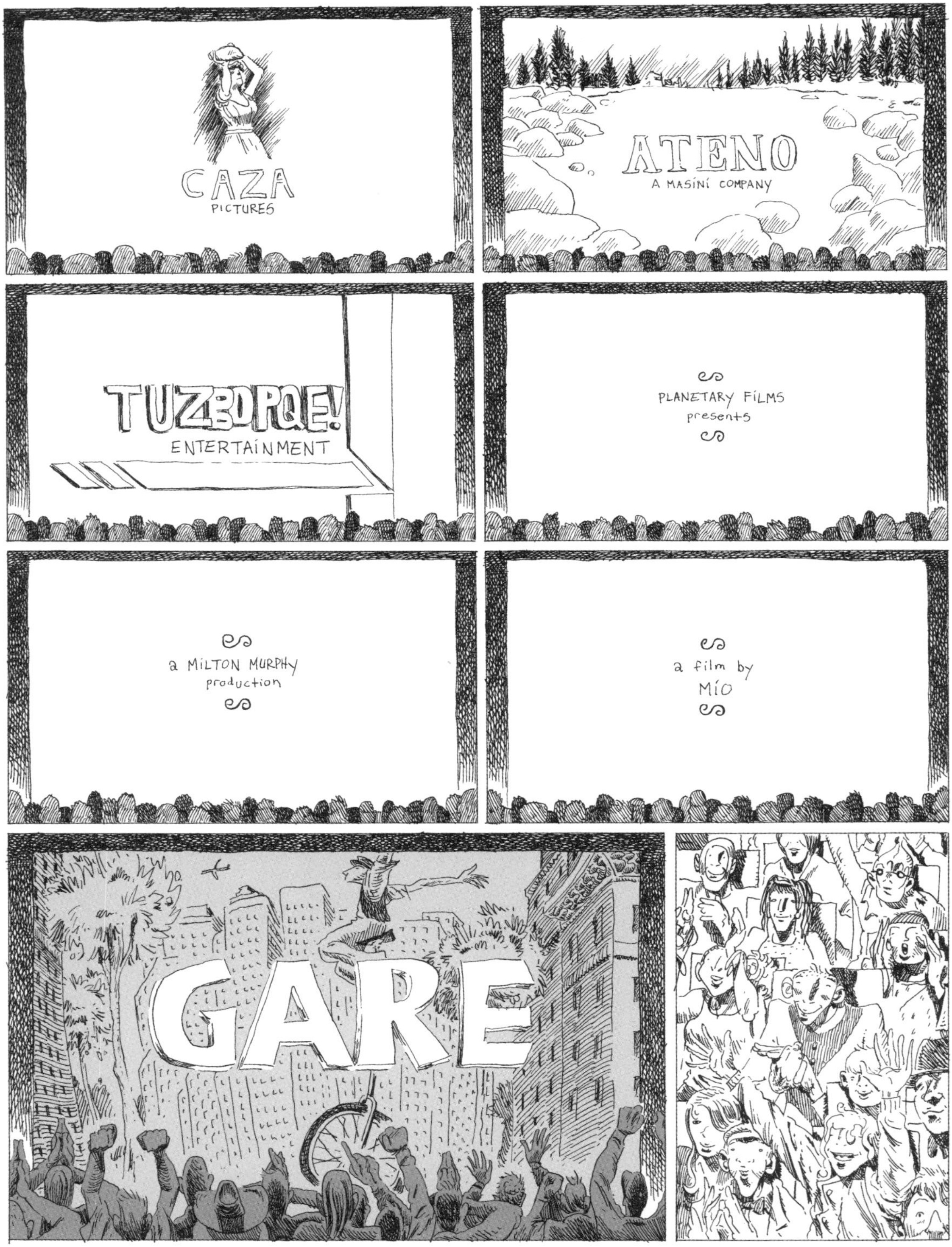
CAZA
PICTURES
ATENO
A MASINÍ COMPANY
TUZBOPQE!
ENTERTAINMENT
PLANETARY FILMS
presents
a MILTON MURPHY
production
a film by
MÍO
GARE

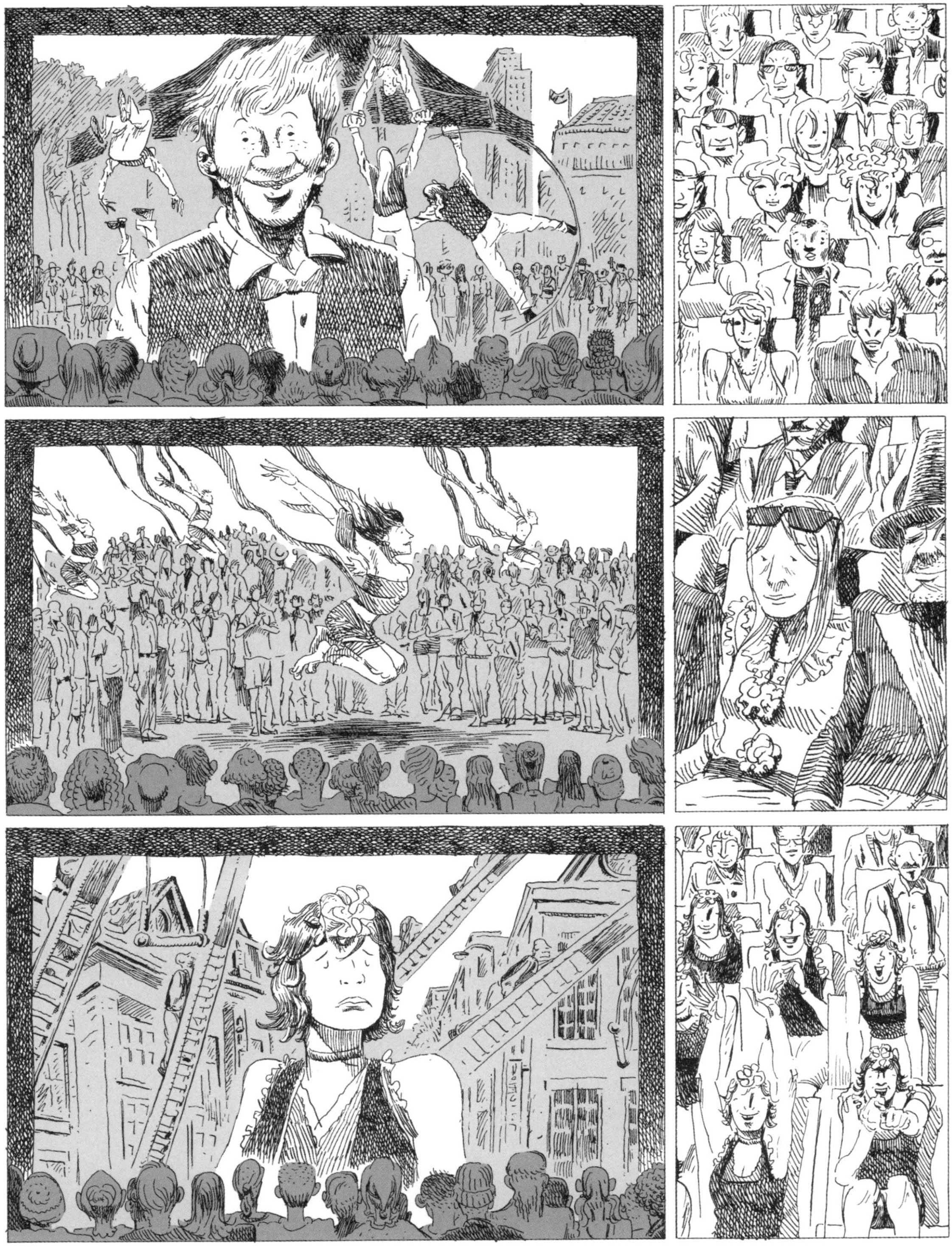

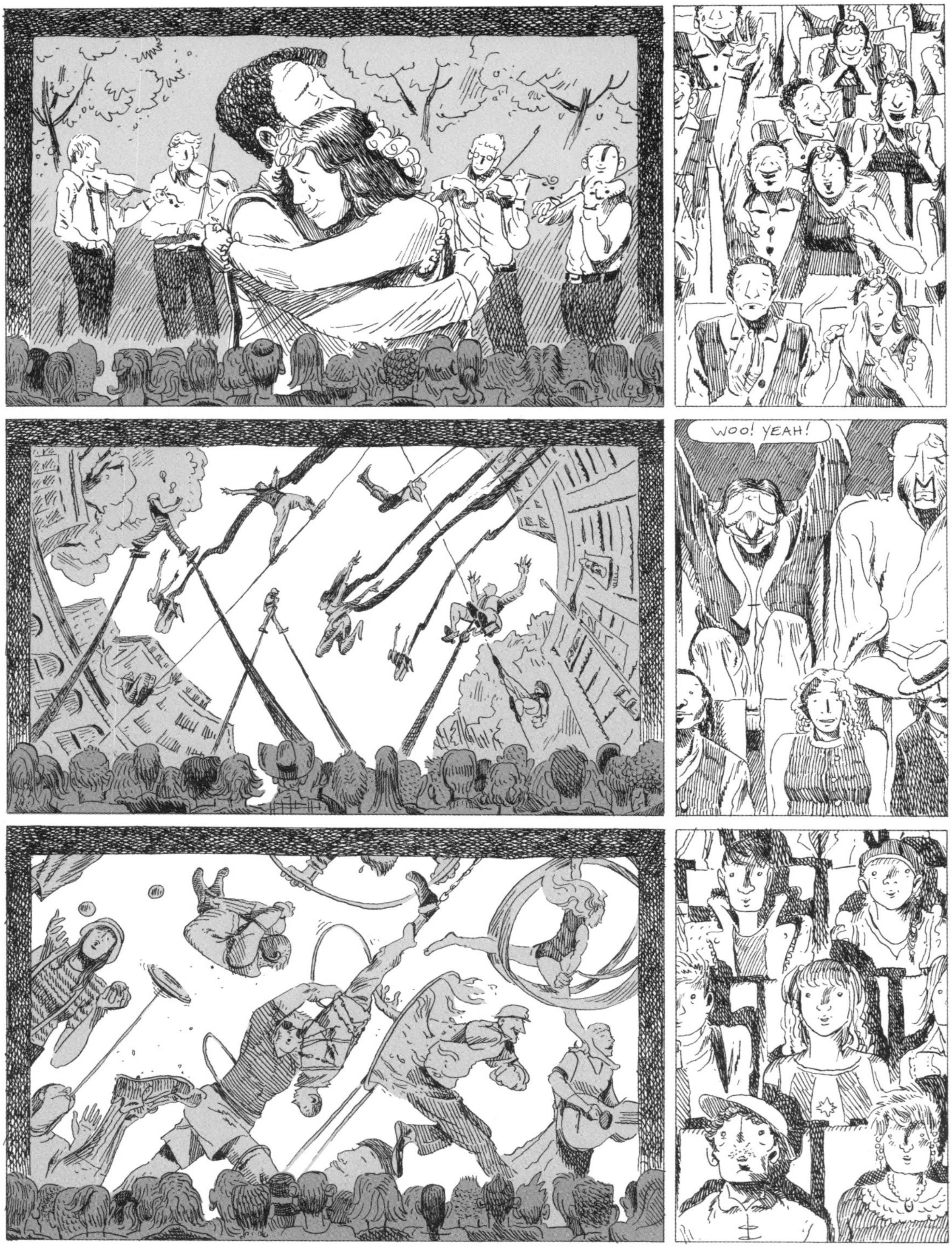
WOO! YEAH!

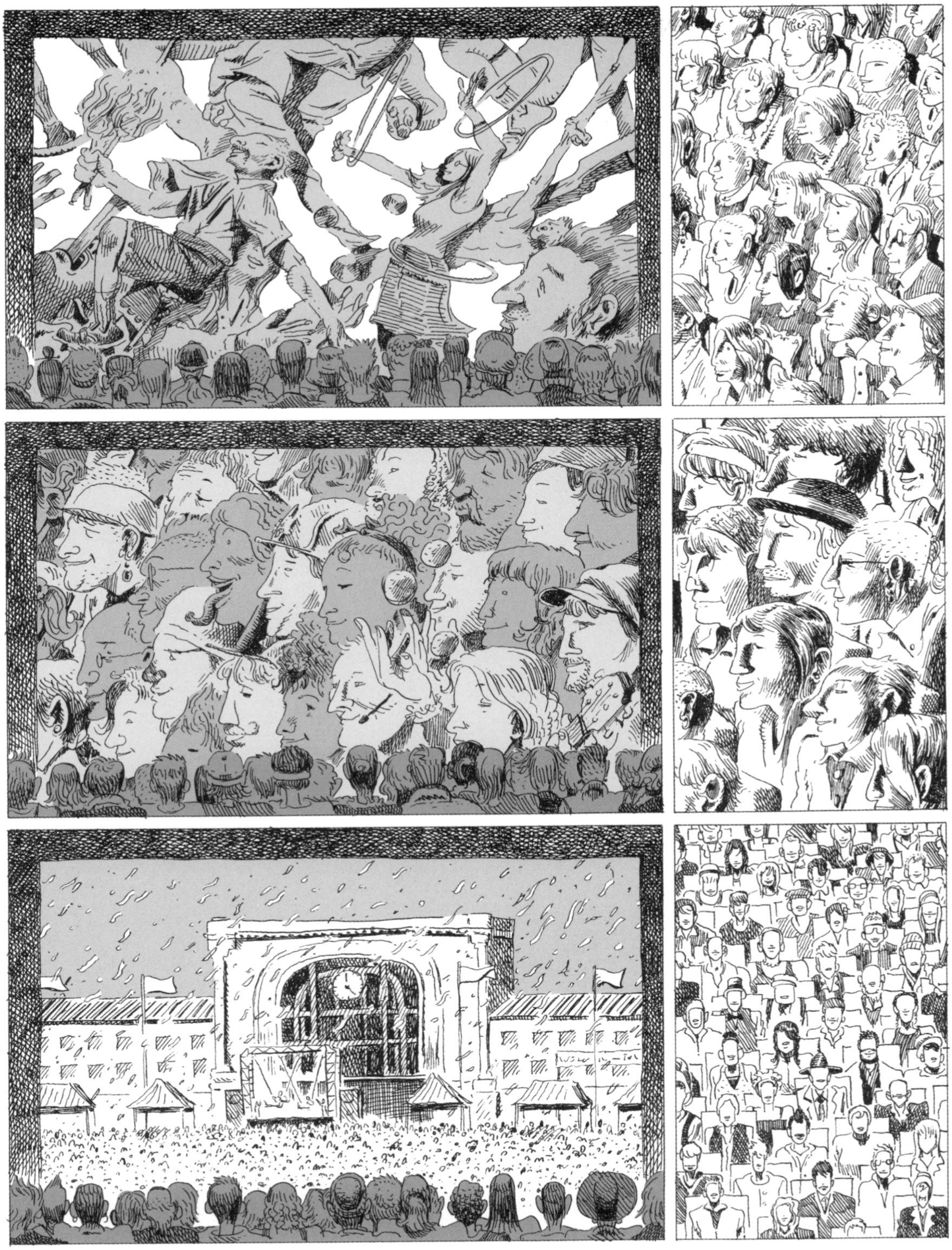

TRANSLATIONS NICOLAS MORITA
CHANTAL DAY
PRODUCTION
ASSISTANTS SANG-HUN LEE
LINDA TOMOV
SUPPLY BOY NIC GAUDI
LEGAL LUIS CHIN
SWING GANG DEAN O'NEIL
MINDY ICER
HUG AMSE

WHAT A FILM!

FOLKS, I CAN SEE THAT YOU'RE
DIE-HARD FANS! THE REAL DEAL!
SO I DON'T HAVE TO TELL YOU TO
PUT YOUR HANDS TOGETHER FOR
THE DIRECTOR OF GARE...

MIO!

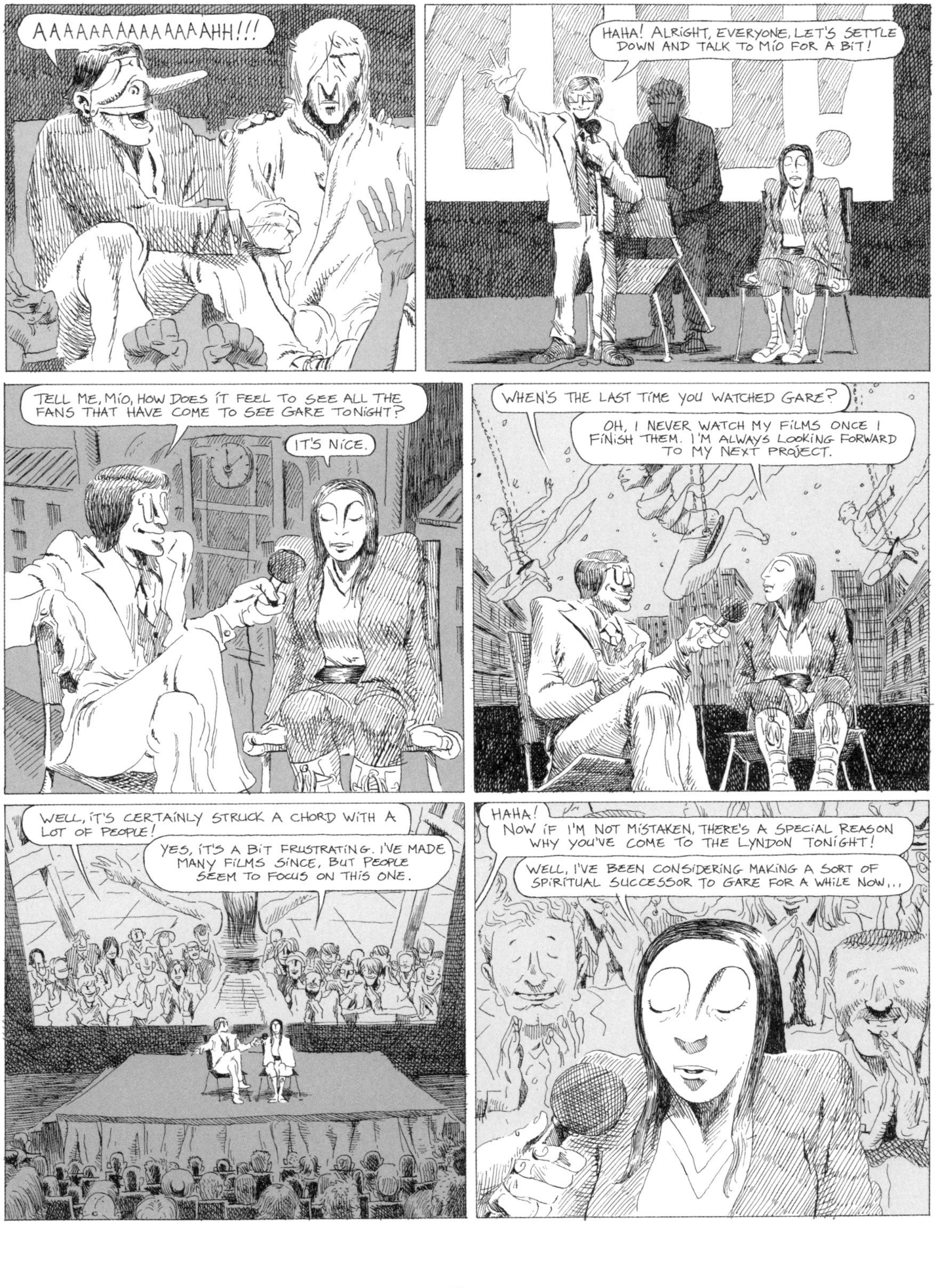
AAAAAAAAAAAAAHH!!!
HAHA! ALRIGHT, EVERYONE, LET'S SETTLE DOWN AND TALK TO MÍO FOR A BIT!
TELL ME, MÍO, HOW DOES IT FEEL TO SEE ALL THE FANS THAT HAVE COME TO SEE GARE TONIGHT?
IT'S NICE.
WHEN'S THE LAST TIME YOU WATCHED GARE?
OH, I NEVER WATCH MY FILMS ONCE I FINISH THEM. I'M ALWAYS LOOKING FORWARD TO MY NEXT PROJECT.
WELL, IT'S CERTAINLY STRUCK A CHORD WITH A LOT OF PEOPLE!
YES, IT'S A BIT FRUSTRATING. I'VE MADE MANY FILMS SINCE, BUT PEOPLE SEEM TO FOCUS ON THIS ONE.
HAHA!
NOW IF I'M NOT MISTAKEN, THERE'S A SPECIAL REASON WHY YOU'VE COME TO THE LYNDON TONIGHT!
WELL, I'VE BEEN CONSIDERING MAKING A SORT OF SPIRITUAL SUCCESSOR TO GARE FOR A WHILE NOW...

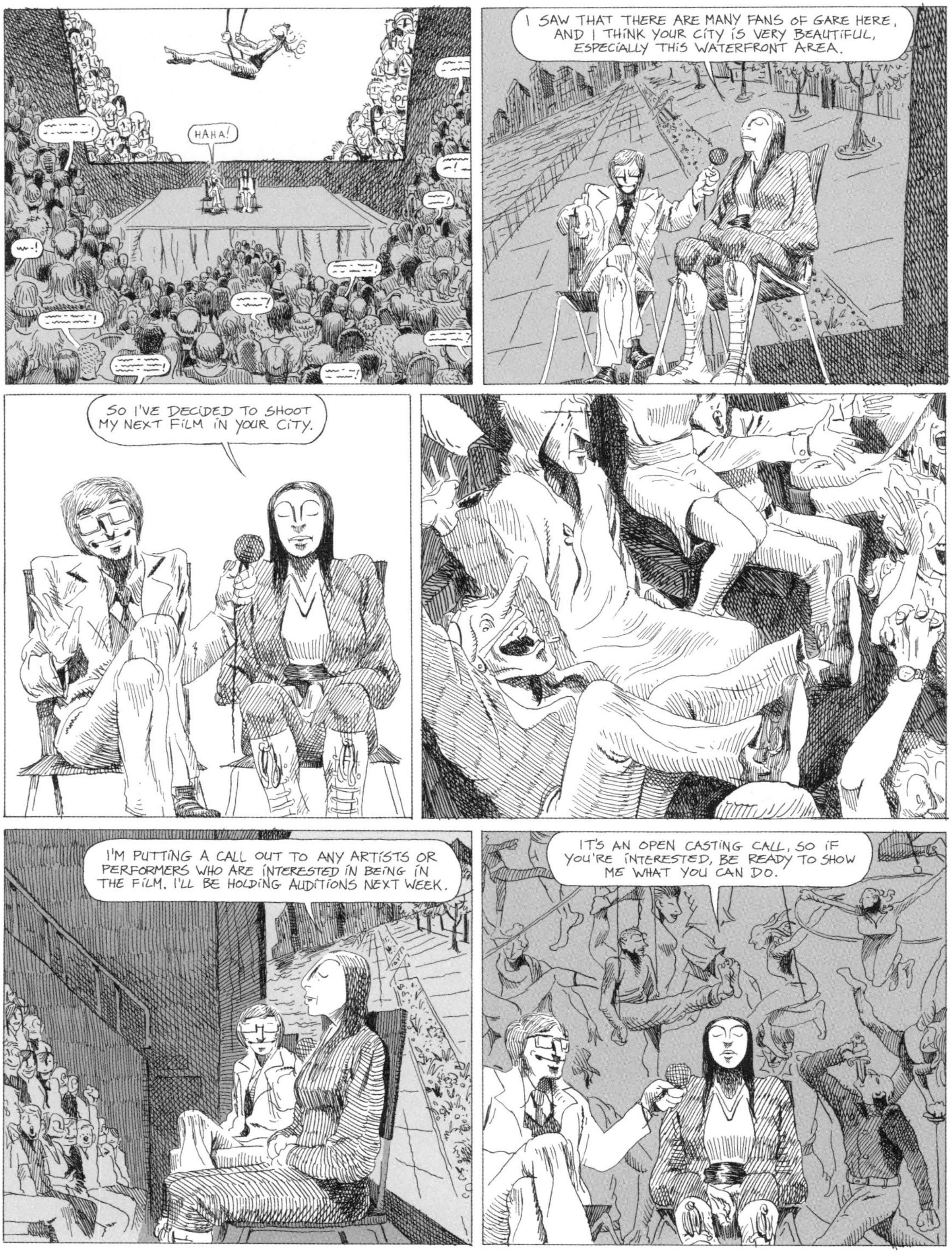
HAHA!
I SAW THAT THERE ARE MANY FANS OF GARE HERE, AND I THINK YOUR CITY IS VERY BEAUTIFUL, ESPECIALLY THIS WATERFRONT AREA.
SO I'VE DECIDED TO SHOOT MY NEXT FILM IN YOUR CITY.
I'M PUTTING A CALL OUT TO ANY ARTISTS OR PERFORMERS WHO ARE INTERESTED IN BEING IN THE FILM. I'LL BE HOLDING AUDITIONS NEXT WEEK.
IT'S AN OPEN CASTING CALL, SO IF YOU'RE INTERESTED, BE READY TO SHOW ME WHAT YOU CAN DO.

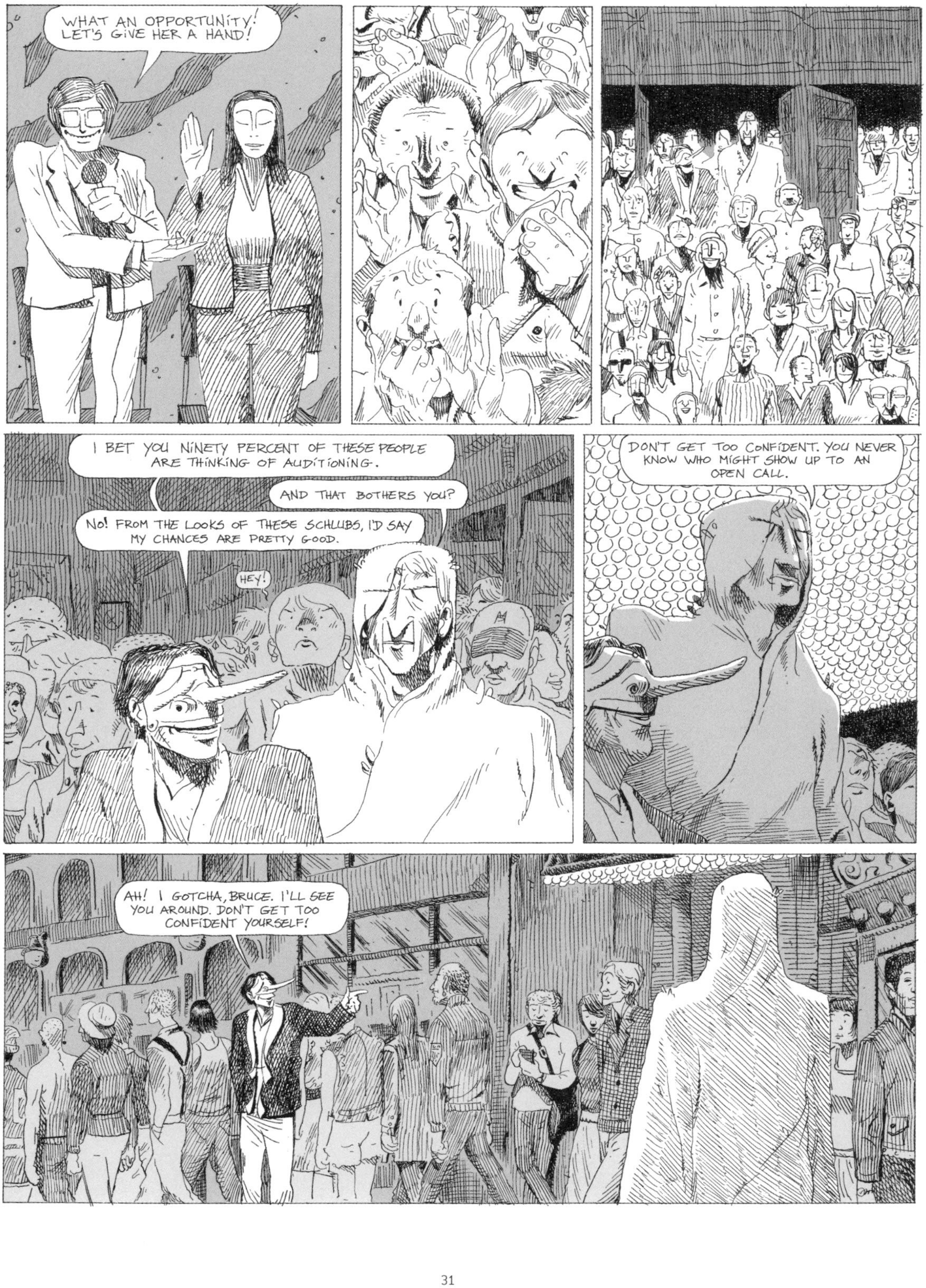
WHAT AN OPPORTUNITY! LET'S GIVE HER A HAND!
I BET YOU NINETY PERCENT OF THESE PEOPLE ARE THINKING OF AUDITIONING.
AND THAT BOTHERS YOU?
NO! FROM THE LOOKS OF THESE SCHLUBS, I'D SAY MY CHANCES ARE PRETTY GOOD.
HEY!
DON'T GET TOO CONFIDENT. YOU NEVER KNOW WHO MIGHT SHOW UP TO AN OPEN CALL.
AH! I GOTCHA, BRUCE. I'LL SEE YOU AROUND. DON'T GET TOO CONFIDENT YOURSELF!

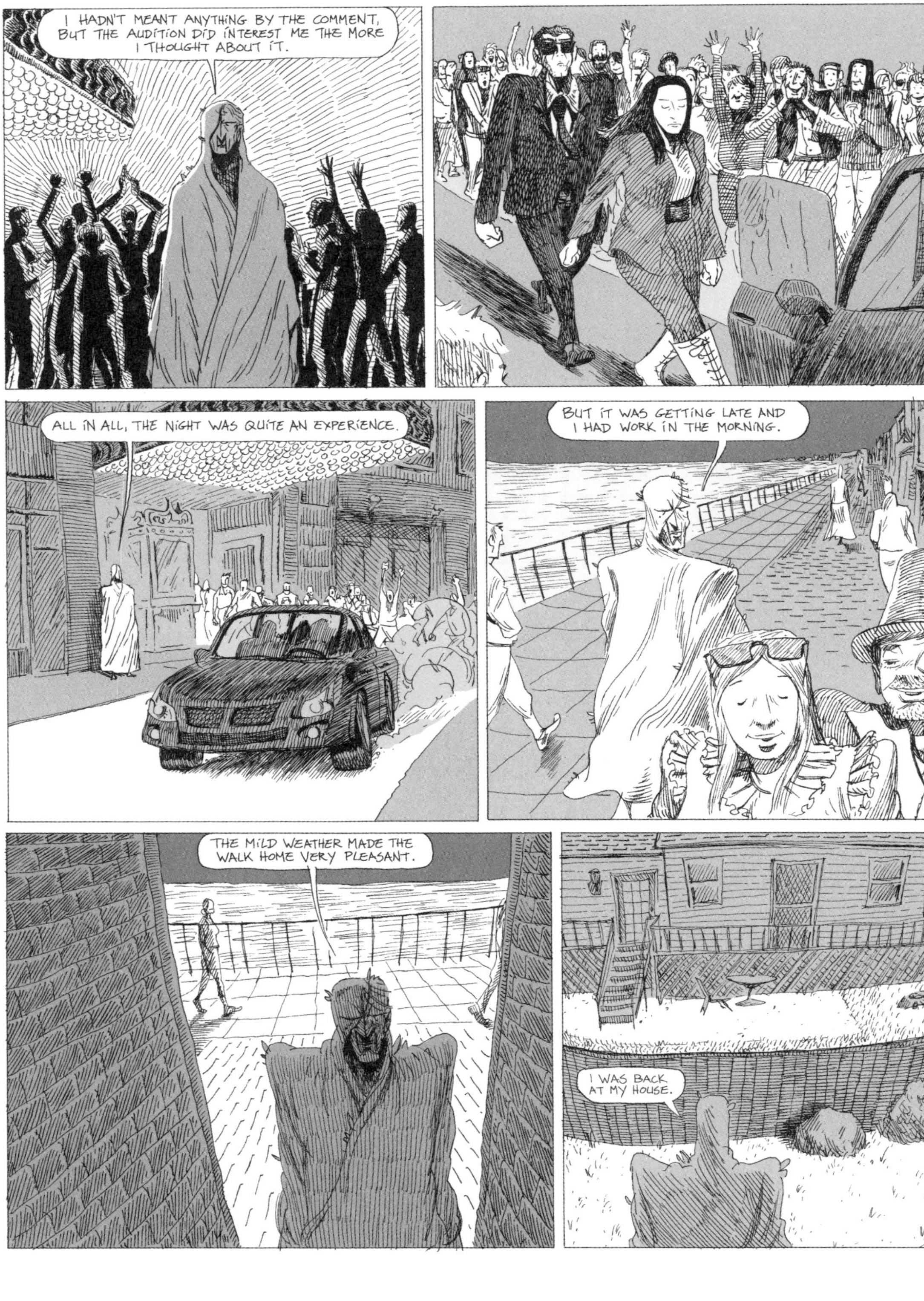
I HADN'T MEANT ANYTHING BY THE COMMENT, BUT THE AUDITION DID INTEREST ME THE MORE I THOUGHT ABOUT IT.
ALL IN ALL, THE NIGHT WAS QUITE AN EXPERIENCE.
BUT IT WAS GETTING LATE AND I HAD WORK IN THE MORNING.
THE MILD WEATHER MADE THE WALK HOME VERY PLEASANT.
I WAS BACK AT MY HOUSE.

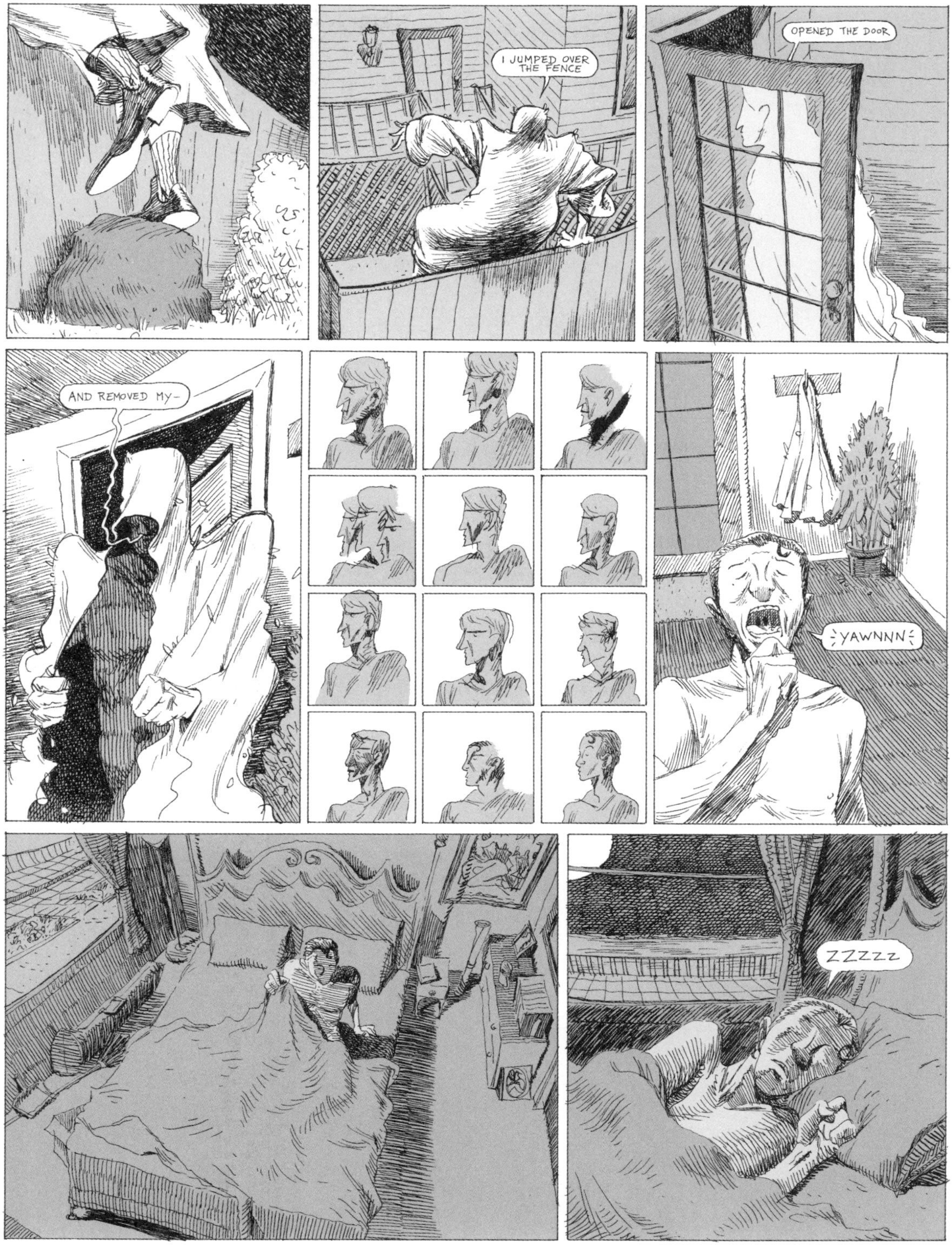
I JUMPED OVER THE FENCE
OPENED THE DOOR
AND REMOVED MY-
YAWNNN
ZZZZZ

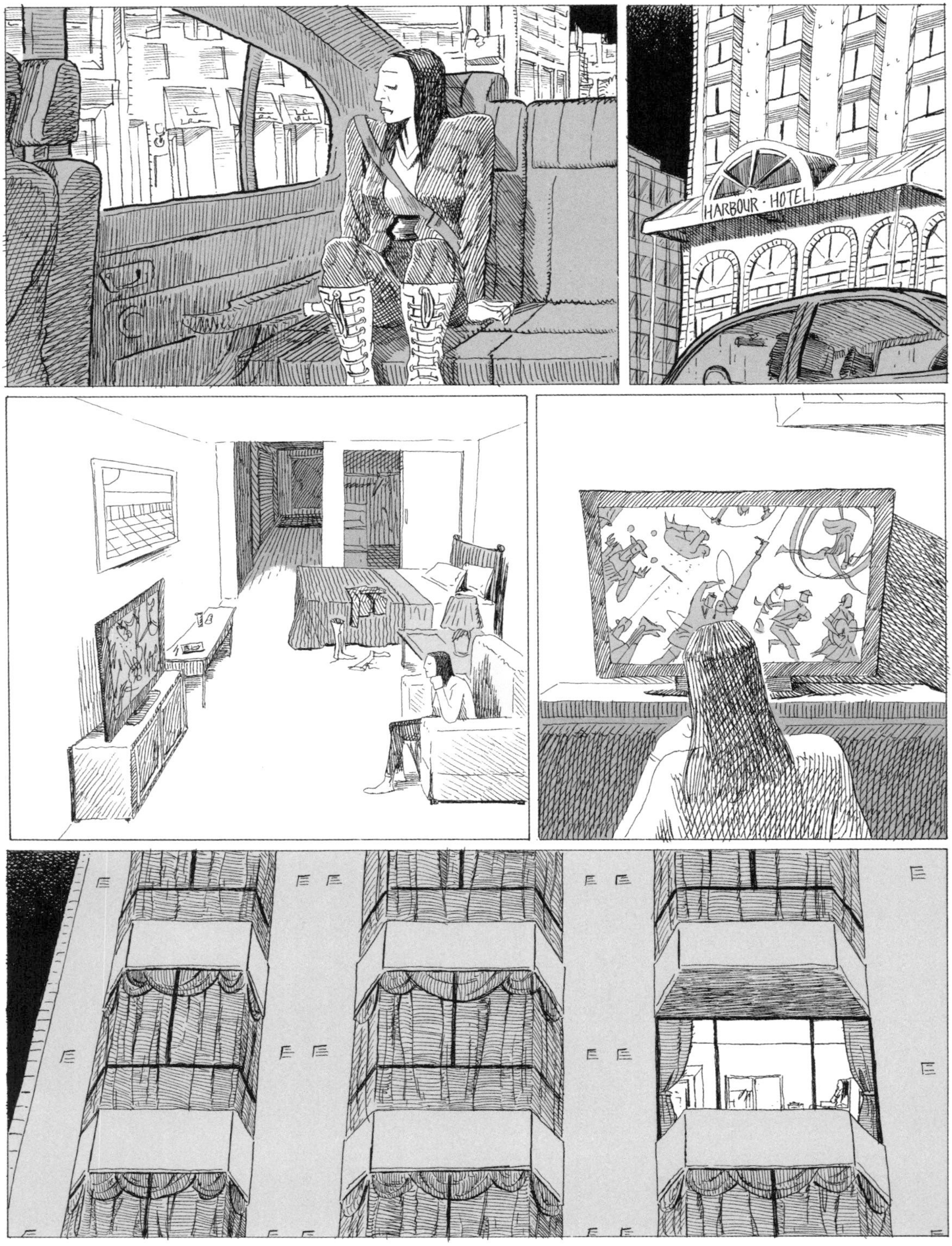
HARBOUR · HOTEL

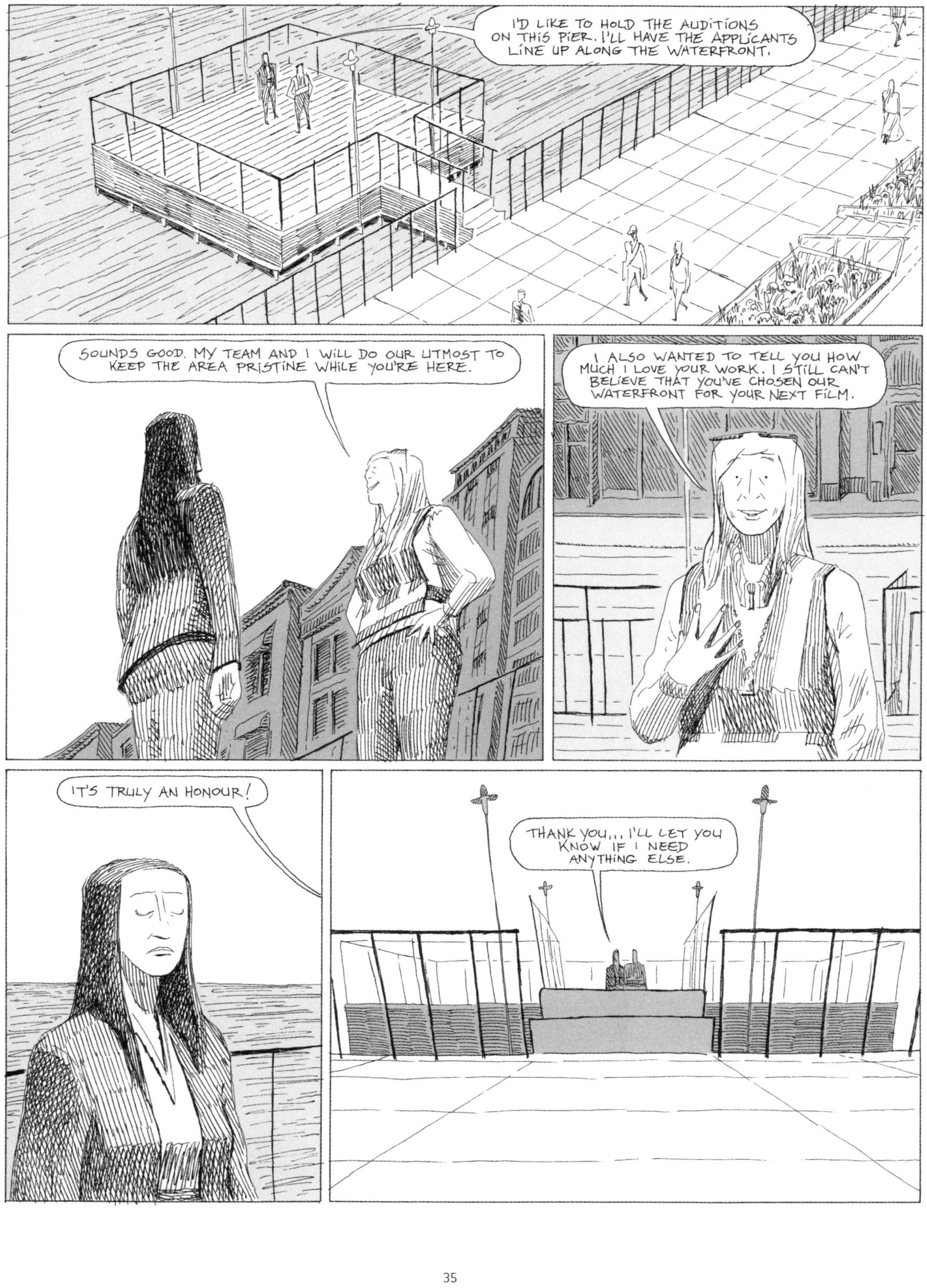
I'D LIKE TO HOLD THE AUDITIONS ON THIS PIER. I'LL HAVE THE APPLICANTS LINE UP ALONG THE WATERFRONT.
SOUNDS GOOD. MY TEAM AND I WILL DO OUR UTMOST TO KEEP THE AREA PRISTINE WHILE YOU'RE HERE.
I ALSO WANTED TO TELL YOU HOW MUCH I LOVE YOUR WORK. I STILL CAN'T BELIEVE THAT YOU'VE CHOSEN OUR WATERFRONT FOR YOUR NEXT FILM.
IT'S TRULY AN HONOUR!
THANK YOU... I'LL LET YOU KNOW IF I NEED ANYTHING ELSE.

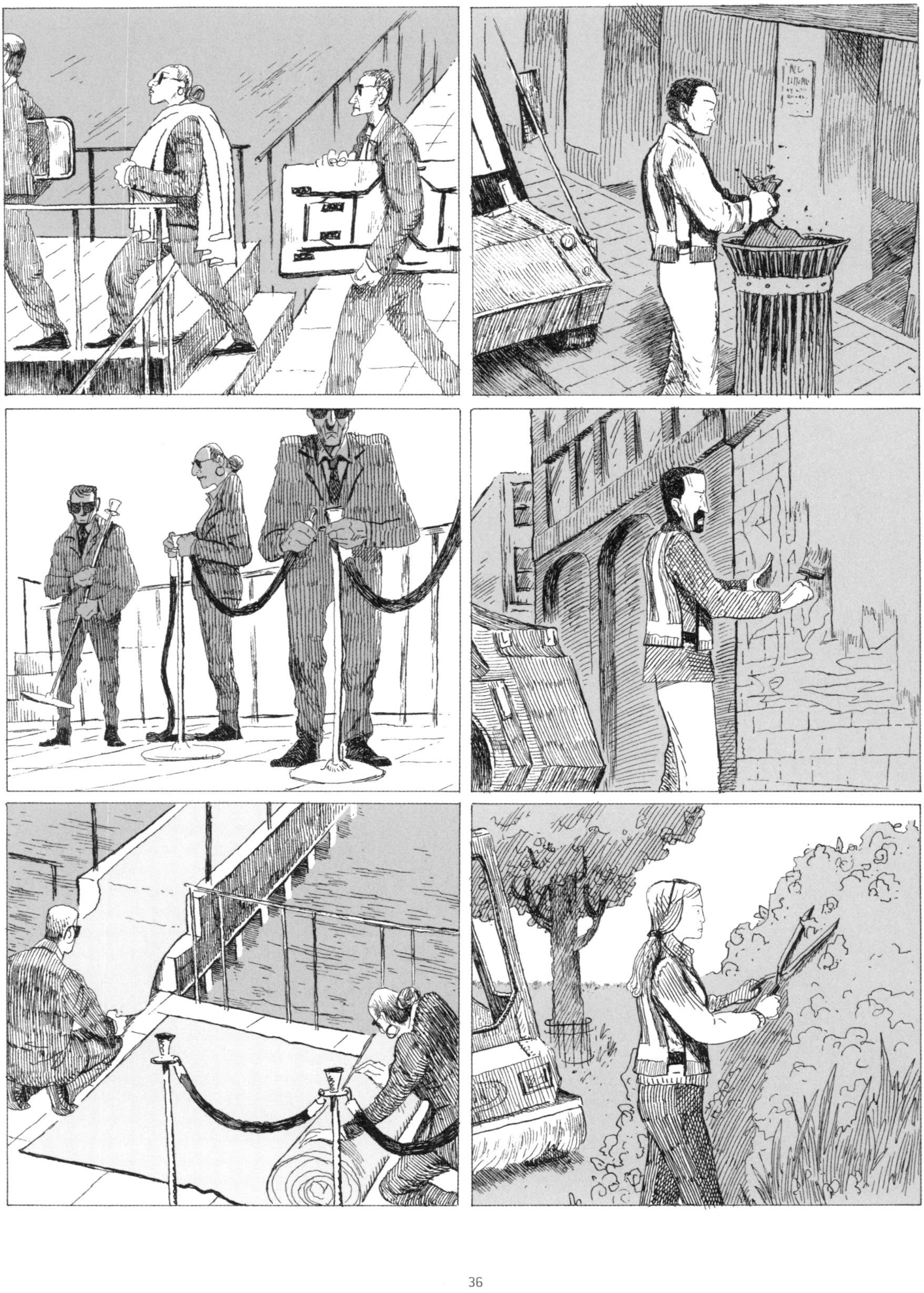

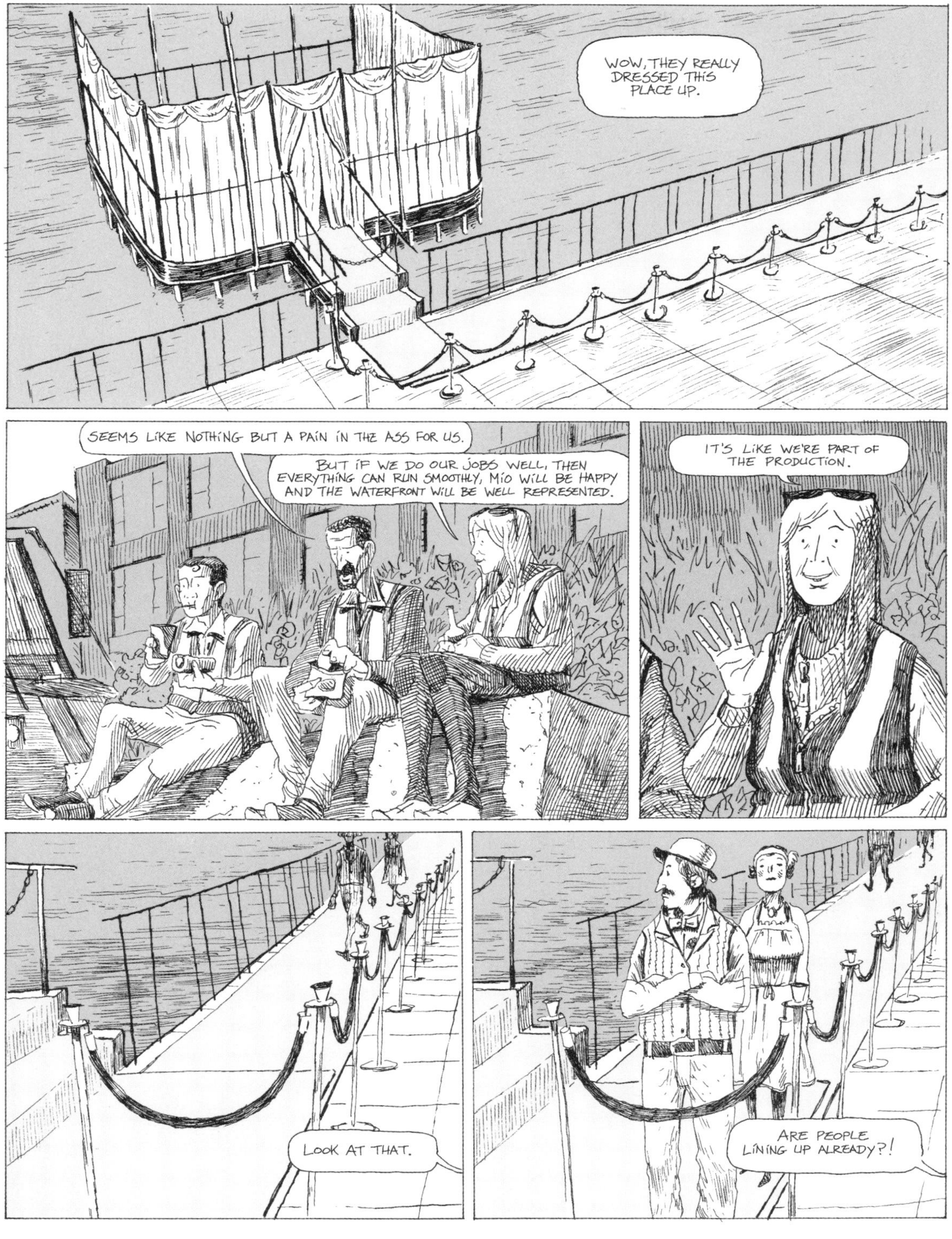
WOW, THEY REALLY DRESSED THIS PLACE UP.
SEEMS LIKE NOTHING BUT A PAIN IN THE ASS FOR US.
BUT IF WE DO OUR JOBS WELL, THEN EVERYTHING CAN RUN SMOOTHLY, MIO WILL BE HAPPY AND THE WATERFRONT WILL BE WELL REPRESENTED.
IT'S LIKE WE'RE PART OF THE PRODUCTION.
LOOK AT THAT.
ARE PEOPLE LINING UP ALREADY?!

COME ON, GUYS. LET'S GET BACK TO WORK.
LUNATICS!

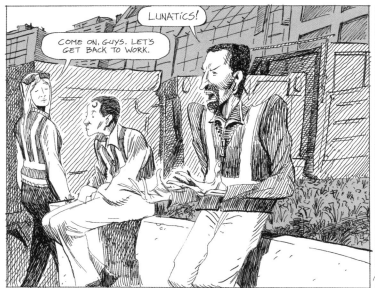

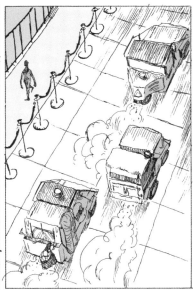

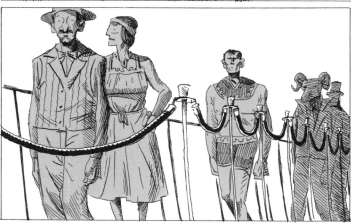

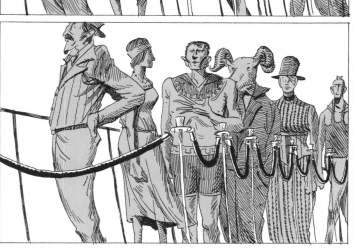

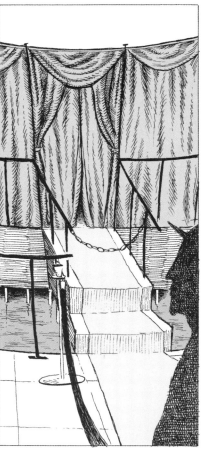

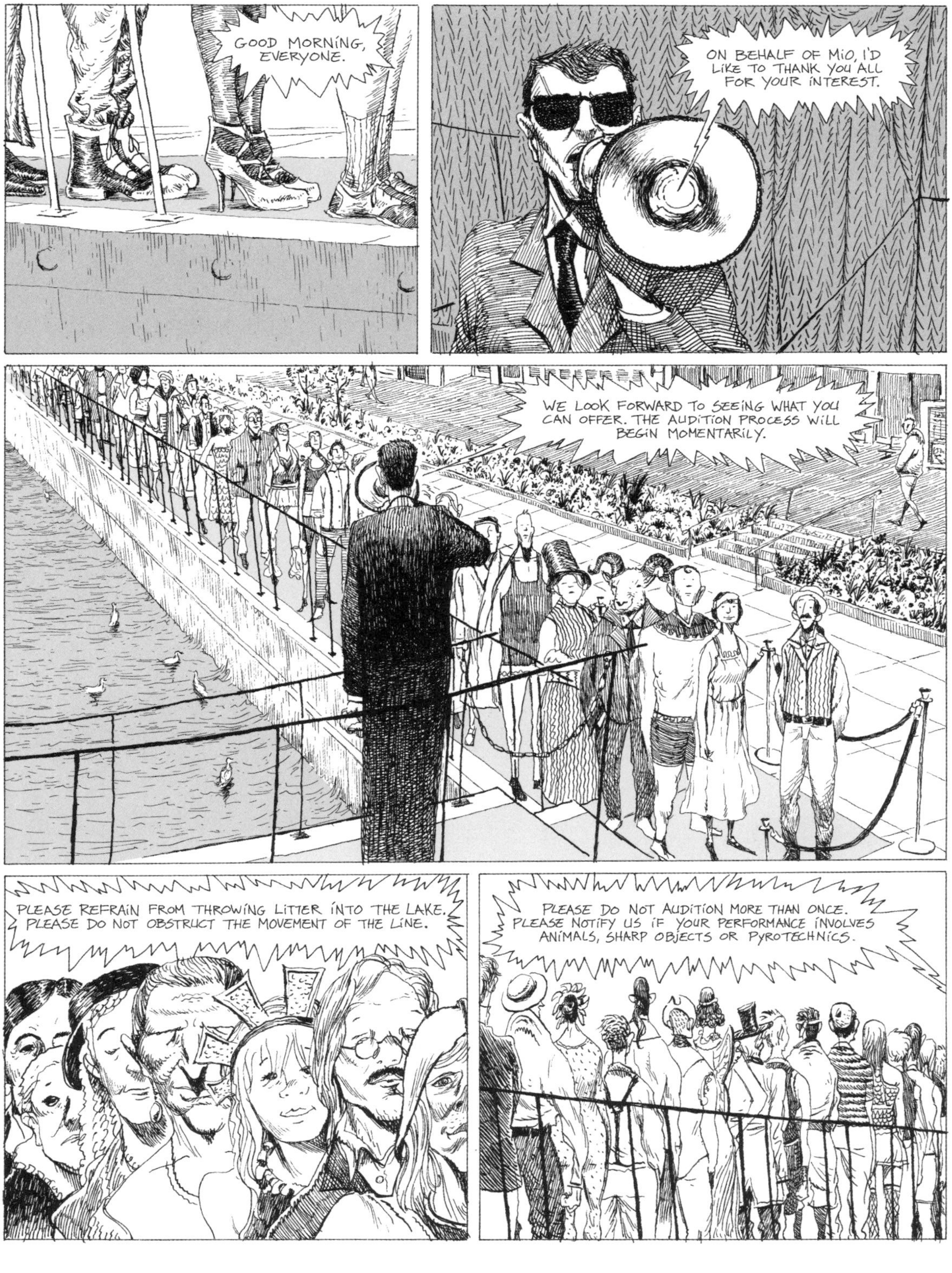
GOOD MORNING, EVERYONE.
ON BEHALF OF MIO, I'D LIKE TO THANK YOU ALL FOR YOUR INTEREST.
WE LOOK FORWARD TO SEEING WHAT YOU CAN OFFER. THE AUDITION PROCESS WILL BEGIN MOMENTARILY.
PLEASE REFRAIN FROM THROWING LITTER INTO THE LAKE. PLEASE DO NOT OBSTRUCT THE MOVEMENT OF THE LINE.
PLEASE DO NOT AUDITION MORE THAN ONCE. PLEASE NOTIFY US IF YOUR PERFORMANCE INVOLVES ANIMALS, SHARP OBJECTS OR PYROTECHNICS.

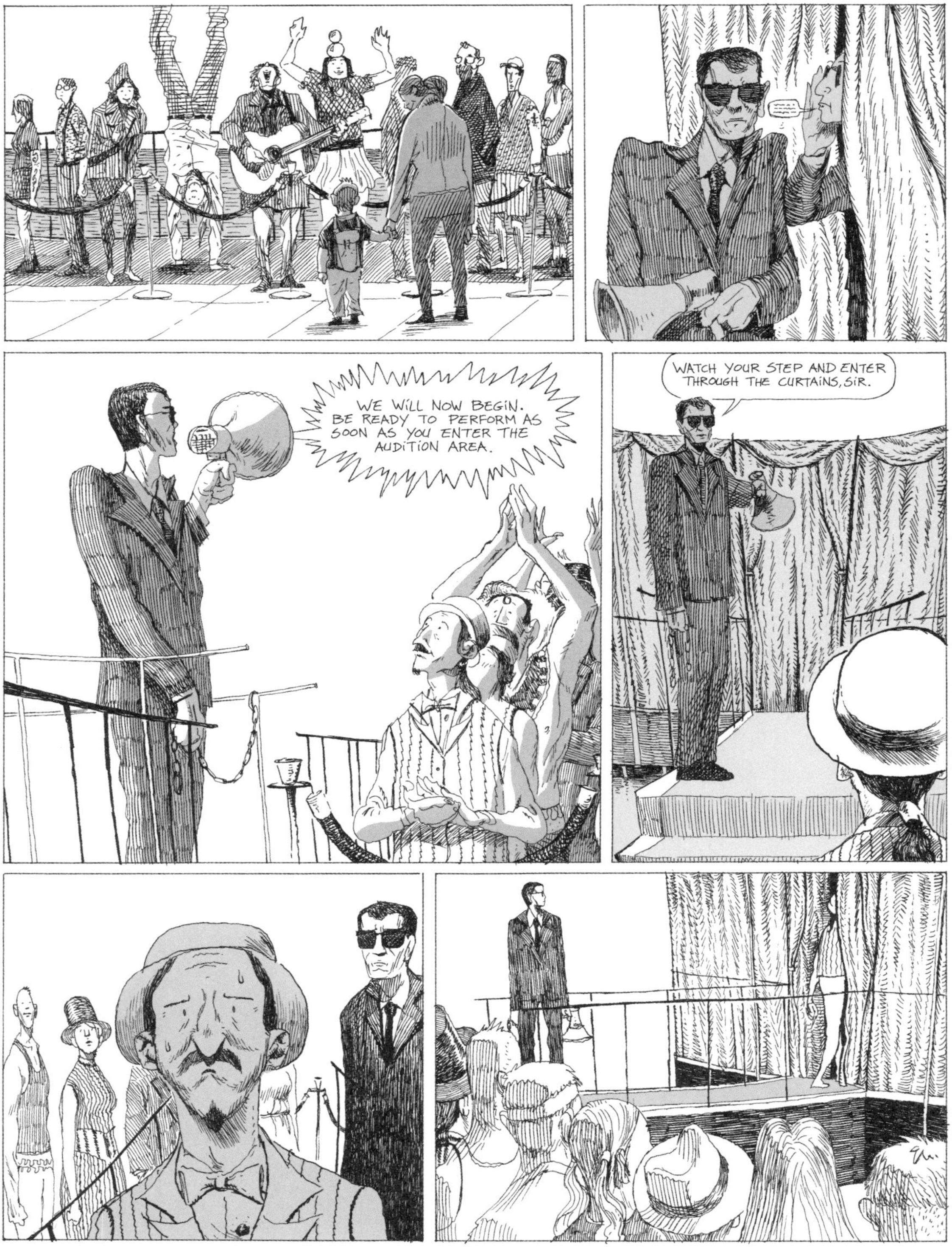
WE WILL NOW BEGIN. BE READY TO PERFORM AS SOON AS YOU ENTER THE AUDITION AREA.
WATCH YOUR STEP AND ENTER THROUGH THE CURTAINS, SIR.

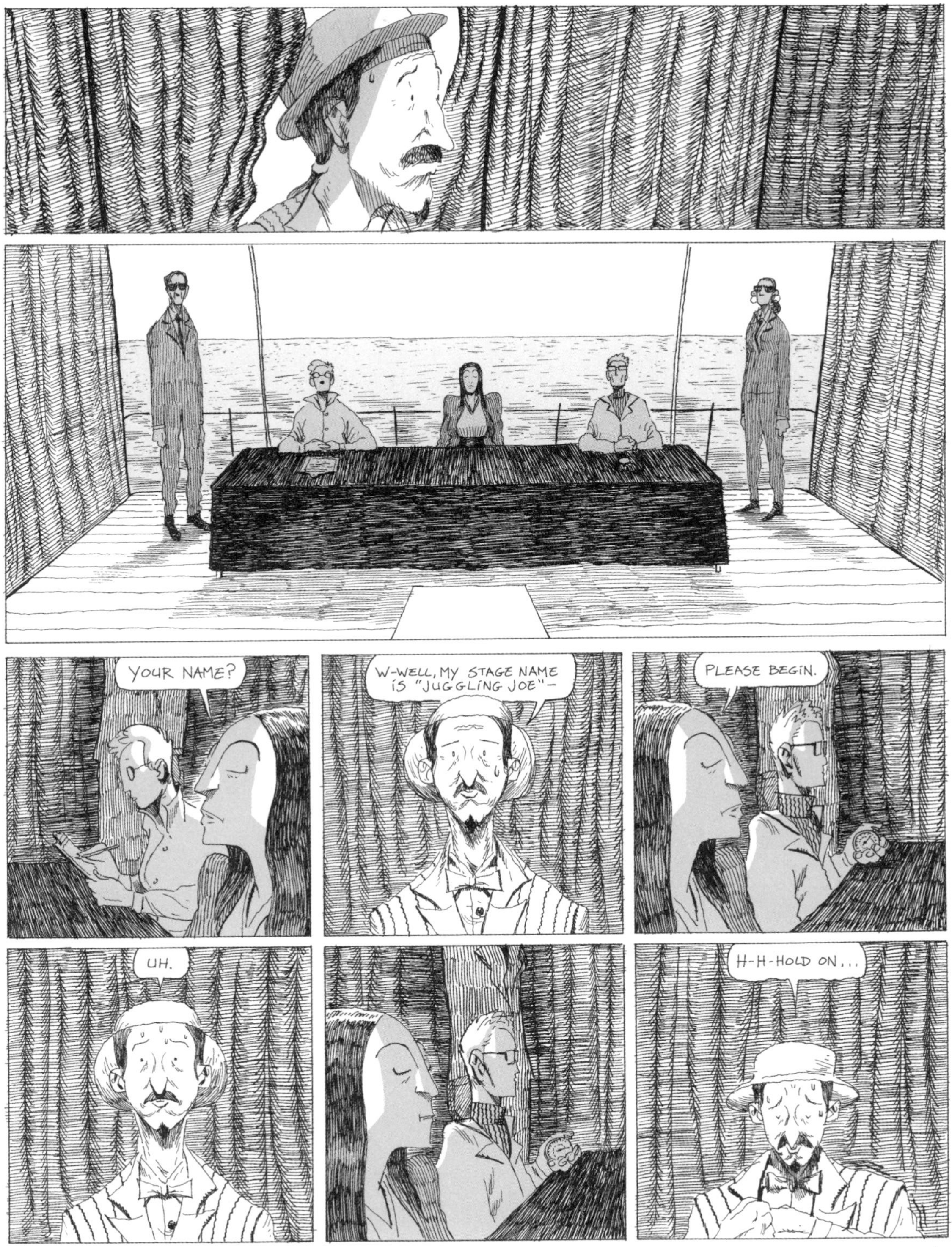
YOUR NAME?
W-WELL, MY STAGE NAME IS "JUGGLING JOE"–
PLEASE BEGIN.
UH.
H-H-HOLD ON...

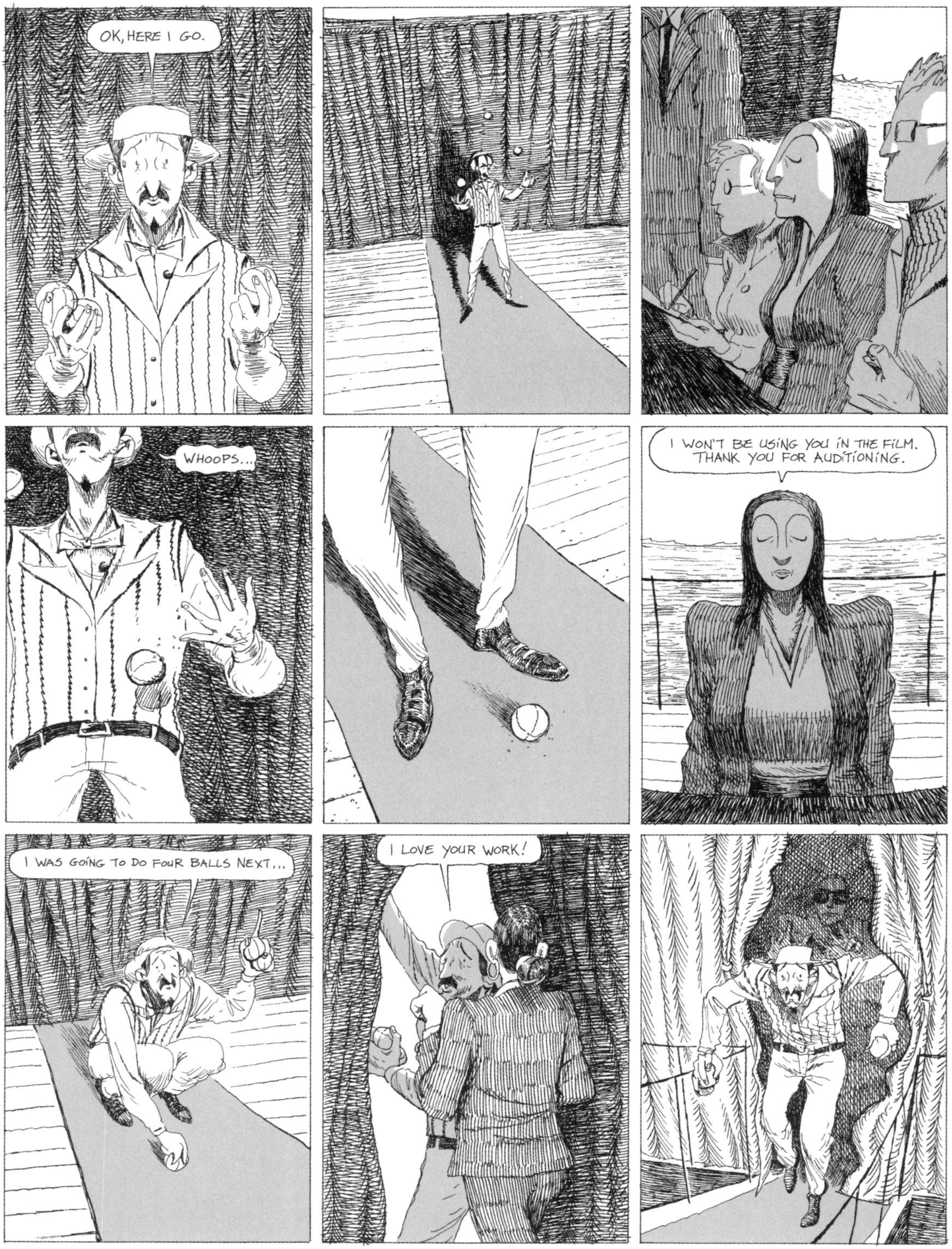
OK, HERE I GO.
WHOOPS....
I WON'T BE USING YOU IN THE FILM. THANK YOU FOR AUDITIONING.
I WAS GOING TO DO FOUR BALLS NEXT...
I LOVE YOUR WORK!

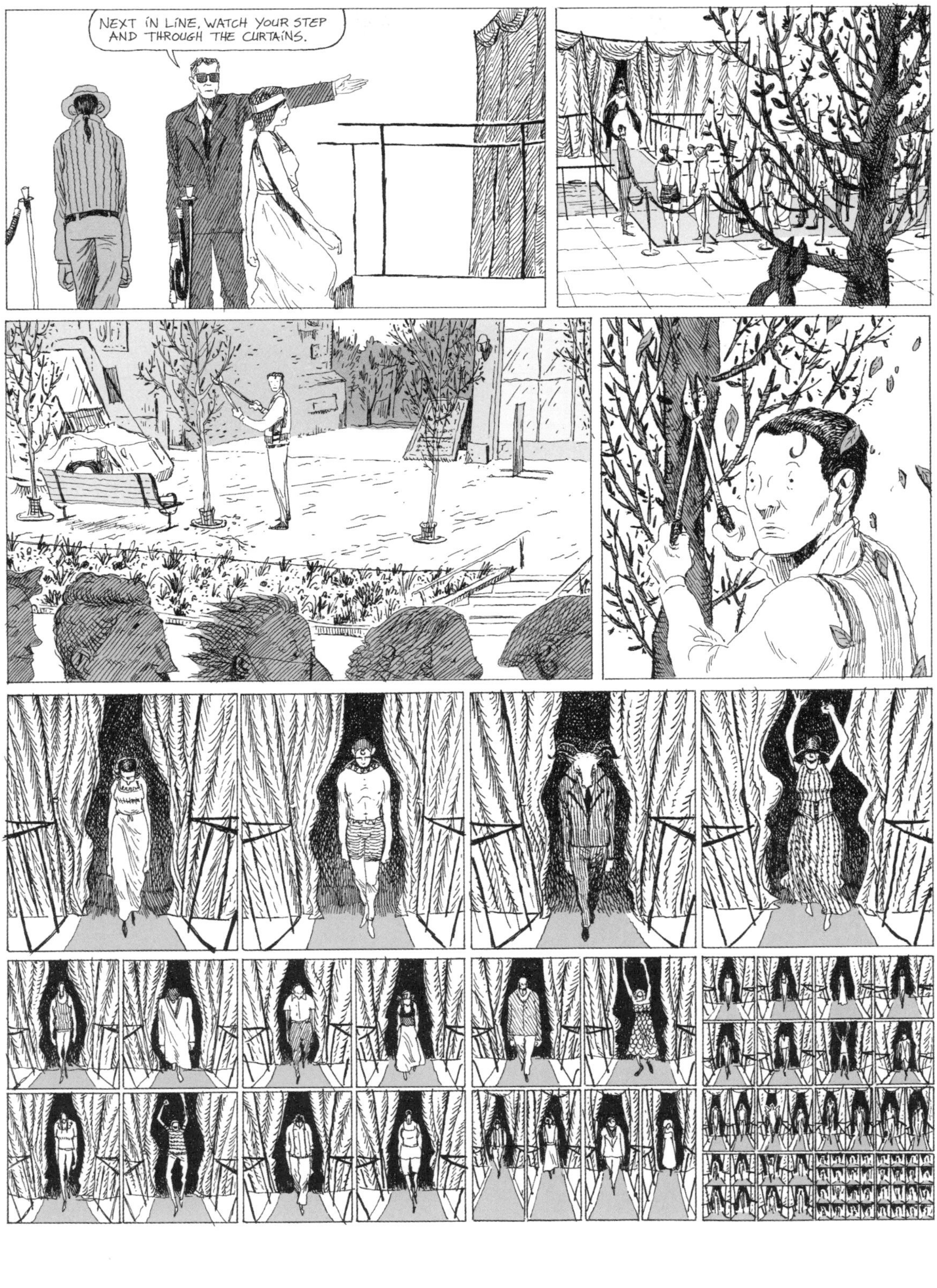
NEXT IN LINE, WATCH YOUR STEP AND THROUGH THE CURTAINS.

I'VE BEEN PLAYING THIS FOR OVER A DECADE NOW!
ALL I'M SAYING IS THAT IT'S ON THEM IF THEY'RE NOT IMPRESSED.
THIS IS IT!
DUM DA-DUM
DA-DUM, DUM
DA-DA-DUM
HA! I'M IN!

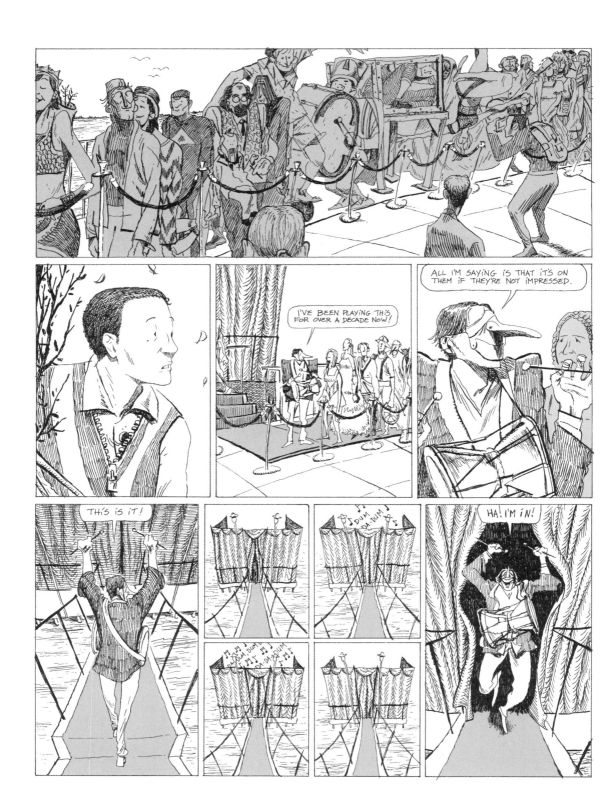

HAHA!

TODAY'S AUDITIONS ARE OVER. WE WILL HAND OUT NUMBERED TICKETS SO YOU CAN RESUME YOUR POSITION IN LINE AT 10 AM TOMORROW.

CAN YOU BELIEVE HOW MANY PEOPLE SHOWED UP?

THEY DIDN'T EVEN GET THROUGH HALF OF THEM TODAY.

ALRIGHT, LET'S CLEAN UP THEIR CRAP...

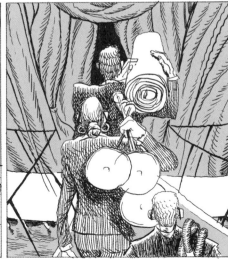

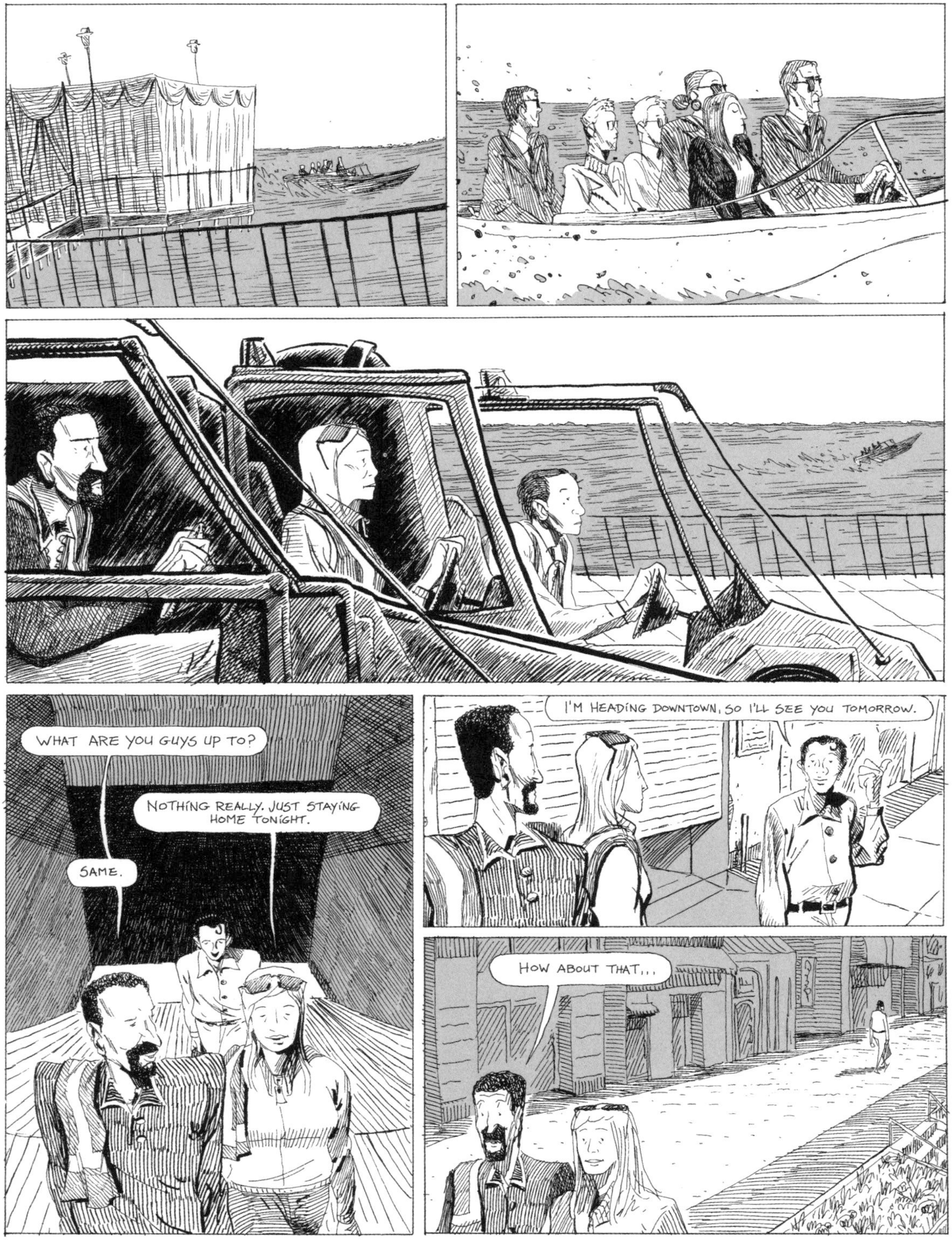
WHAT ARE YOU GUYS UP TO?
NOTHING REALLY. JUST STAYING HOME TONIGHT.
SAME.
I'M HEADING DOWNTOWN, SO I'LL SEE YOU TOMORROW.
HOW ABOUT THAT...

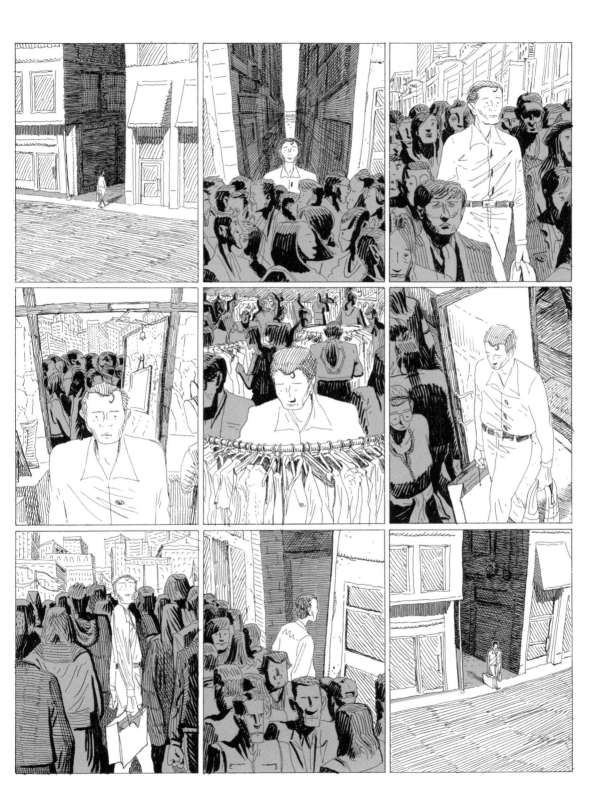

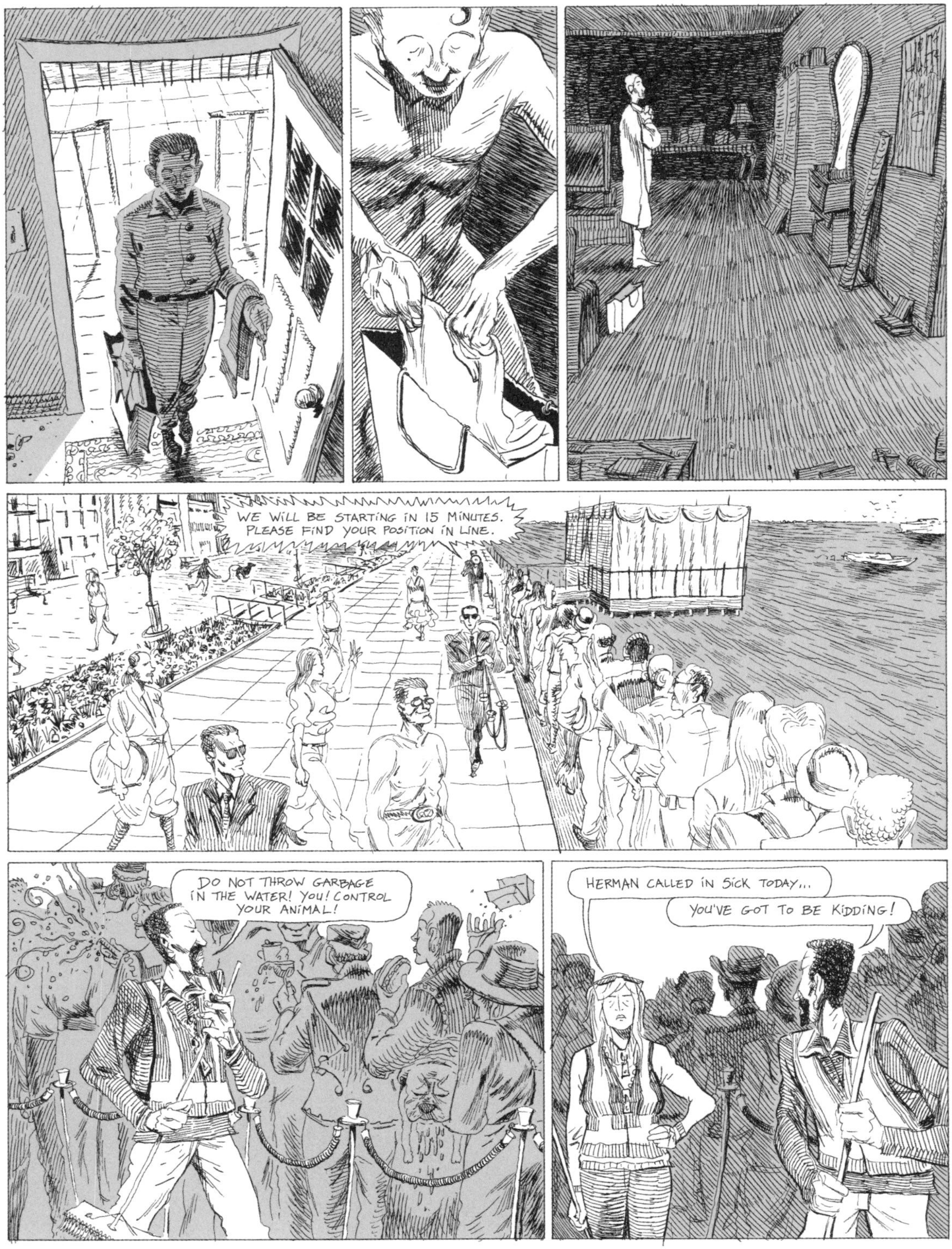
WE WILL BE STARTING IN 15 MINUTES. PLEASE FIND YOUR POSITION IN LINE.
DO NOT THROW GARBAGE IN THE WATER! YOU! CONTROL YOUR ANIMAL!
HERMAN CALLED IN SICK TODAY...
YOU'VE GOT TO BE KIDDING!

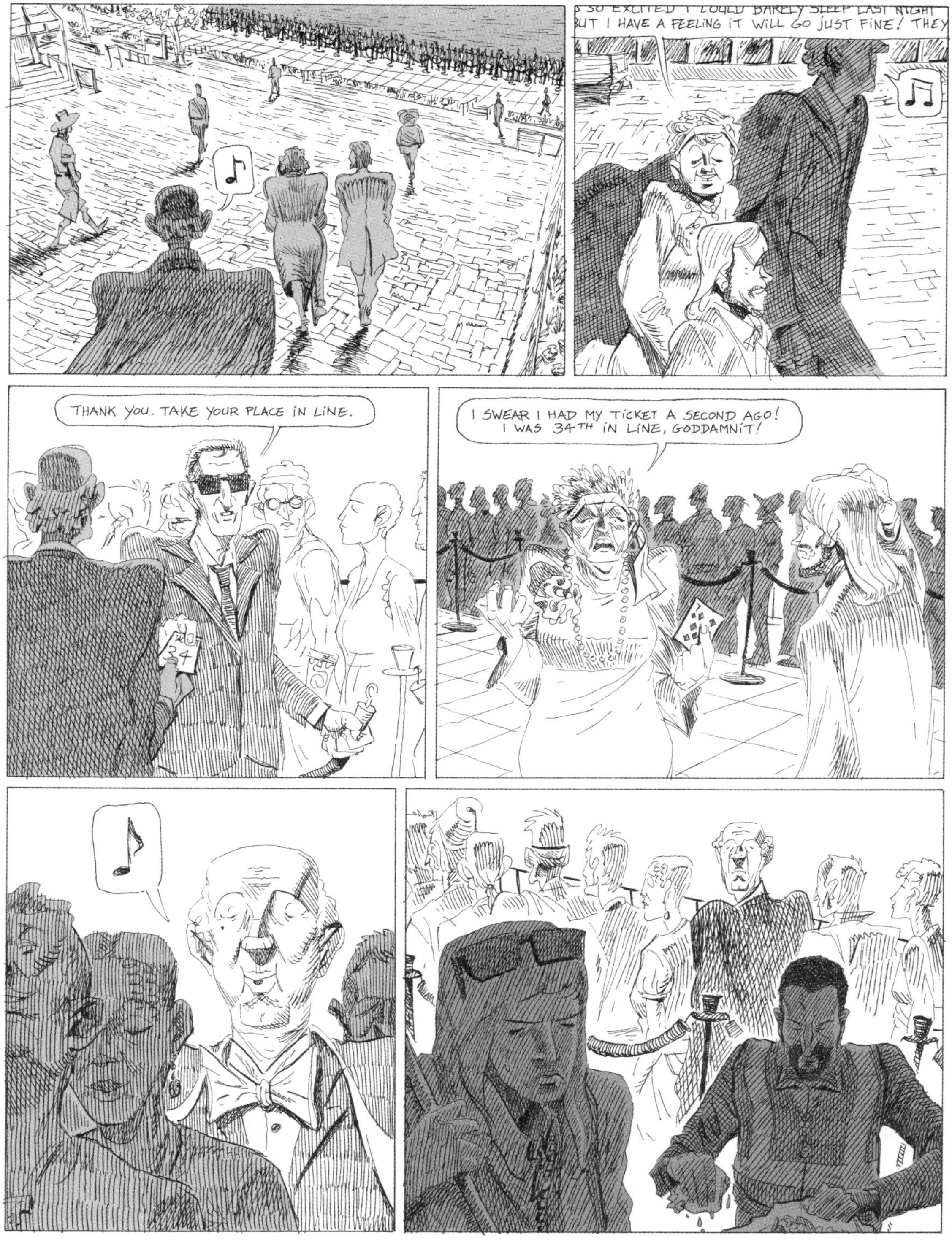
SO EXCITED I COULD BARELY SLEEP LAST NIGHT
BUT I HAVE A FEELING IT WILL GO JUST FINE! THEY
THANK YOU. TAKE YOUR PLACE IN LINE.
34
I SWEAR I HAD MY TICKET A SECOND AGO! I WAS 34TH IN LINE, GODDAMNIT!

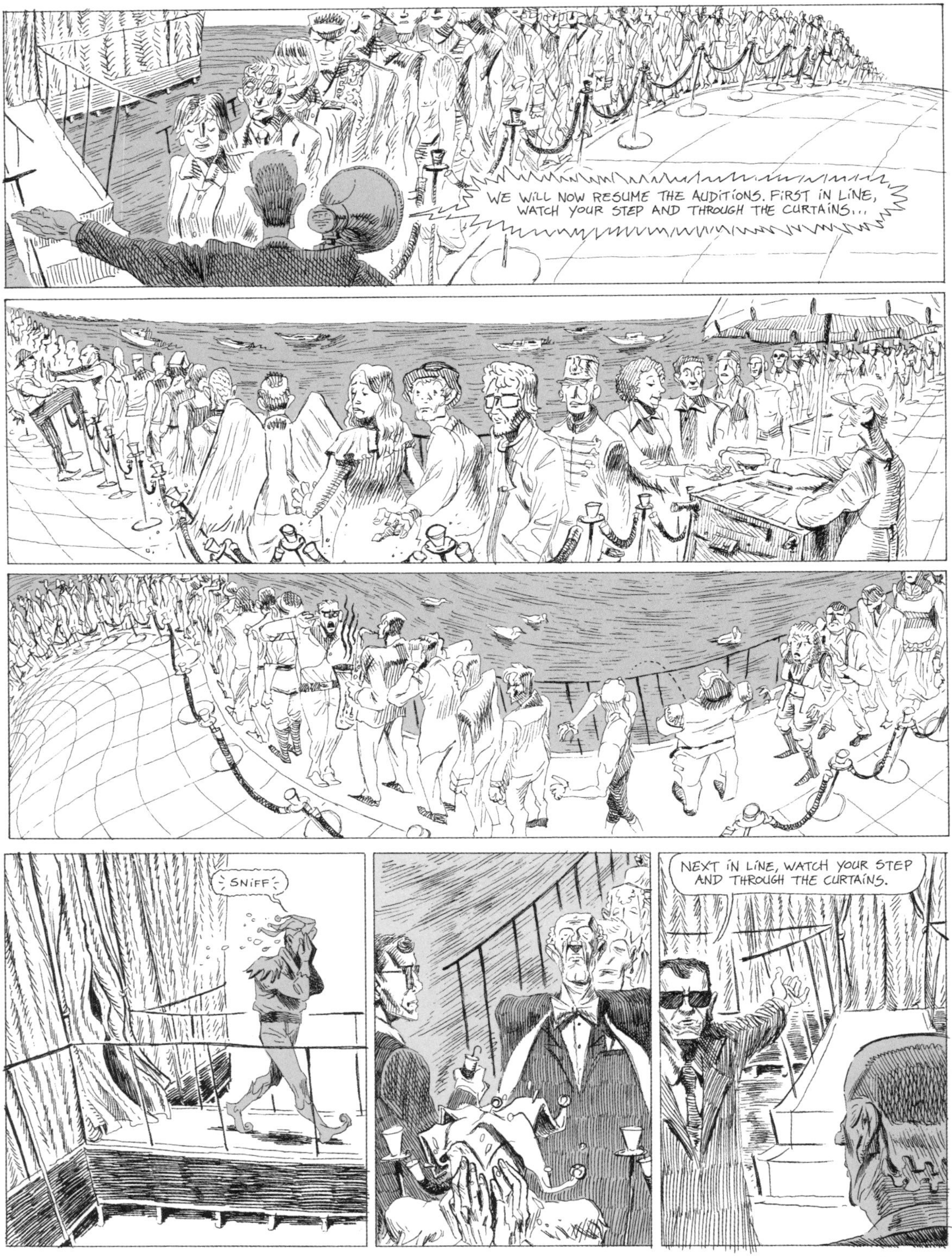
WE WILL NOW RESUME THE AUDITIONS. FIRST IN LINE, WATCH YOUR STEP AND THROUGH THE CURTAINS...
SNIFF
NEXT IN LINE, WATCH YOUR STEP AND THROUGH THE CURTAINS.

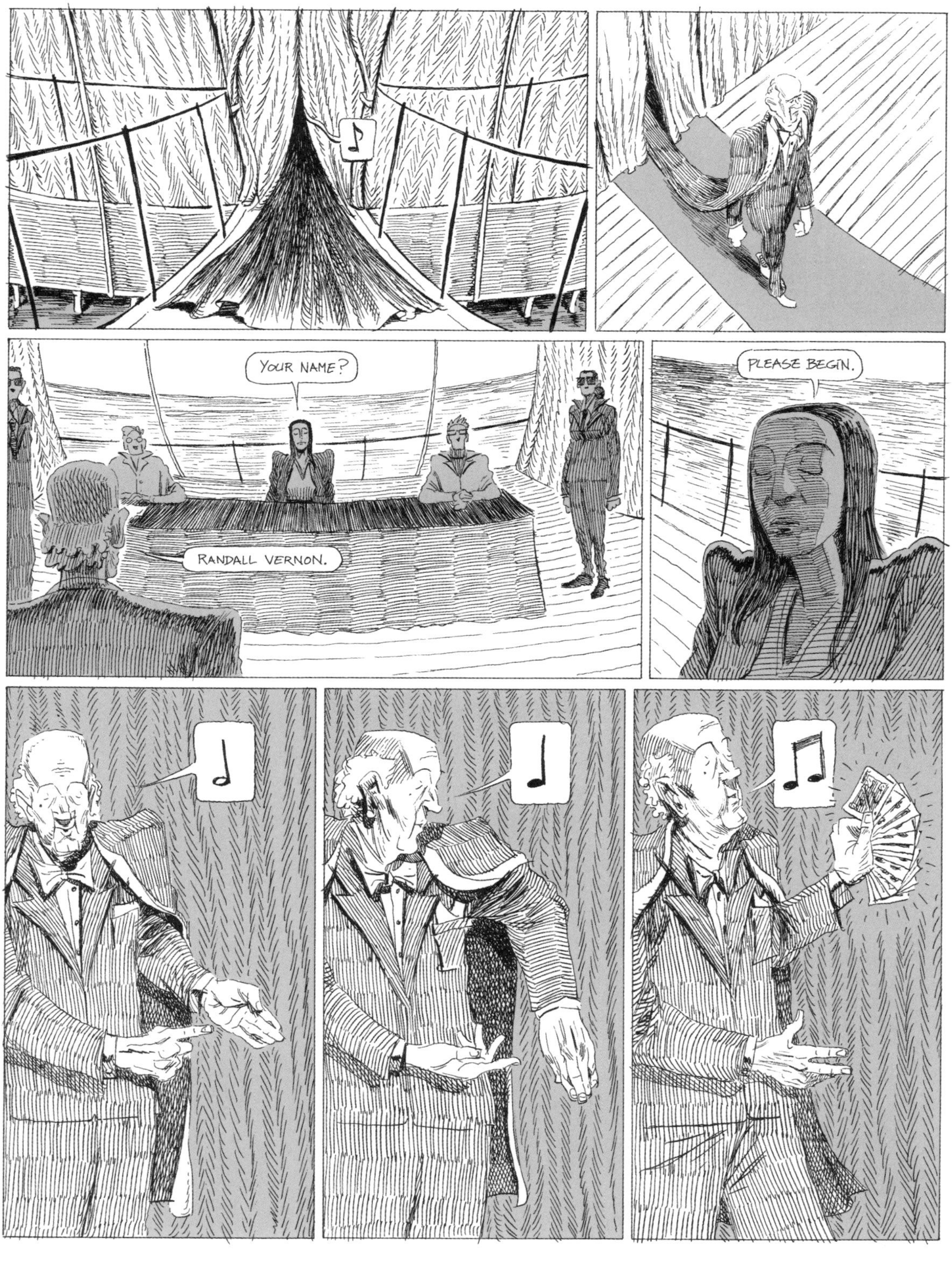
YOUR NAME?
RANDALL VERNON.
PLEASE BEGIN.

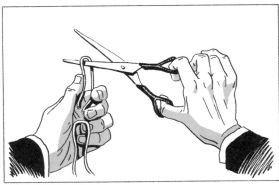

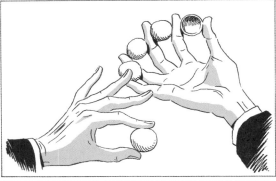

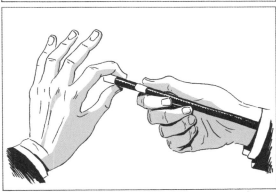

OK, OK. THANK YOU.

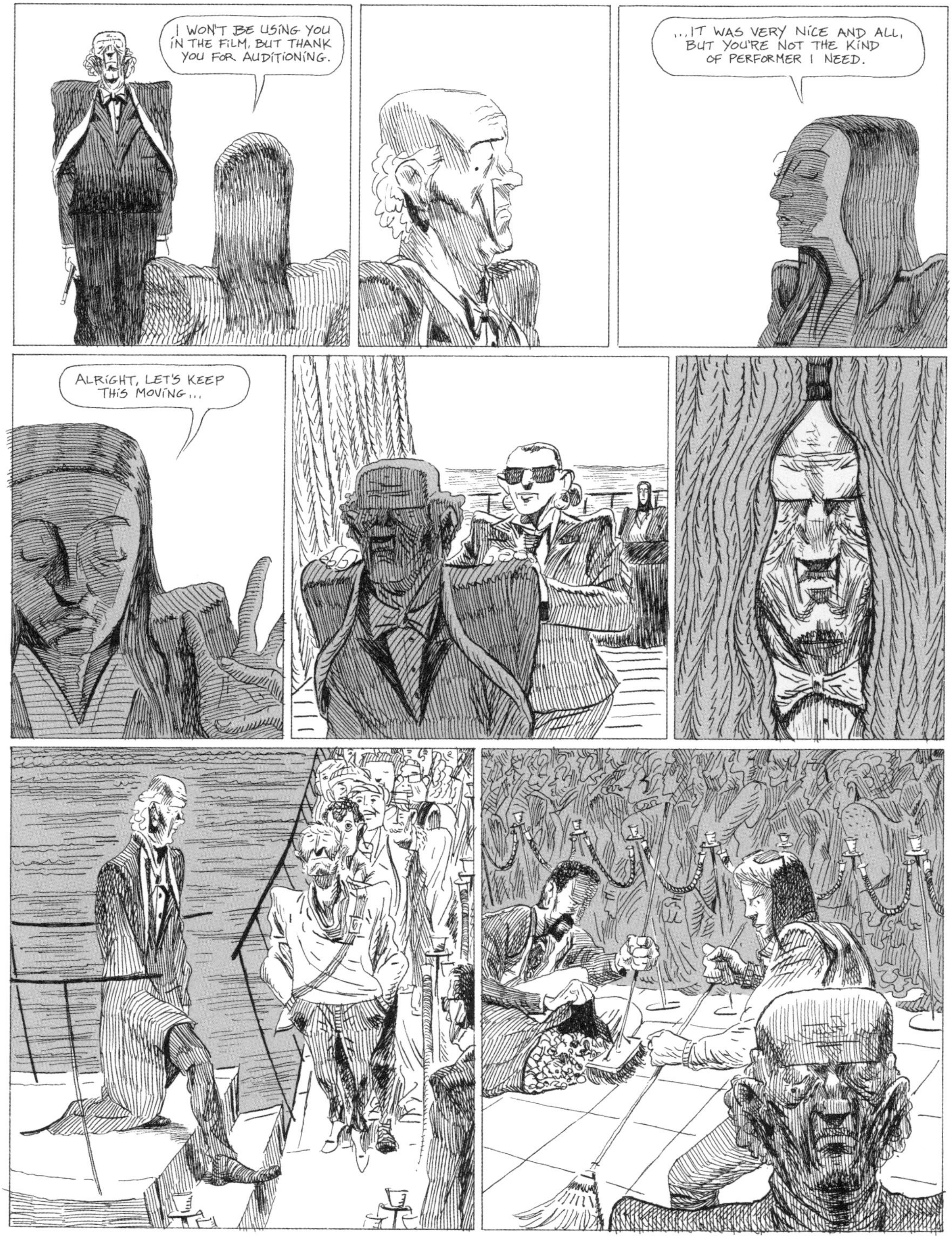
I WON'T BE USING YOU IN THE FILM, BUT THANK YOU FOR AUDITIONING.
...IT WAS VERY NICE AND ALL, BUT YOU'RE NOT THE KIND OF PERFORMER I NEED.
ALRIGHT, LET'S KEEP THIS MOVING...

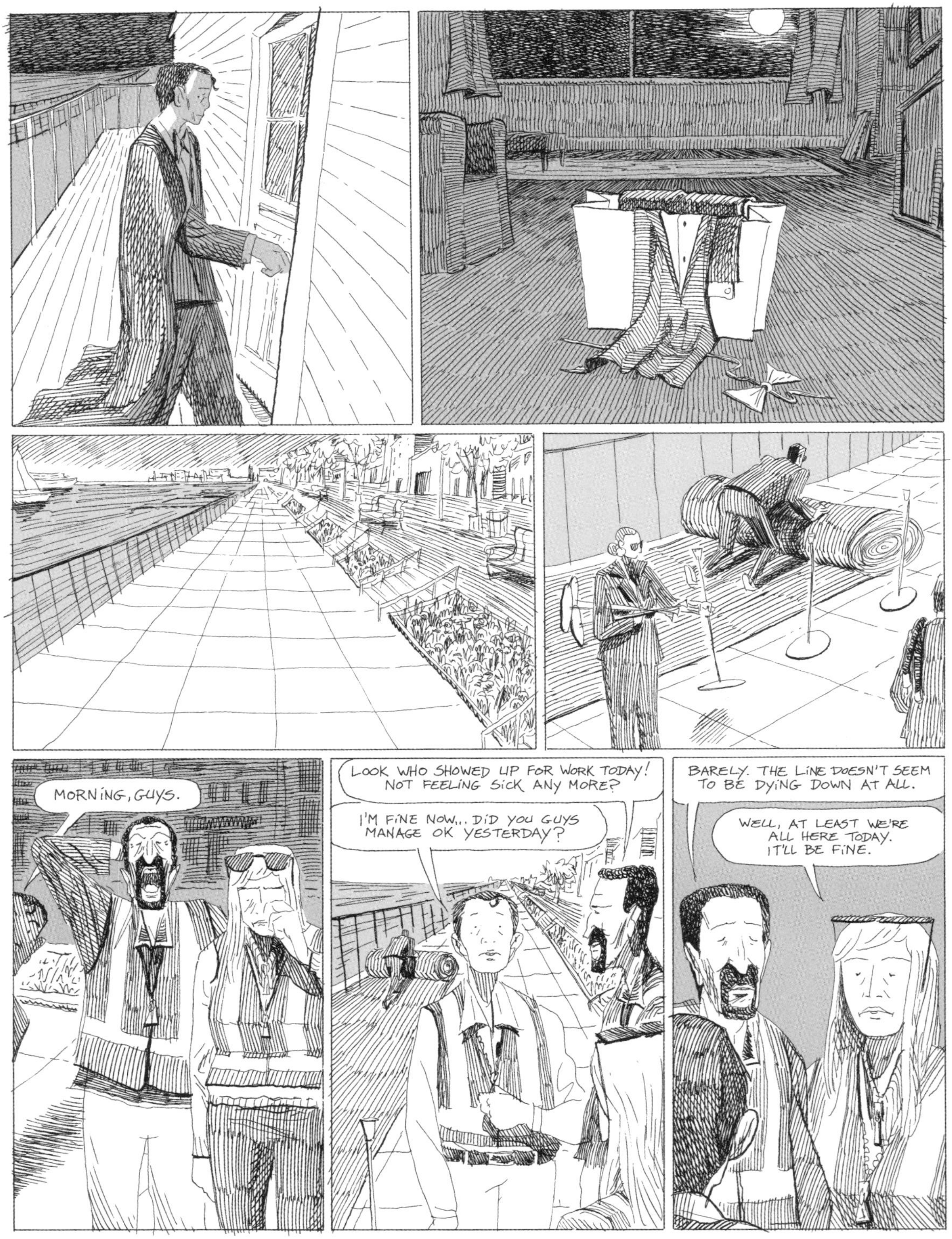
MORNING, GUYS.
LOOK WHO SHOWED UP FOR WORK TODAY! NOT FEELING SICK ANY MORE?
I'M FINE NOW... DID YOU GUYS MANAGE OK YESTERDAY?
BARELY. THE LINE DOESN'T SEEM TO BE DYING DOWN AT ALL.
WELL, AT LEAST WE'RE ALL HERE TODAY. IT'LL BE FINE.

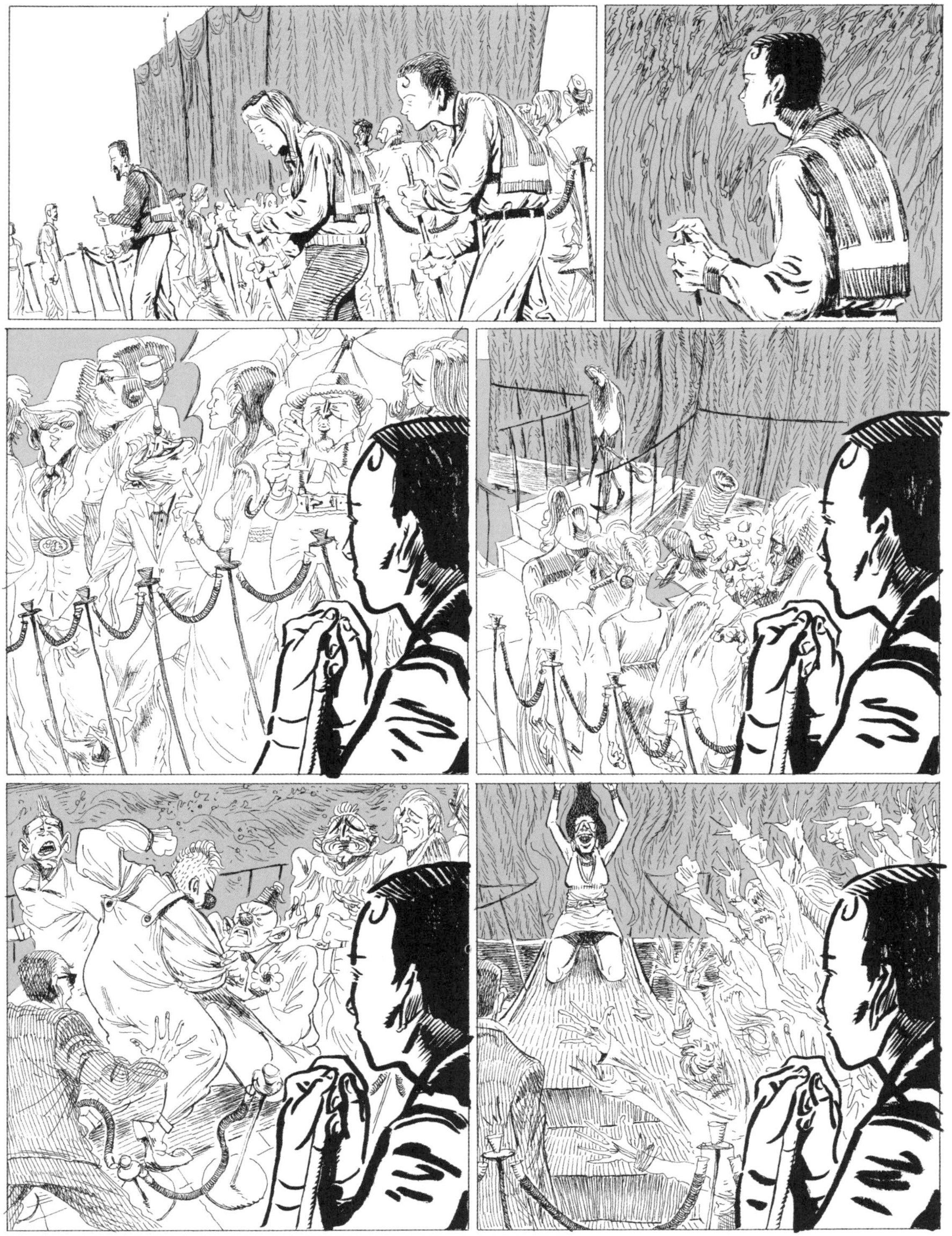

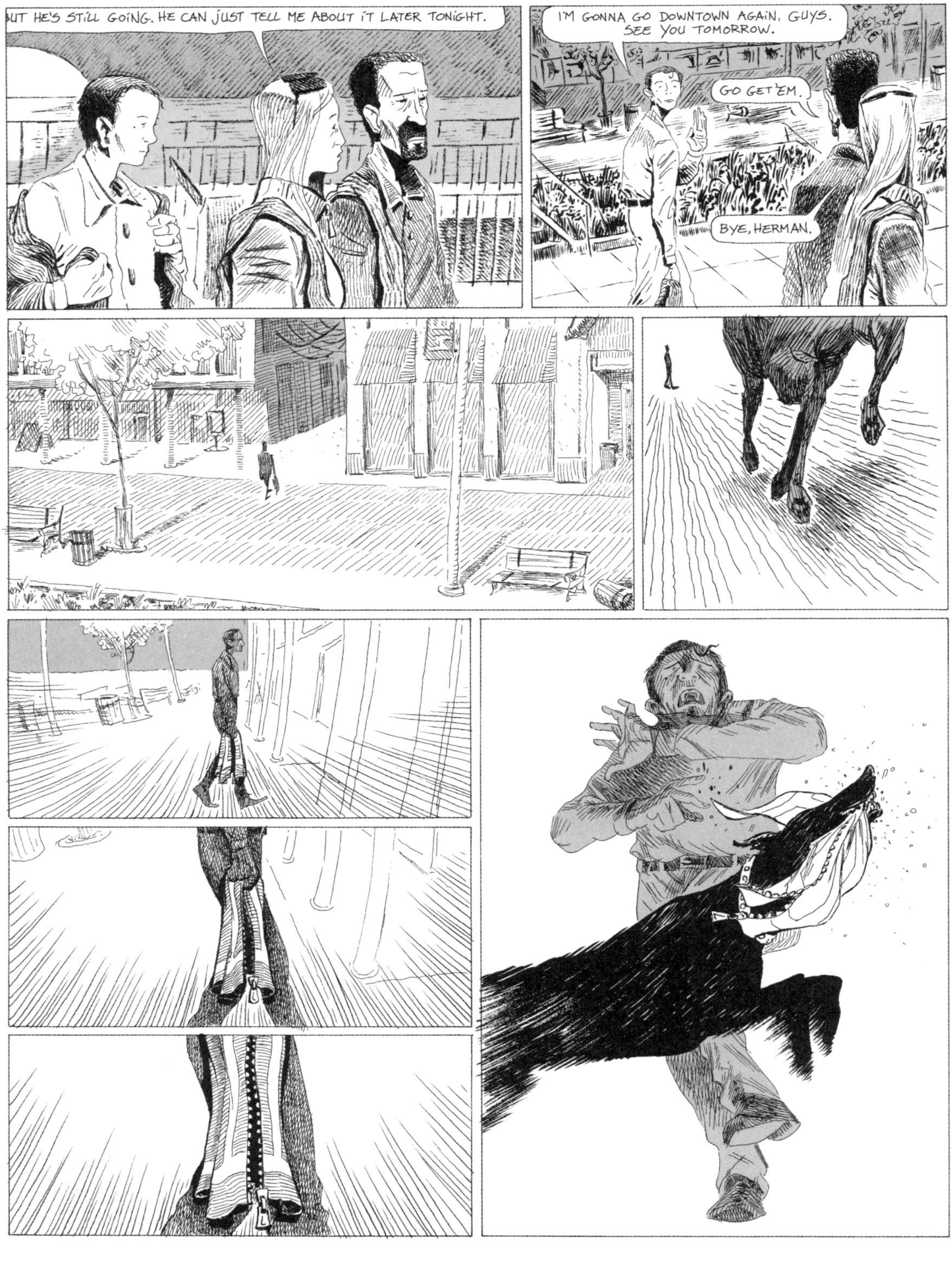
BUT HE'S STILL GOING. HE CAN JUST TELL ME ABOUT IT LATER TONIGHT.
I'M GONNA GO DOWNTOWN AGAIN, GUYS. SEE YOU TOMORROW.
GO GET 'EM.
BYE, HERMAN.

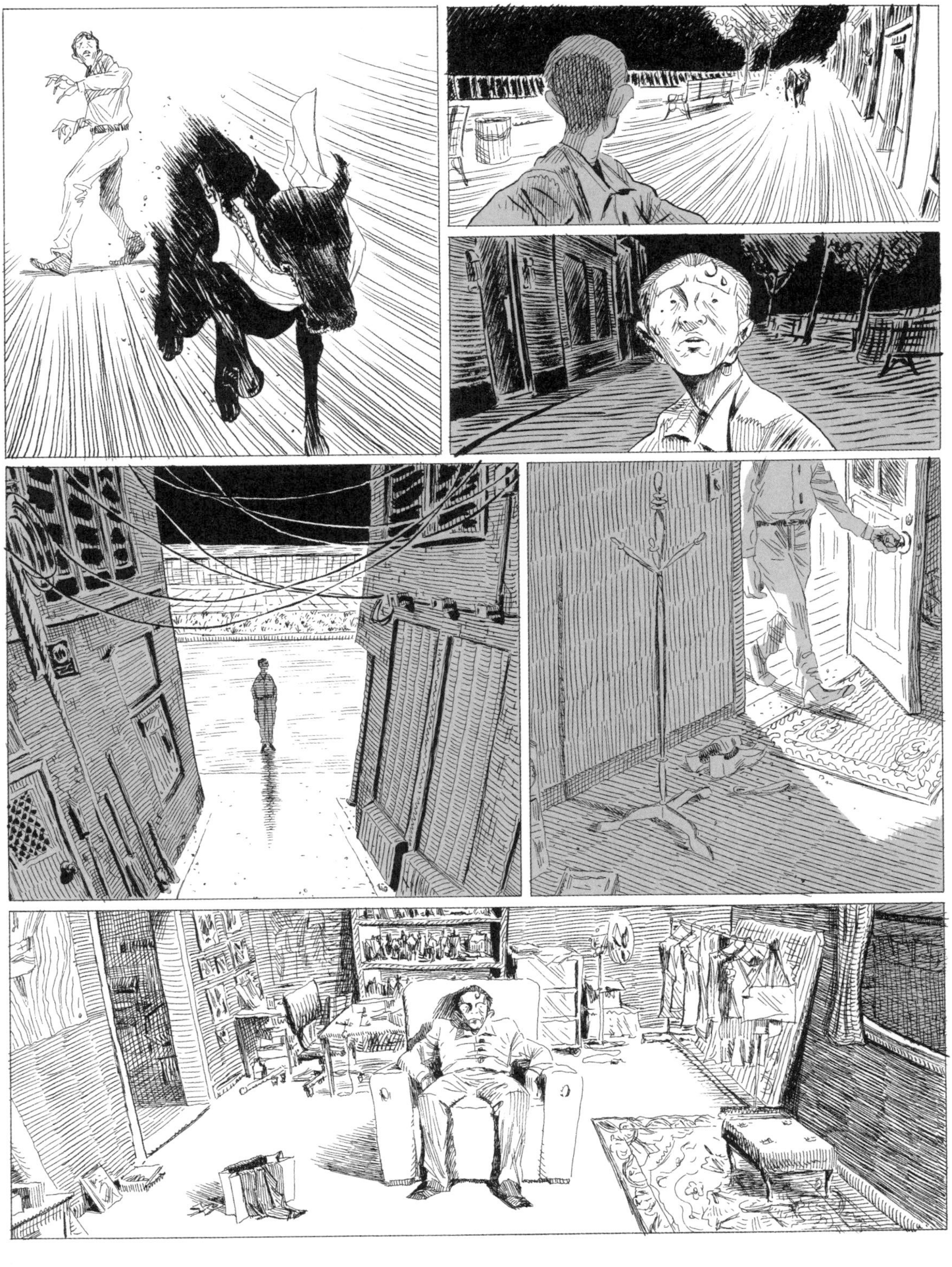

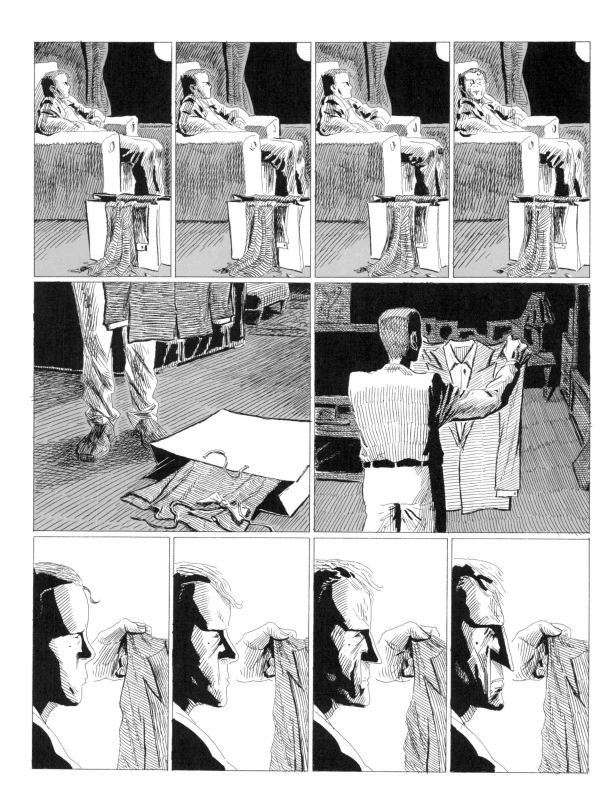

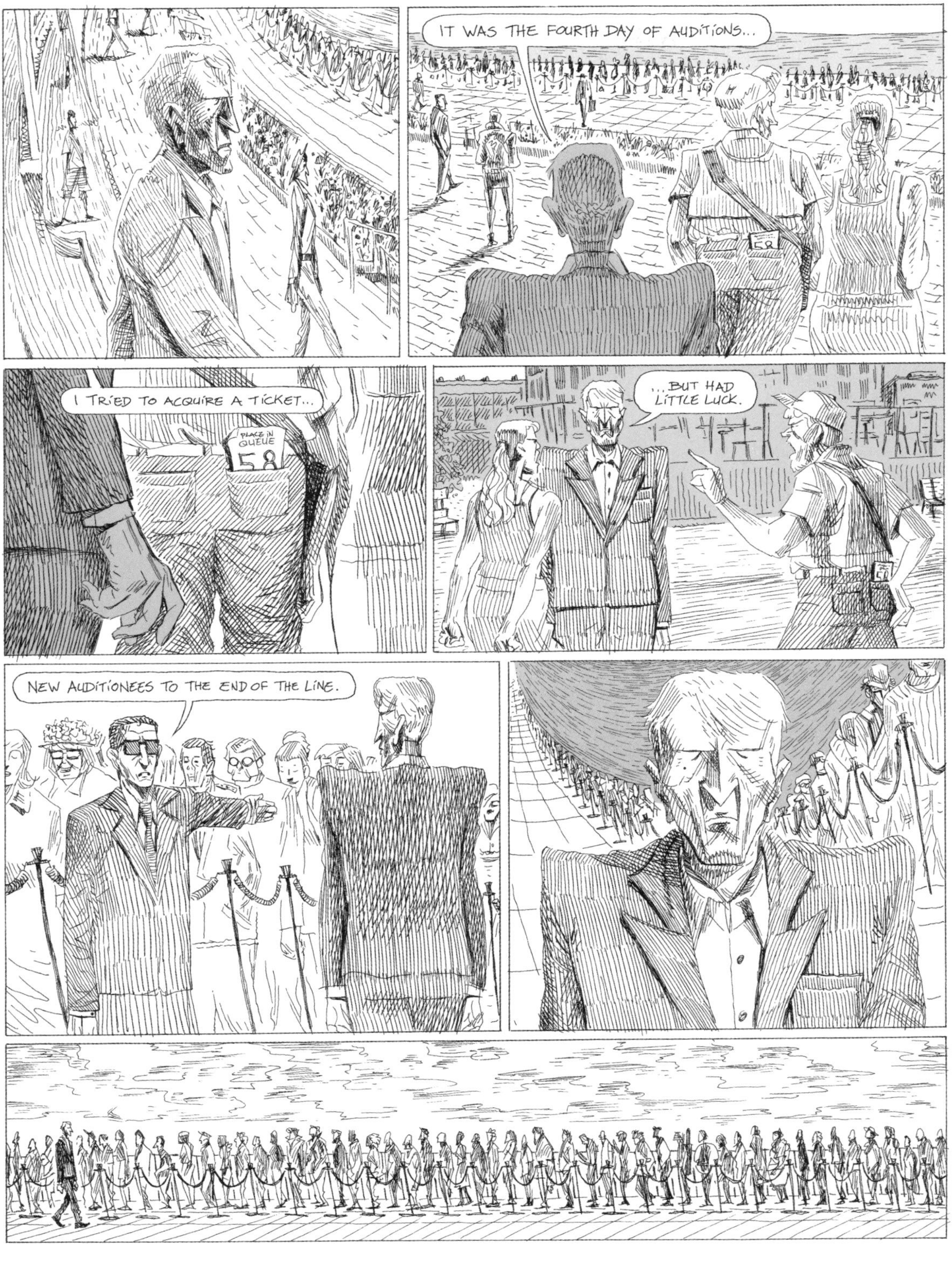
IT WAS THE FOURTH DAY OF AUDITIONS...
58
I TRIED TO ACQUIRE A TICKET...
PLACE IN QUEUE
58
...BUT HAD LITTLE LUCK.
NEW AUDITIONEES TO THE END OF THE LINE.

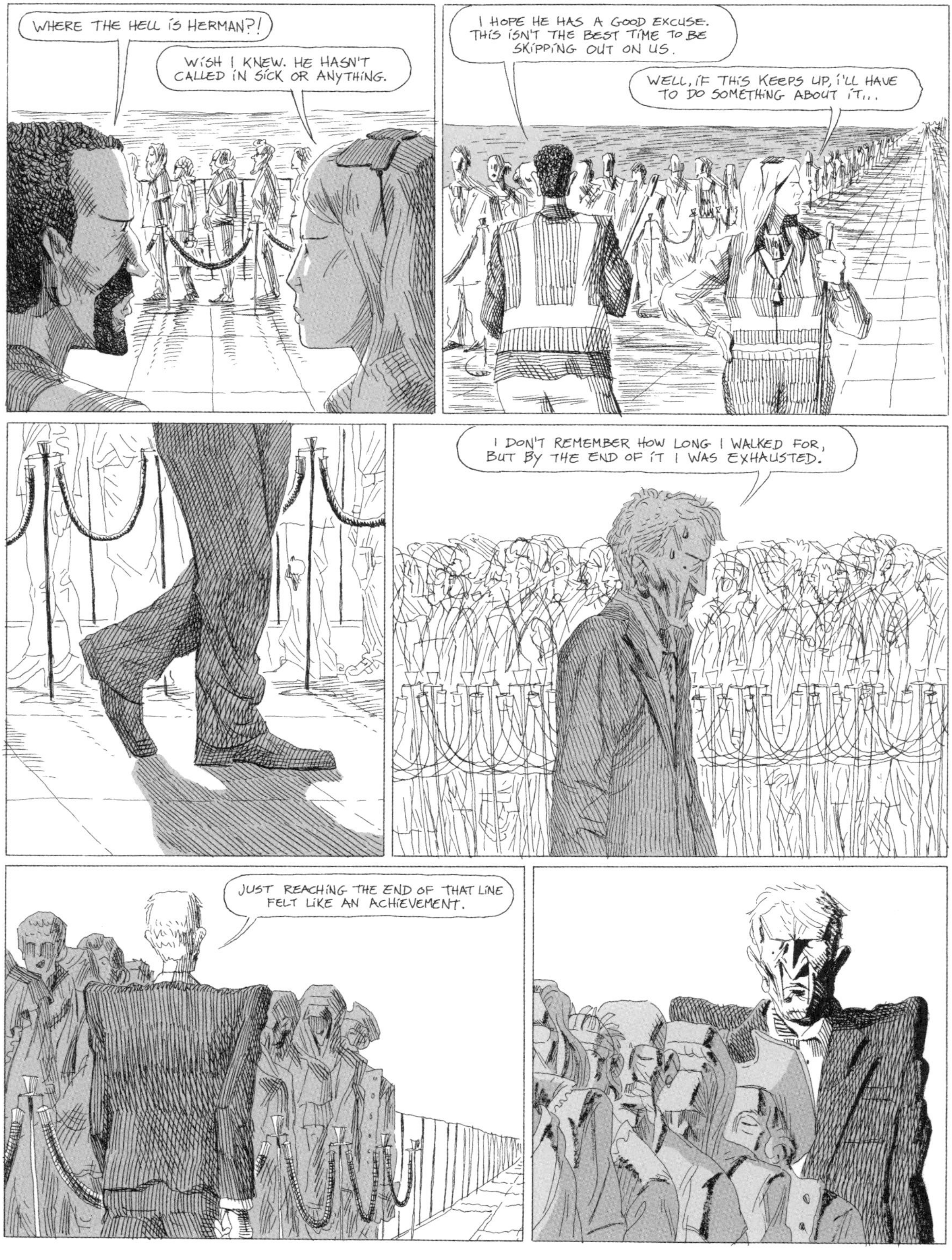
WHERE THE HELL IS HERMAN?!
WISH I KNEW. HE HASN'T CALLED IN SICK OR ANYTHING.
I HOPE HE HAS A GOOD EXCUSE. THIS ISN'T THE BEST TIME TO BE SKIPPING OUT ON US.
WELL, IF THIS KEEPS UP, I'LL HAVE TO DO SOMETHING ABOUT IT...
I DON'T REMEMBER HOW LONG I WALKED FOR, BUT BY THE END OF IT I WAS EXHAUSTED.
JUST REACHING THE END OF THAT LINE FELT LIKE AN ACHIEVEMENT.

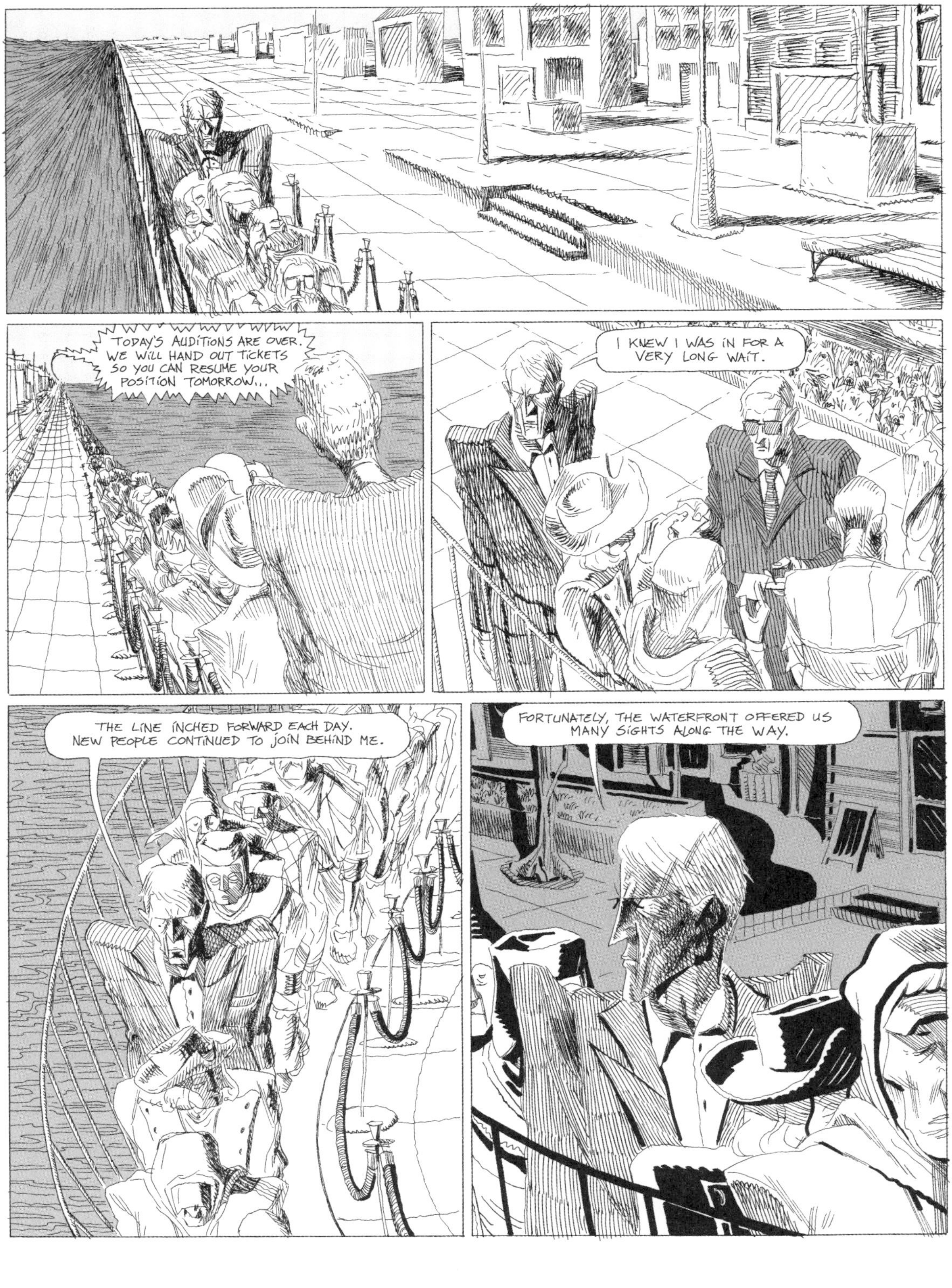
TODAY'S AUDITIONS ARE OVER. WE WILL HAND OUT TICKETS SO YOU CAN RESUME YOUR POSITION TOMORROW...
I KNEW I WAS IN FOR A VERY LONG WAIT.
THE LINE INCHED FORWARD EACH DAY. NEW PEOPLE CONTINUED TO JOIN BEHIND ME.
FORTUNATELY, THE WATERFRONT OFFERED US MANY SIGHTS ALONG THE WAY.

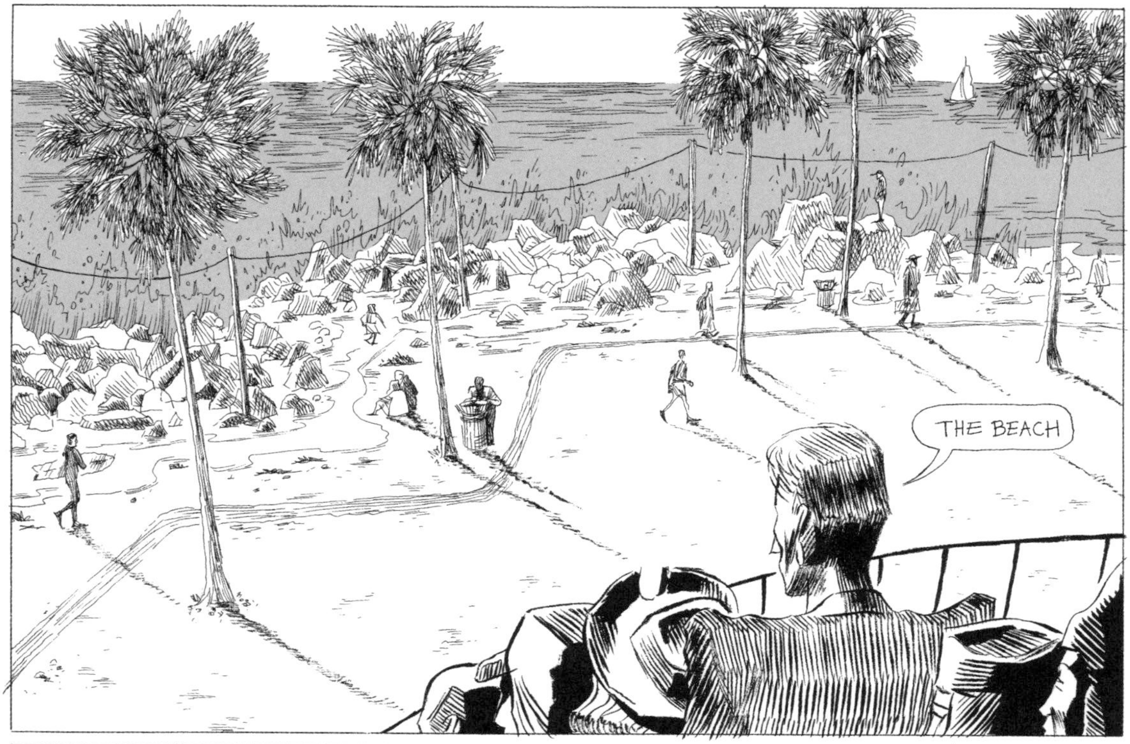
THE BEACH

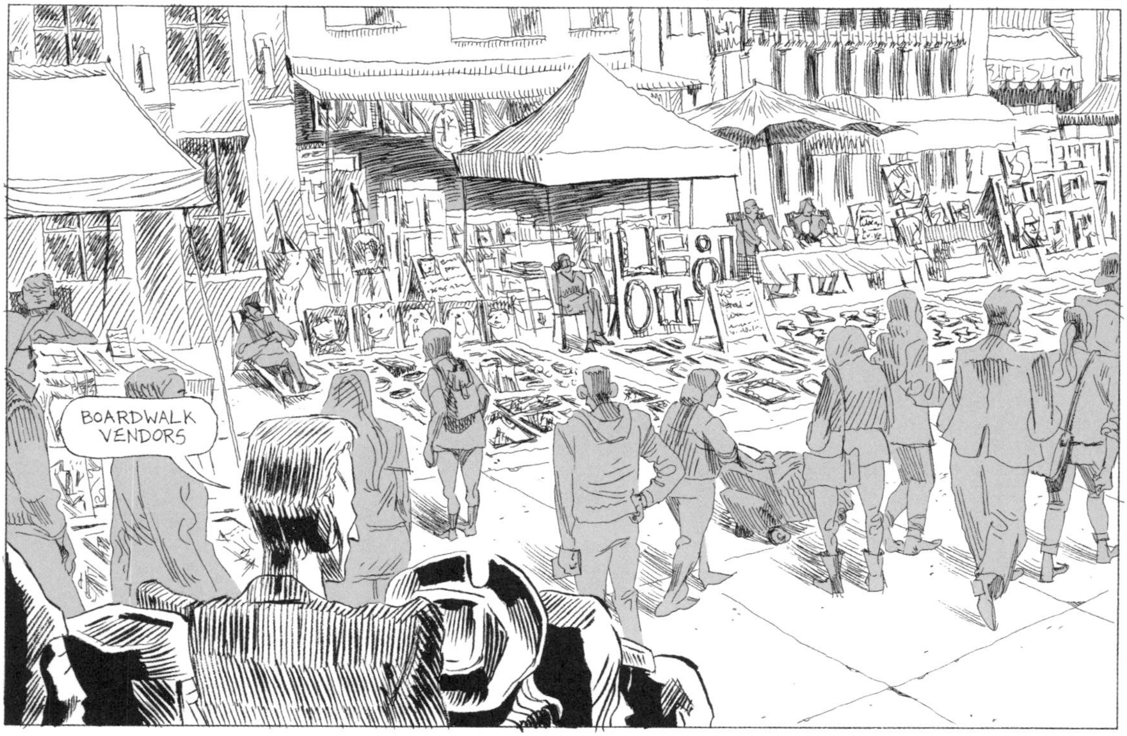
BOARDWALK VENDORS

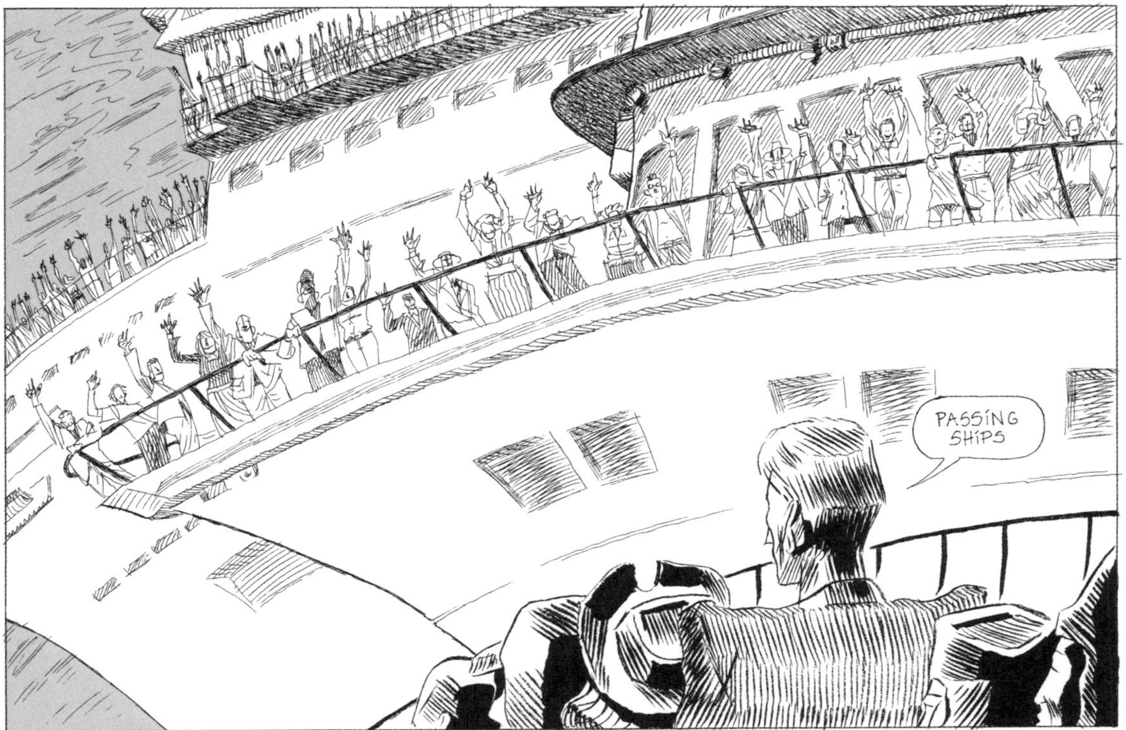
PASSING SHIPS

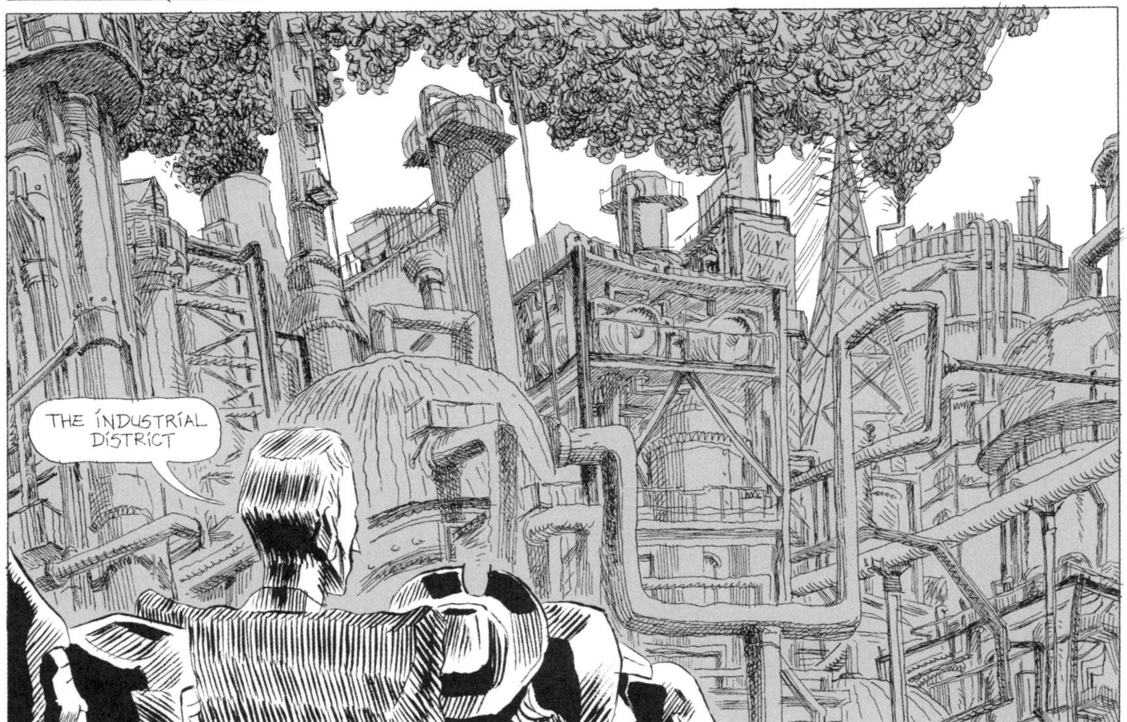
THE INDUSTRIAL DISTRICT

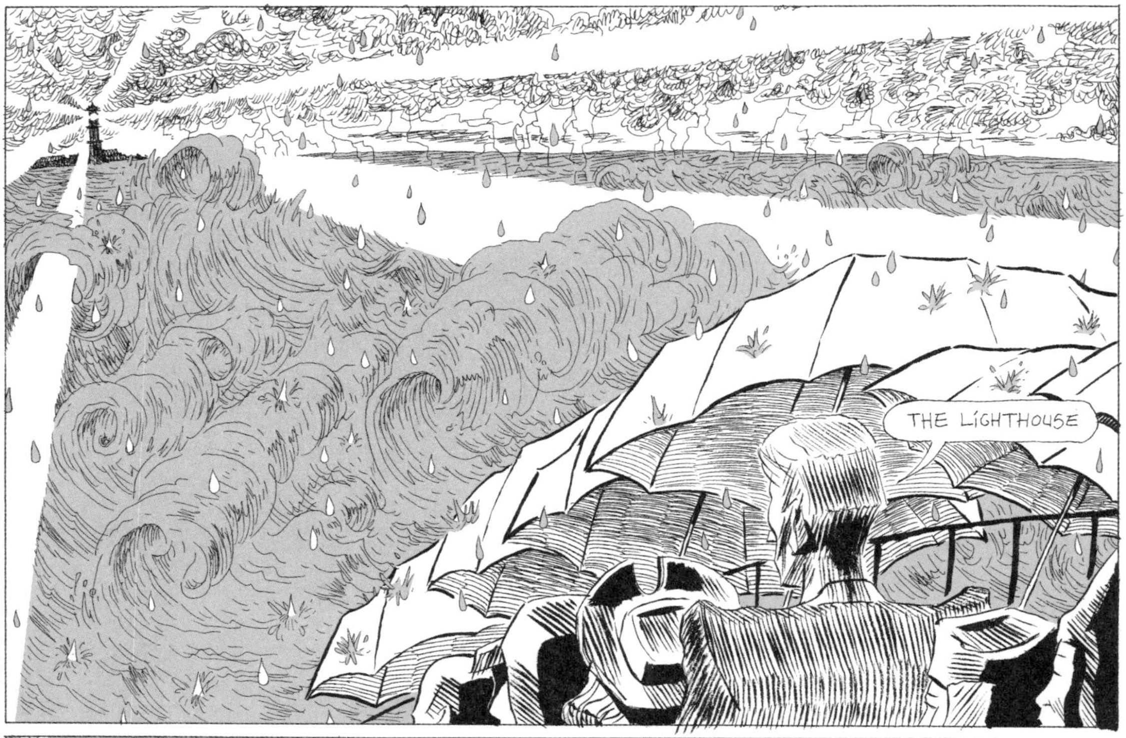
THE LIGHTHOUSE

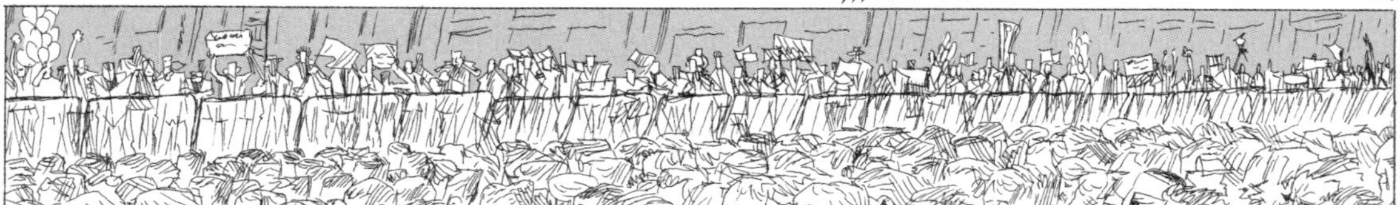
MARATHONERS

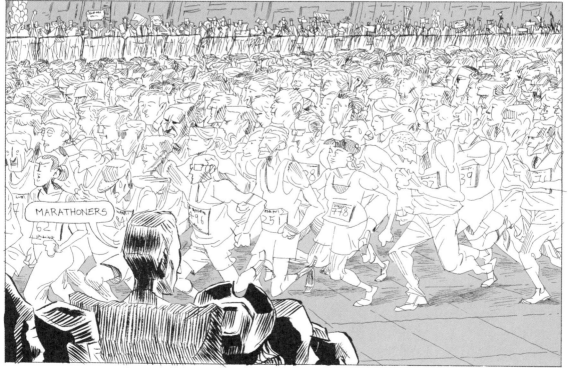

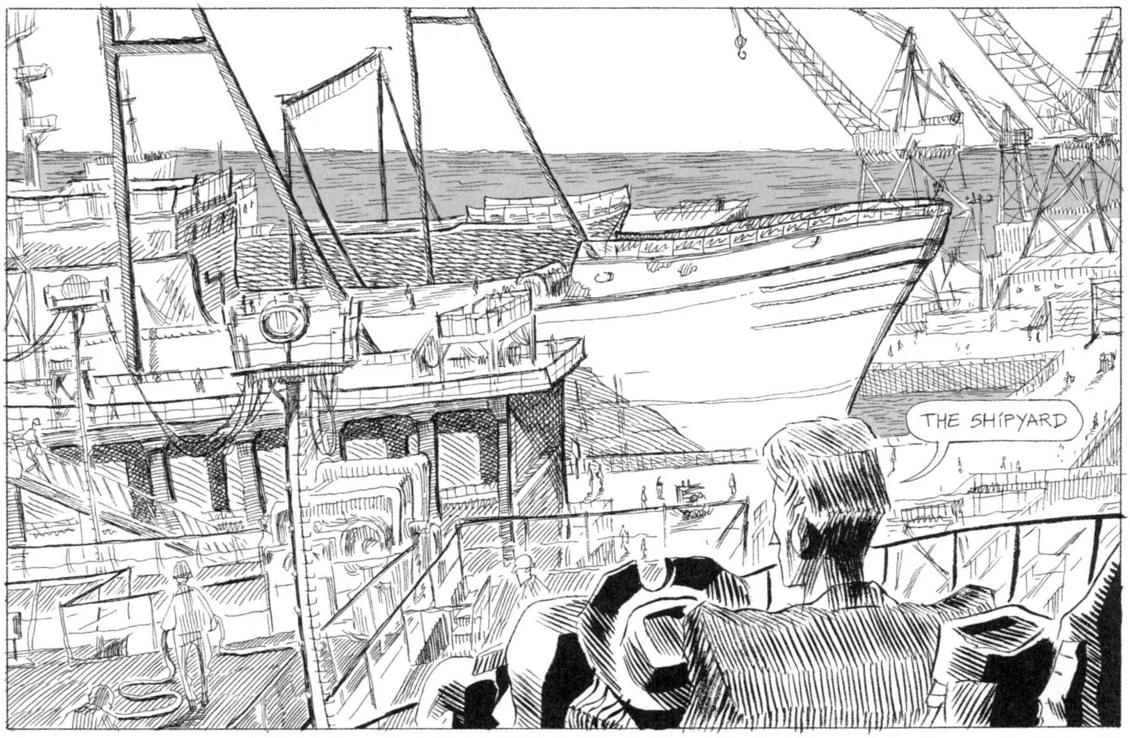
THE SHIPYARD

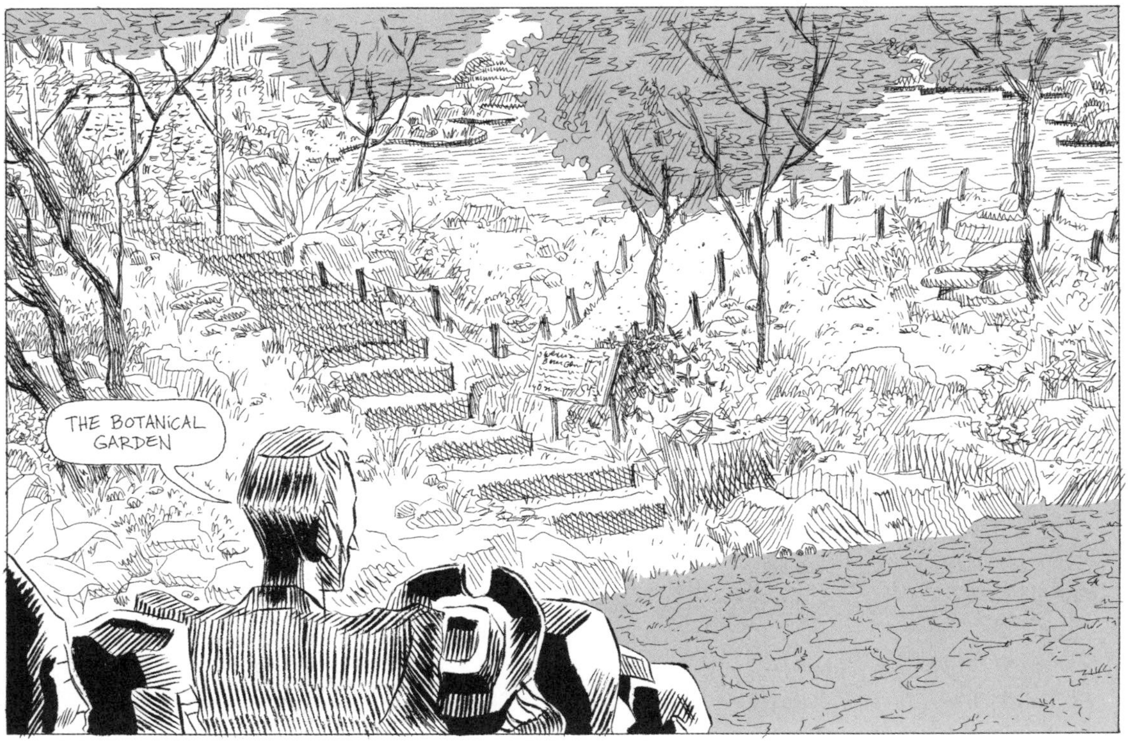
THE BOTANICAL GARDEN

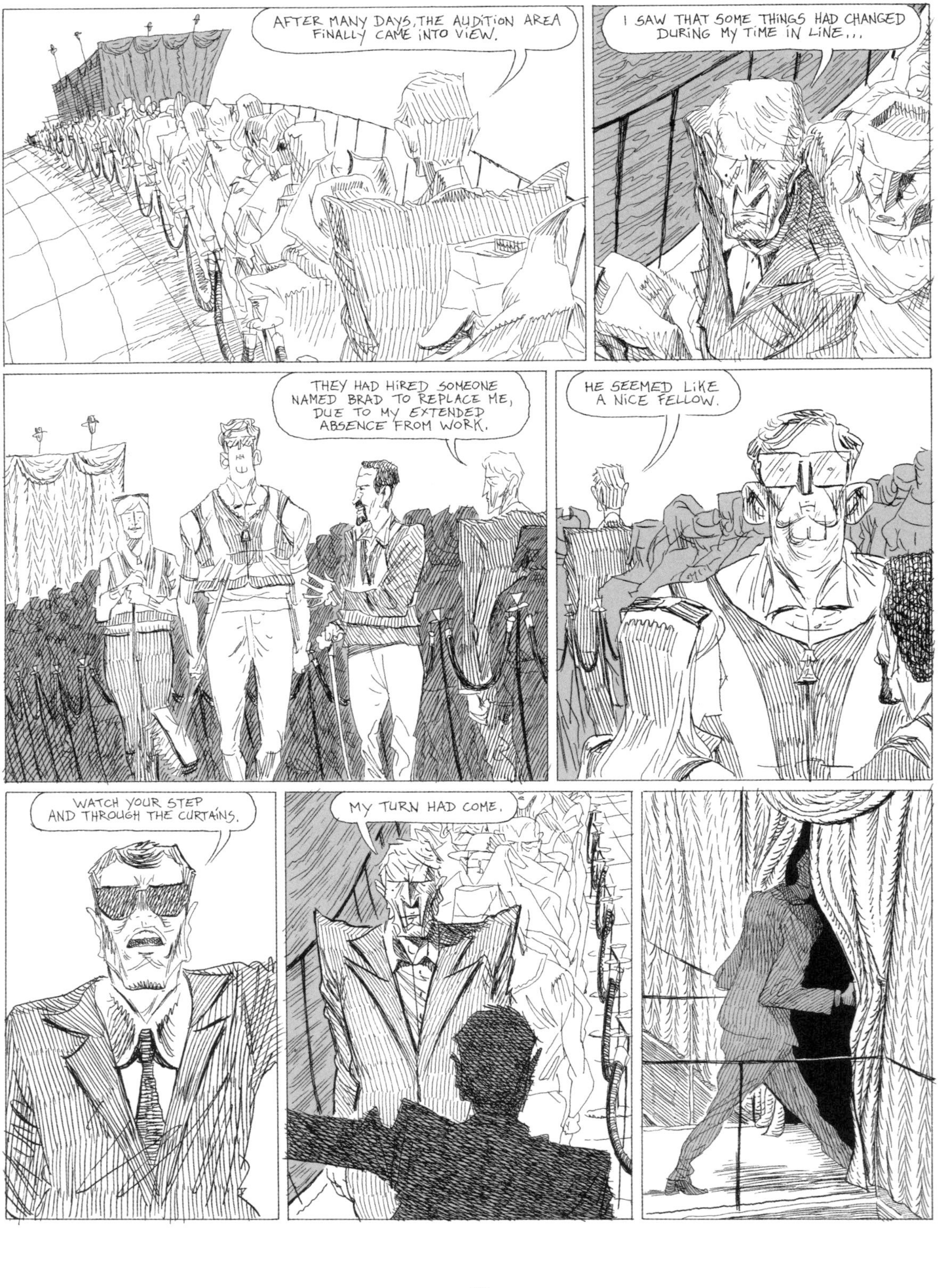
AFTER MANY DAYS, THE AUDITION AREA FINALLY CAME INTO VIEW.
I SAW THAT SOME THINGS HAD CHANGED DURING MY TIME IN LINE...
THEY HAD HIRED SOMEONE NAMED BRAD TO REPLACE ME, DUE TO MY EXTENDED ABSENCE FROM WORK.
HE SEEMED LIKE A NICE FELLOW.
WATCH YOUR STEP AND THROUGH THE CURTAINS.
MY TURN HAD COME.

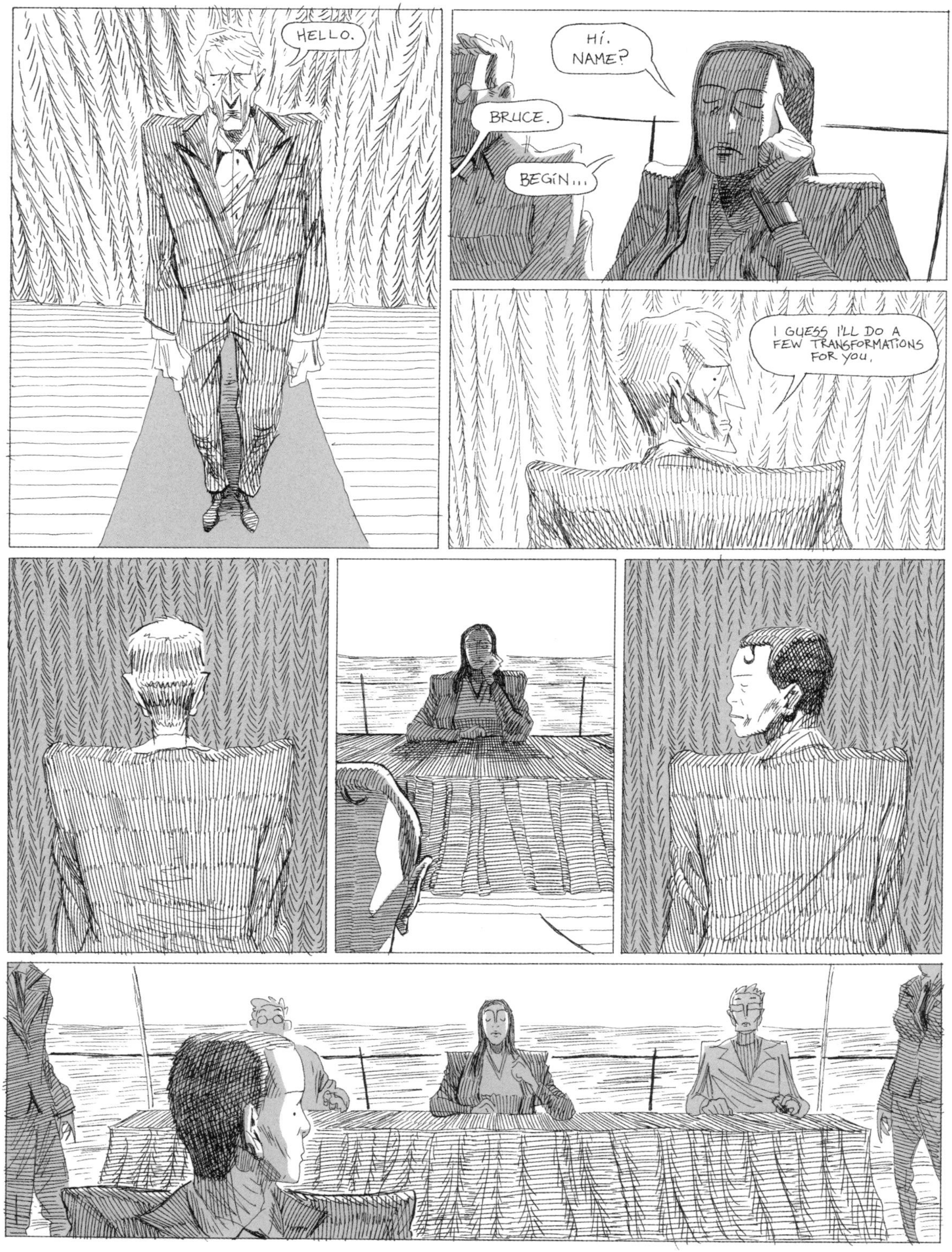
HELLO.
Hi. NAME?
BRUCE.
BEGIN...
I GUESS I'LL DO A FEW TRANSFORMATIONS FOR YOU.

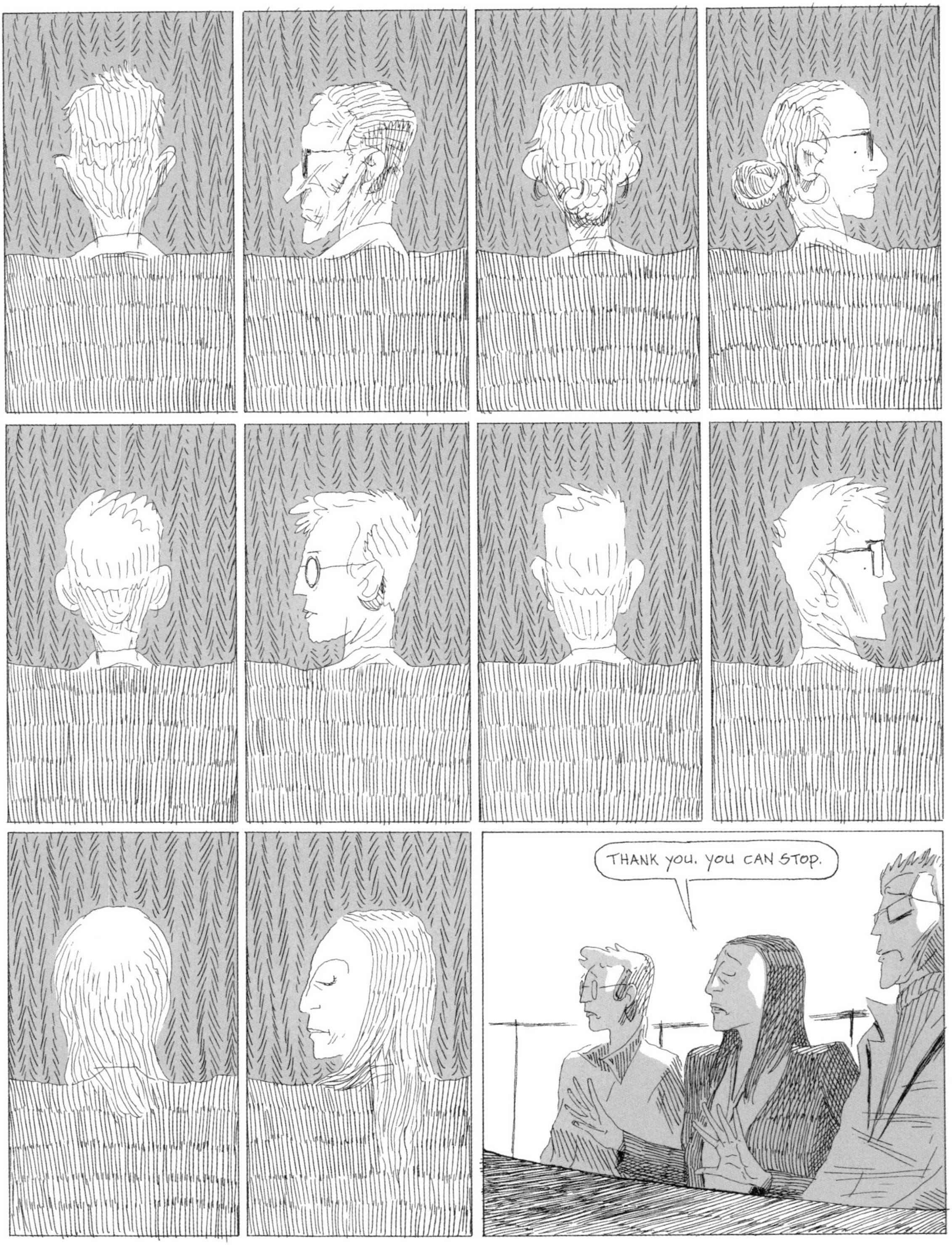
THANK YOU. YOU CAN STOP.

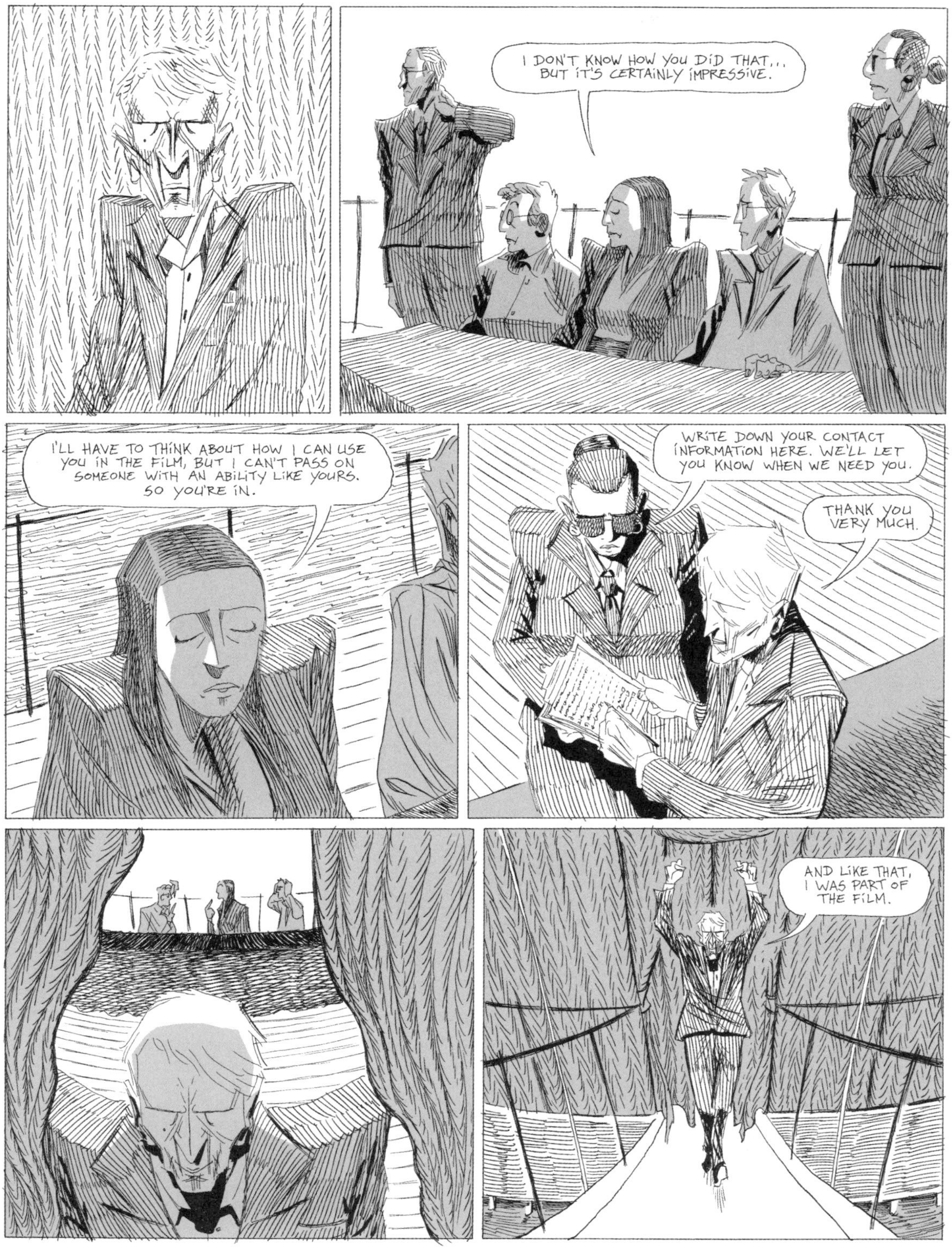
I DON'T KNOW HOW YOU DID THAT... BUT IT'S CERTAINLY IMPRESSIVE.
I'LL HAVE TO THINK ABOUT HOW I CAN USE YOU IN THE FILM, BUT I CAN'T PASS ON SOMEONE WITH AN ABILITY LIKE YOURS. SO YOU'RE IN.
WRITE DOWN YOUR CONTACT INFORMATION HERE. WE'LL LET YOU KNOW WHEN WE NEED YOU.
THANK YOU VERY MUCH.
AND LIKE THAT, I WAS PART OF THE FILM.

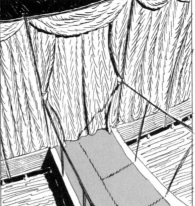

MAY I HAVE YOUR ATTENTION, PLEASE. THIS IS MIO SPEAKING...

I WOULD LIKE TO THANK YOU ALL FOR YOUR HIGH LEVEL OF INTEREST IN MY UPCOMING FILM. HOWEVER, I HAVE FOUND ENOUGH PERFORMERS TO MOVE FORWARD WITH PRODUCTION, SO I WILL BE ENDING THE AUDITIONS TODAY.

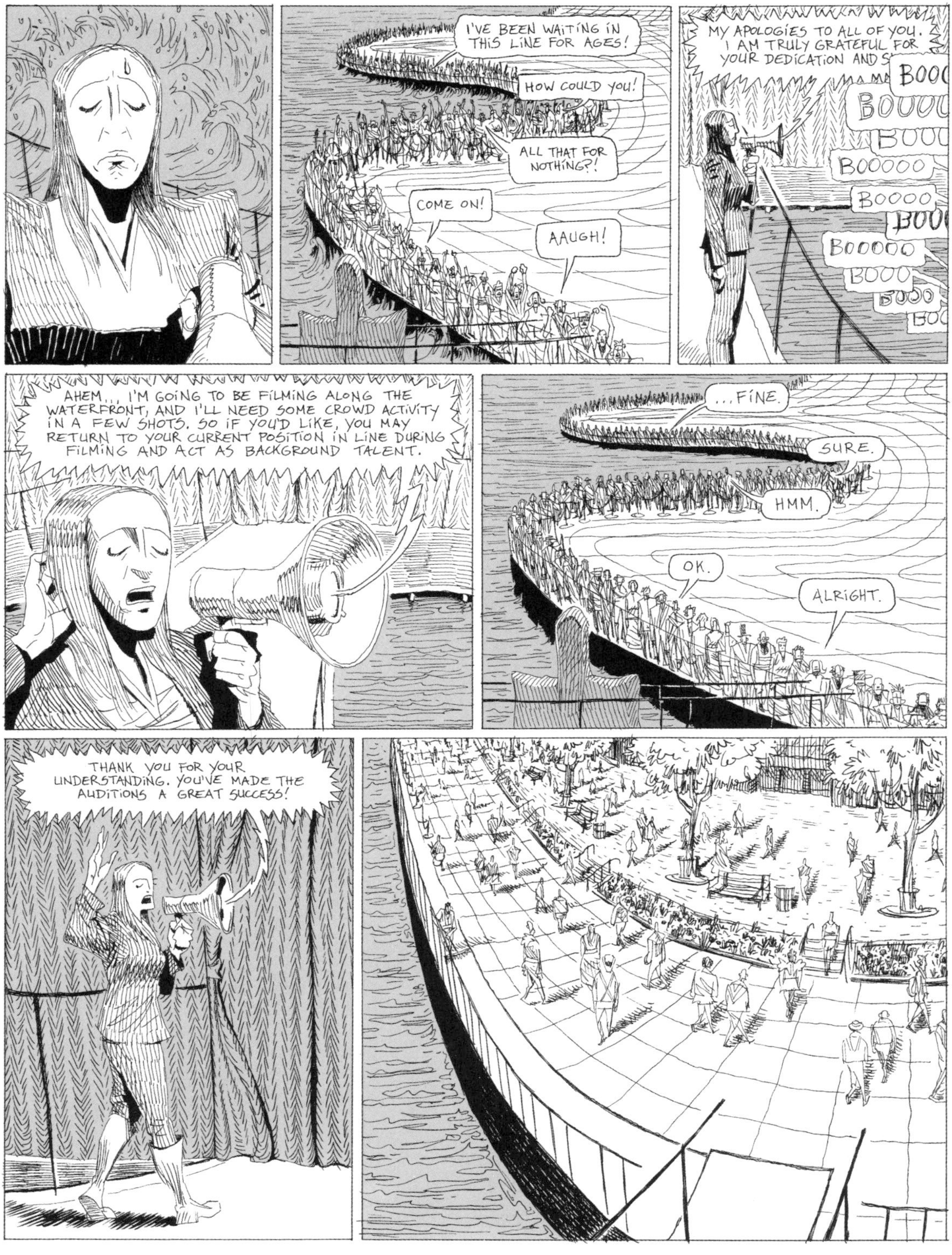
I'VE BEEN WAITING IN THIS LINE FOR AGES!
HOW COULD YOU!
ALL THAT FOR NOTHING?!
COME ON!
AAUGH!
MY APOLOGIES TO ALL OF YOU. I AM TRULY GRATEFUL FOR YOUR DEDICATION AND S
BOOO
BOUUU
BOOO
BOOOOO
BOOOO
BOO
BOOOOO
BOOO
BOOO
BOO
AHEM.., I'M GOING TO BE FILMING ALONG THE WATERFRONT, AND I'LL NEED SOME CROWD ACTIVITY IN A FEW SHOTS. SO IF YOU'D LIKE, YOU MAY RETURN TO YOUR CURRENT POSITION IN LINE DURING FILMING AND ACT AS BACKGROUND TALENT.
...FINE.
SURE.
HMM.
OK.
ALRIGHT.
THANK YOU FOR YOUR UNDERSTANDING. YOU'VE MADE THE AUDITIONS A GREAT SUCCESS!

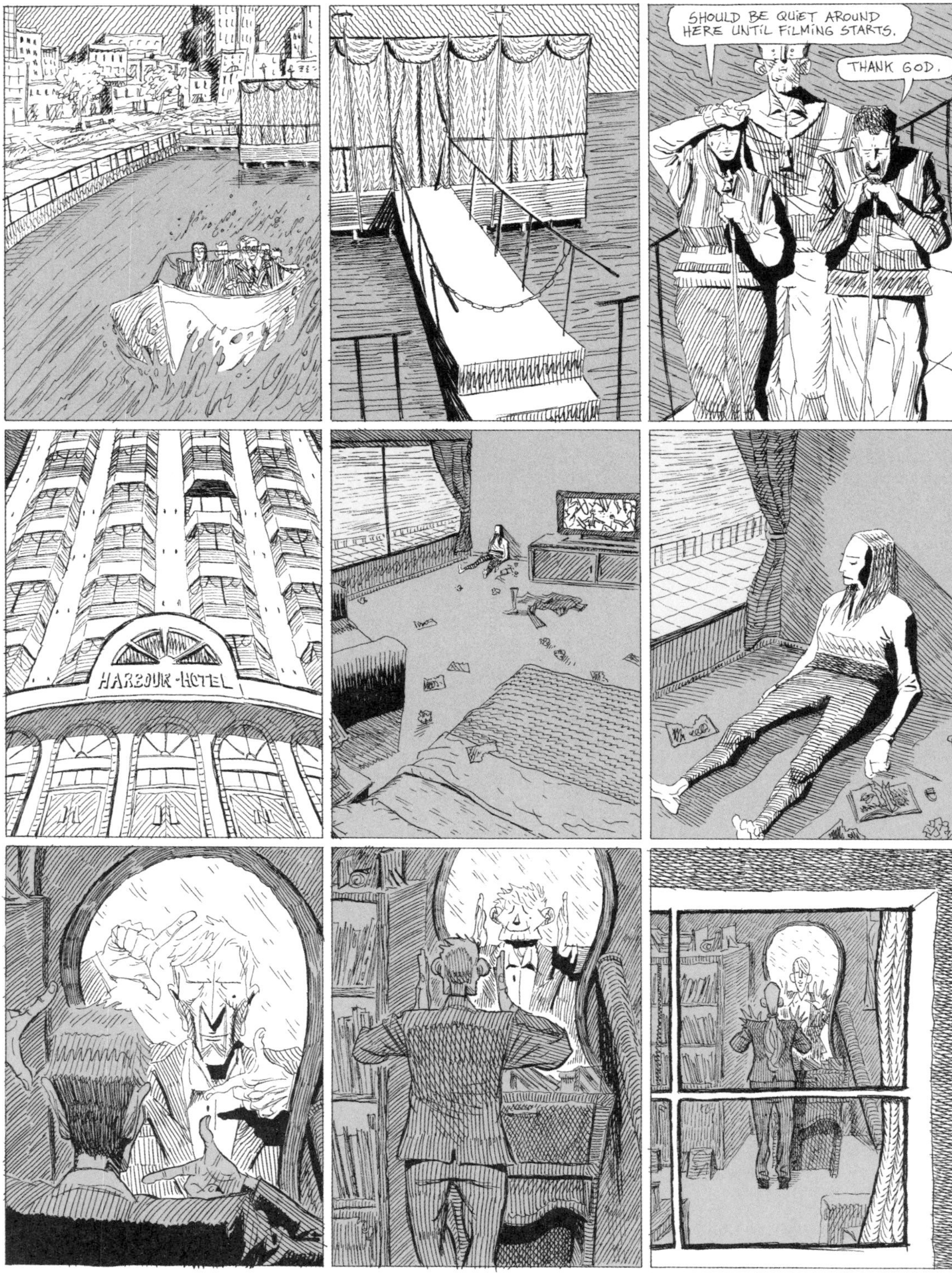
SHOULD BE QUIET AROUND HERE UNTIL FILMING STARTS.
THANK GOD.
HARBOUR-HOTEL

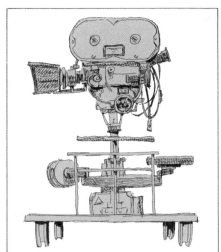

WHAT ARE THEY GOING TO FILM? IT'S JUST RAILINGS AND WATER OVER THERE. ALL THE INTERESTING STUFF IS BEHIND THEM...

MIO'S GOING TO FILL THE WATERFRONT WITH PERFORMERS, AND LOOK—

SHE'S BRINGING IN ROWERS AND SHIPS. IT'S GOING TO BE A SPECTACLE!

ALRIGHT, THEN. GUESS THAT'S WHY I'M NOT A DIRECTOR...

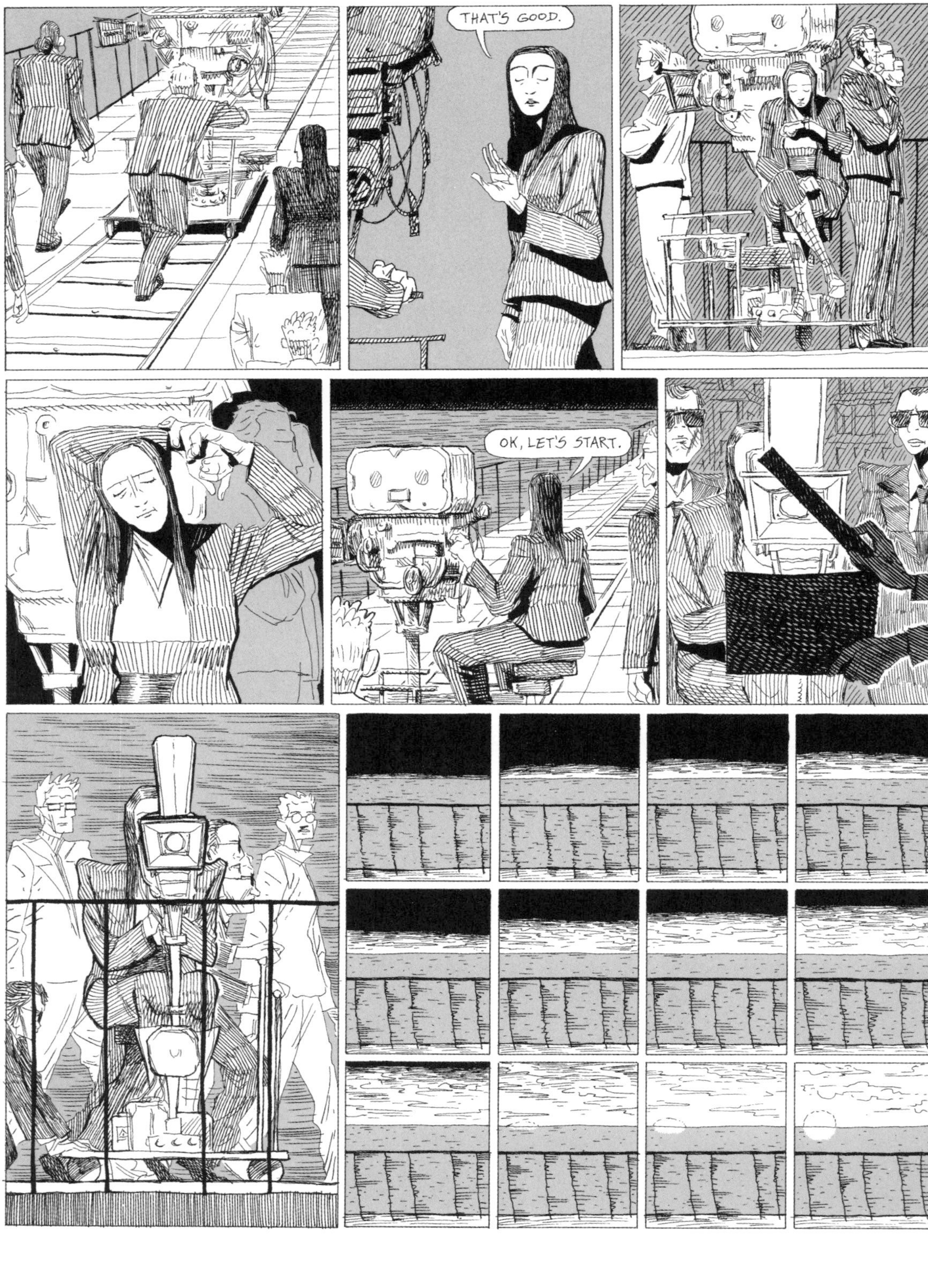
THAT'S GOOD.
OK, LET'S START.

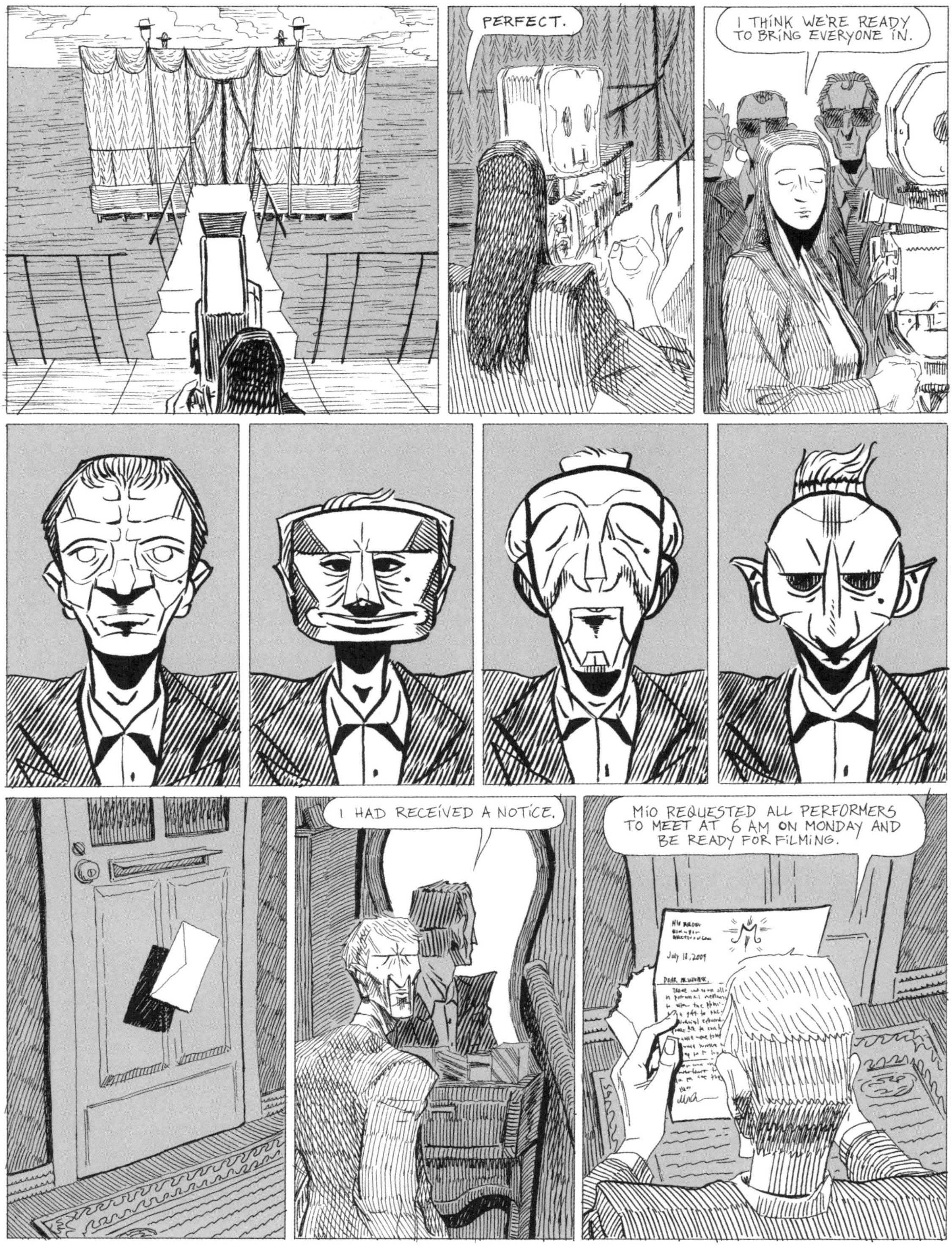
PERFECT.
I THINK WE'RE READY TO BRING EVERYONE IN.
I HAD RECEIVED A NOTICE.
MIO REQUESTED ALL PERFORMERS TO MEET AT 6 AM ON MONDAY AND BE READY FOR FILMING.

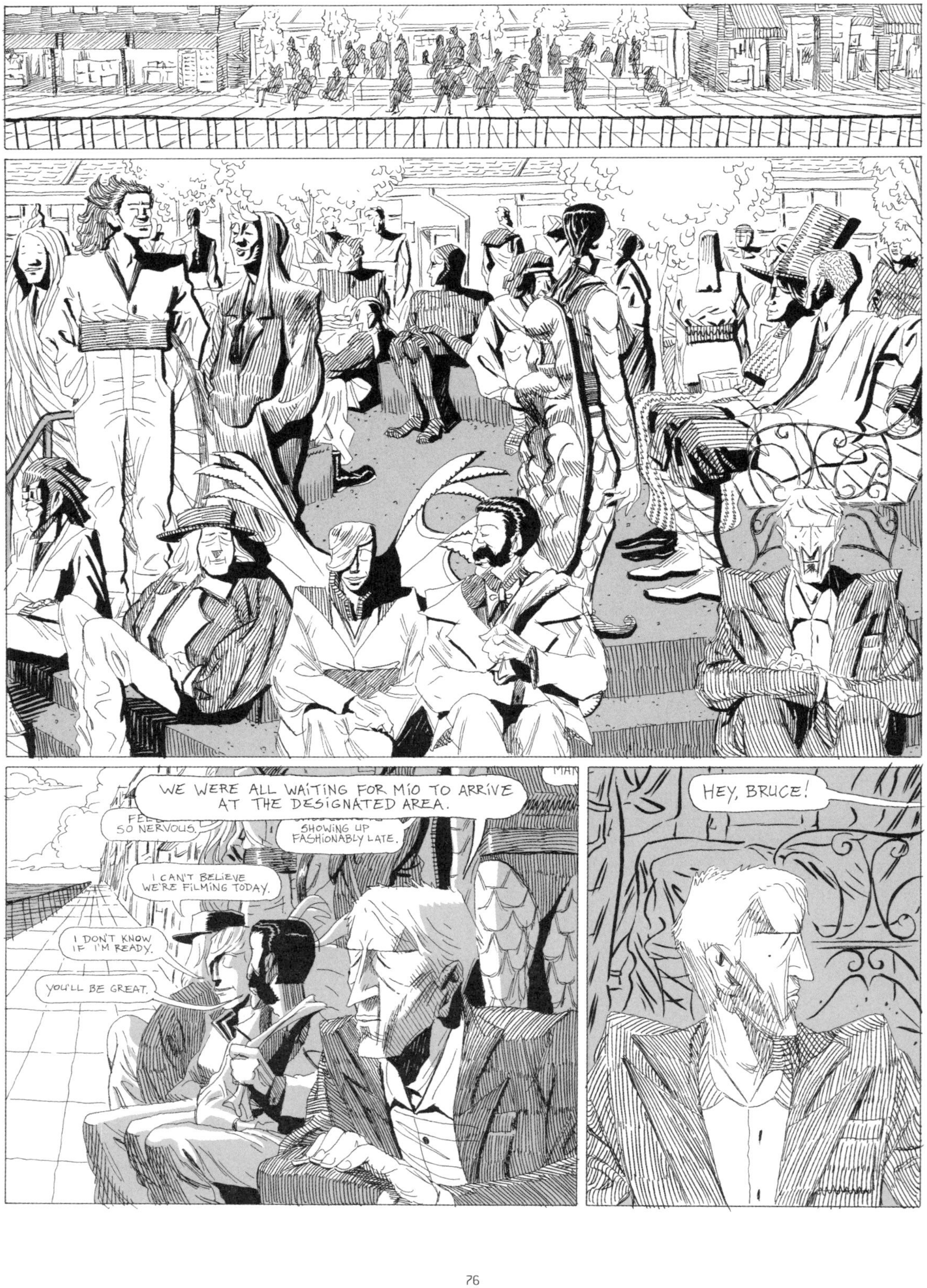

WE WERE ALL WAITING FOR MIO TO ARRIVE AT THE DESIGNATED AREA.
SO NERVOUS.
SHOWING UP FASHIONABLY LATE.
I CAN'T BELIEVE WE'RE FILMING TODAY.
I DON'T KNOW IF I'M READY.
YOU'LL BE GREAT.
HEY, BRUCE!

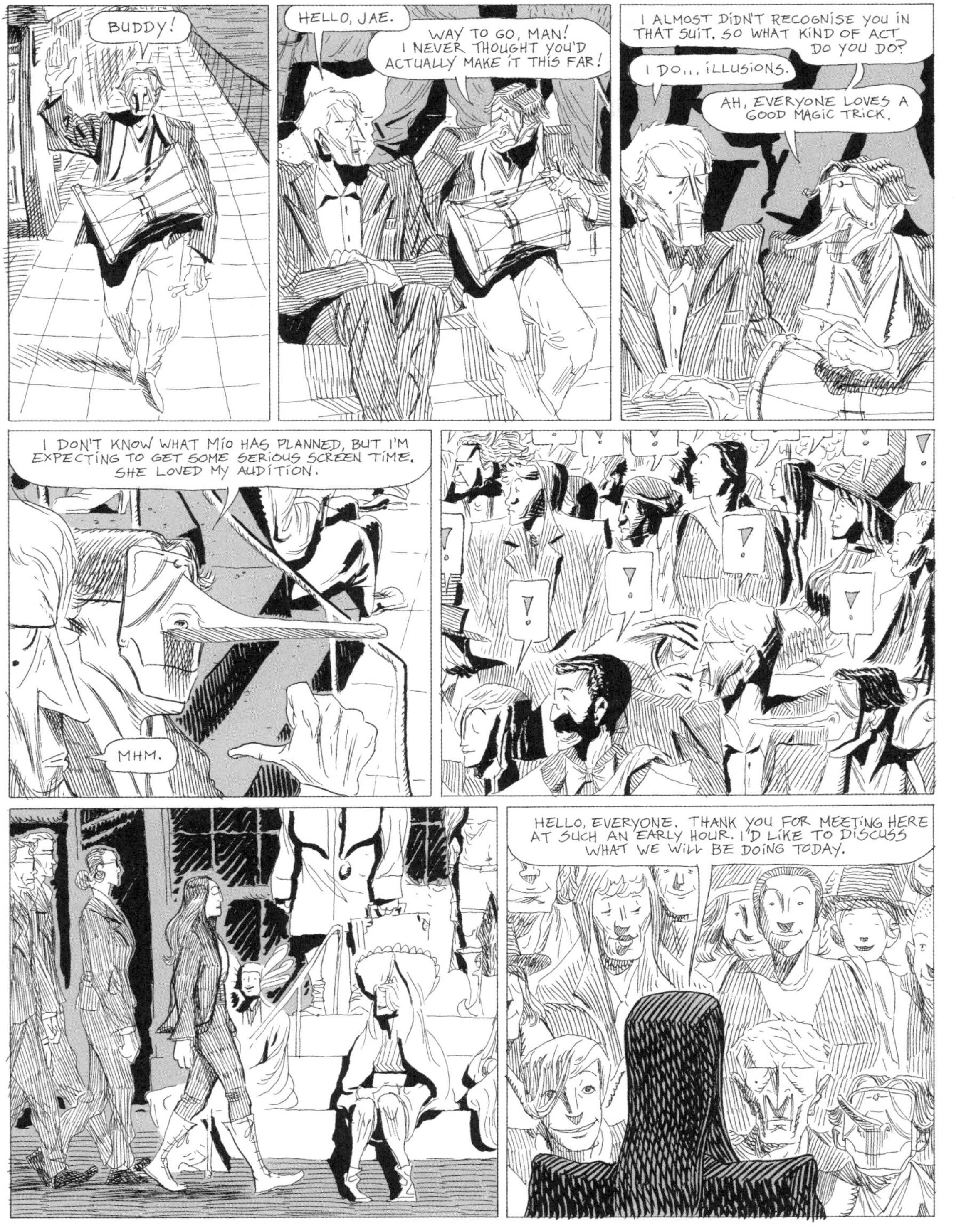
BUDDY!
HELLO, JAE.
WAY TO GO, MAN! I NEVER THOUGHT YOU'D ACTUALLY MAKE IT THIS FAR!
I ALMOST DIDN'T RECOGNISE YOU IN THAT SUIT. SO WHAT KIND OF ACT DO YOU DO?
I DO... ILLUSIONS.
AH, EVERYONE LOVES A GOOD MAGIC TRICK.
I DON'T KNOW WHAT MIO HAS PLANNED, BUT I'M EXPECTING TO GET SOME SERIOUS SCREEN TIME. SHE LOVED MY AUDITION.
MHM.
HELLO, EVERYONE. THANK YOU FOR MEETING HERE AT SUCH AN EARLY HOUR. I'D LIKE TO DISCUSS WHAT WE WILL BE DOING TODAY.

THE AUDITIONS WERE A WONDERFUL EXPERIENCE. I WAS GREATLY INSPIRED BY EVERYONE'S ENERGY AND ENTHUSIASM.

THE FIRST PERSON WILL EMERGE FROM THE CURTAINS.

I WISH TO CAPTURE THAT ENERGY IN THIS FILM. IT WILL BEGIN AT THE AUDITION AREA...

THEY WILL WALK ALONG THE WATERFRONT AS THEY PERFORM THEIR ACT.

I WANT TO CHANGE BETWEEN DIFFERENT PERFORMERS, GIVING YOU ALL A CHANCE TO SHOWCASE YOUR TALENTS.

TRANSITION SHOTS WILL BE USED TO SHOW ONE PERSON CHANGING INTO ANOTHER.

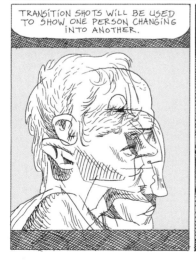

AND I WILL USE YOU TO DO THOSE TRANSITIONS.

SINCE YOU HAVE THE REMARKABLE ABILITY TO TRANSFORM YOUR APPEARANCE AT WILL.

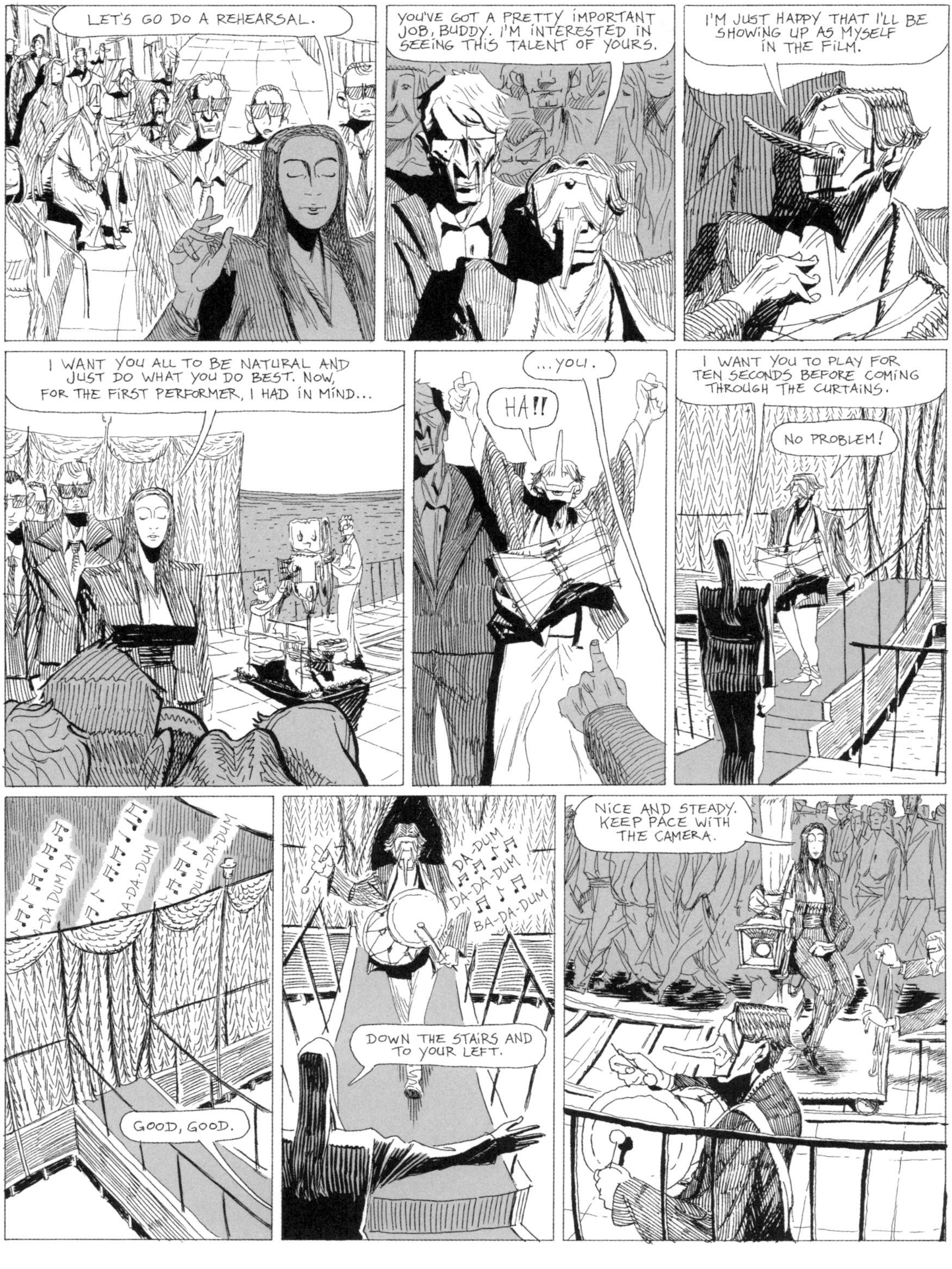

LET'S GO DO A REHEARSAL.
YOU'VE GOT A PRETTY IMPORTANT JOB, BUDDY. I'M INTERESTED IN SEEING THIS TALENT OF YOURS.
I'M JUST HAPPY THAT I'LL BE SHOWING UP AS MYSELF IN THE FILM.
I WANT YOU ALL TO BE NATURAL AND JUST DO WHAT YOU DO BEST. NOW, FOR THE FIRST PERFORMER, I HAD IN MIND...
...YOU.
HA!!
I WANT YOU TO PLAY FOR TEN SECONDS BEFORE COMING THROUGH THE CURTAINS.
NO PROBLEM!
-DA DUM DA
DA-DA-DUM
DUM-DA-DUM
GOOD, GOOD.
DA-DUM
DA-DA-DUM
BA-DA-DUM
DOWN THE STAIRS AND TO YOUR LEFT.
NICE AND STEADY. KEEP PACE WITH THE CAMERA.

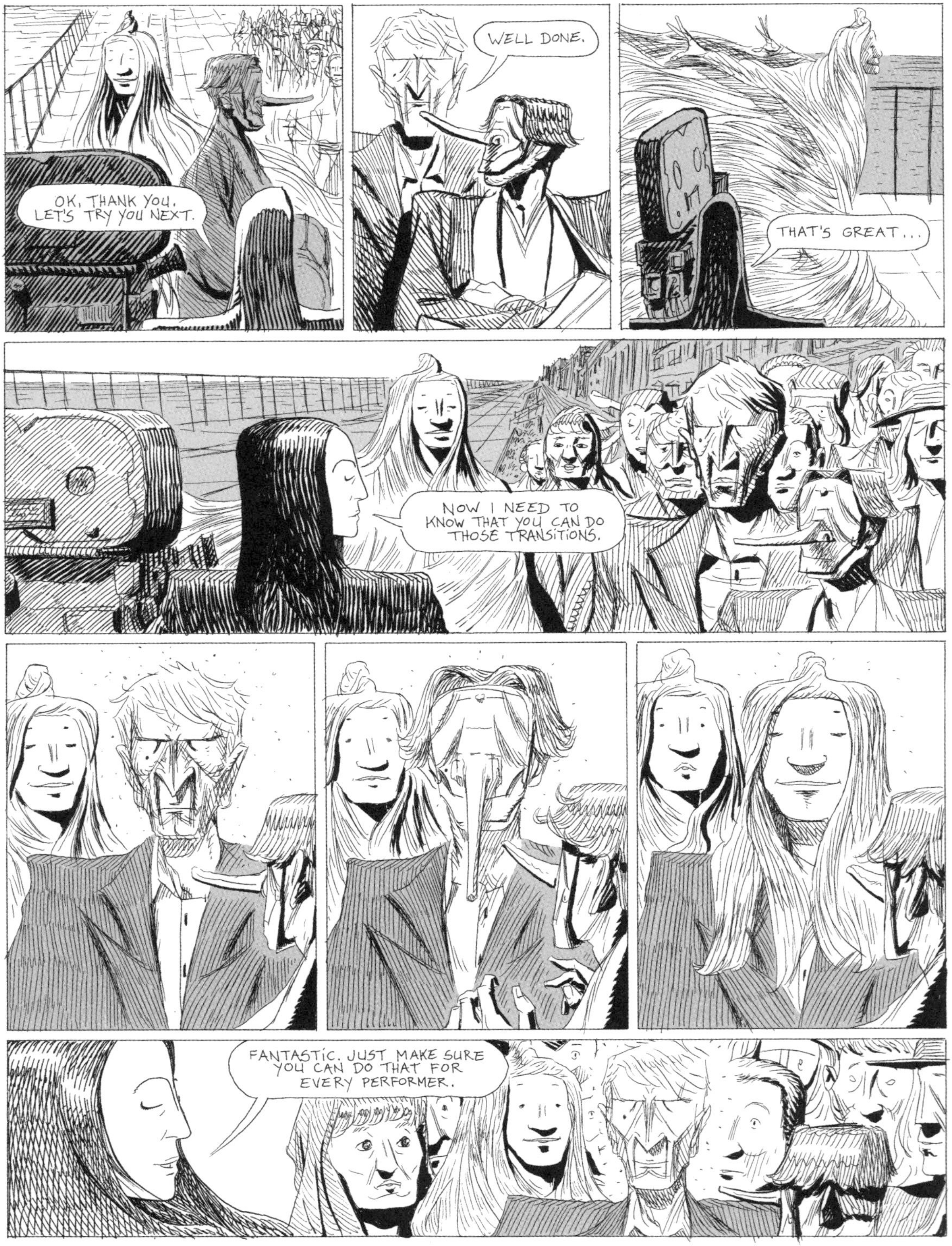
OK, THANK YOU. LET'S TRY YOU NEXT.
WELL DONE.
THAT'S GREAT...
NOW I NEED TO KNOW THAT YOU CAN DO THOSE TRANSITIONS.
FANTASTIC. JUST MAKE SURE YOU CAN DO THAT FOR EVERY PERFORMER.

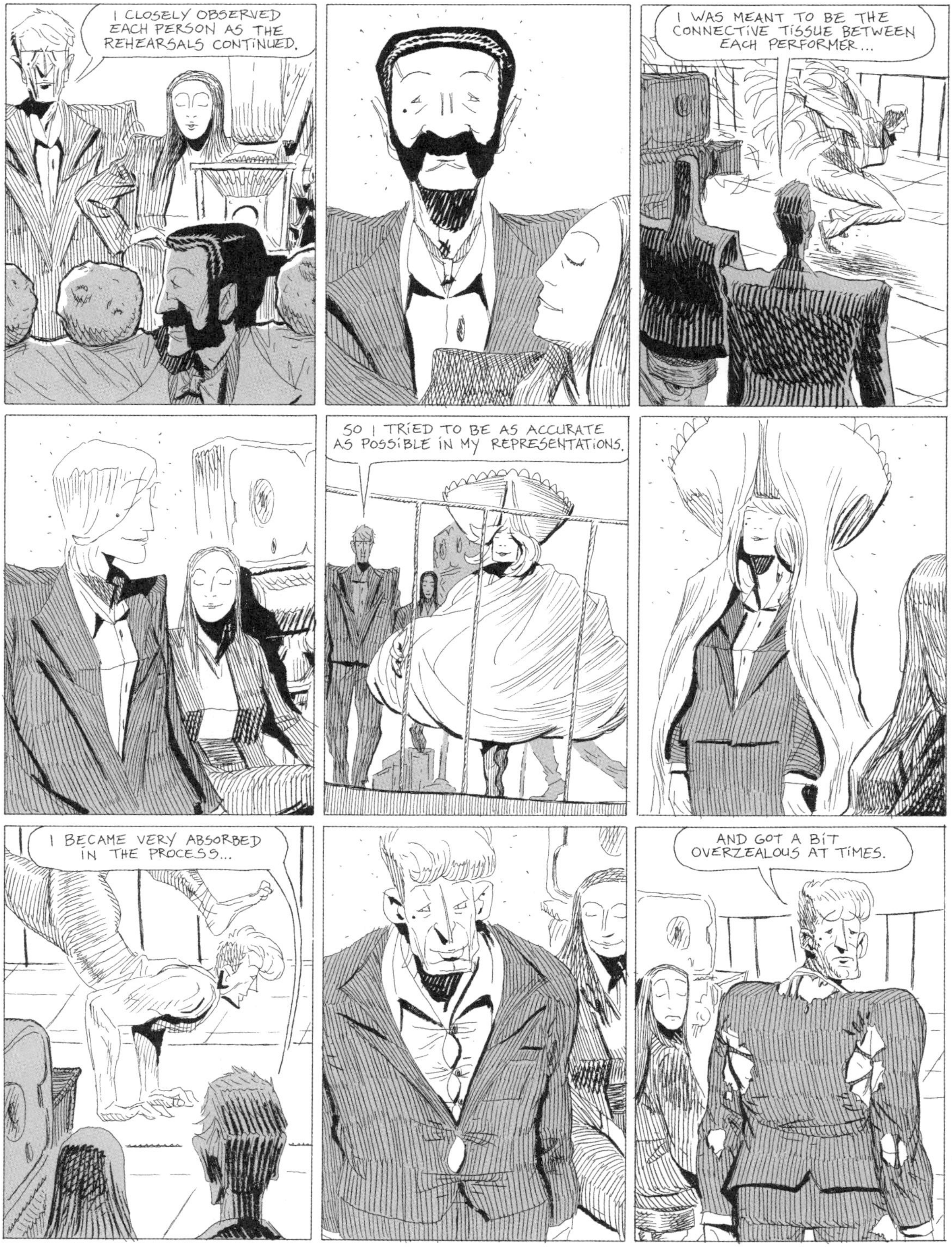
I CLOSELY OBSERVED EACH PERSON AS THE REHEARSALS CONTINUED.
I WAS MEANT TO BE THE CONNECTIVE TISSUE BETWEEN EACH PERFORMER...
SO I TRIED TO BE AS ACCURATE AS POSSIBLE IN MY REPRESENTATIONS.
I BECAME VERY ABSORBED IN THE PROCESS...
AND GOT A BIT OVERZEALOUS AT TIMES.

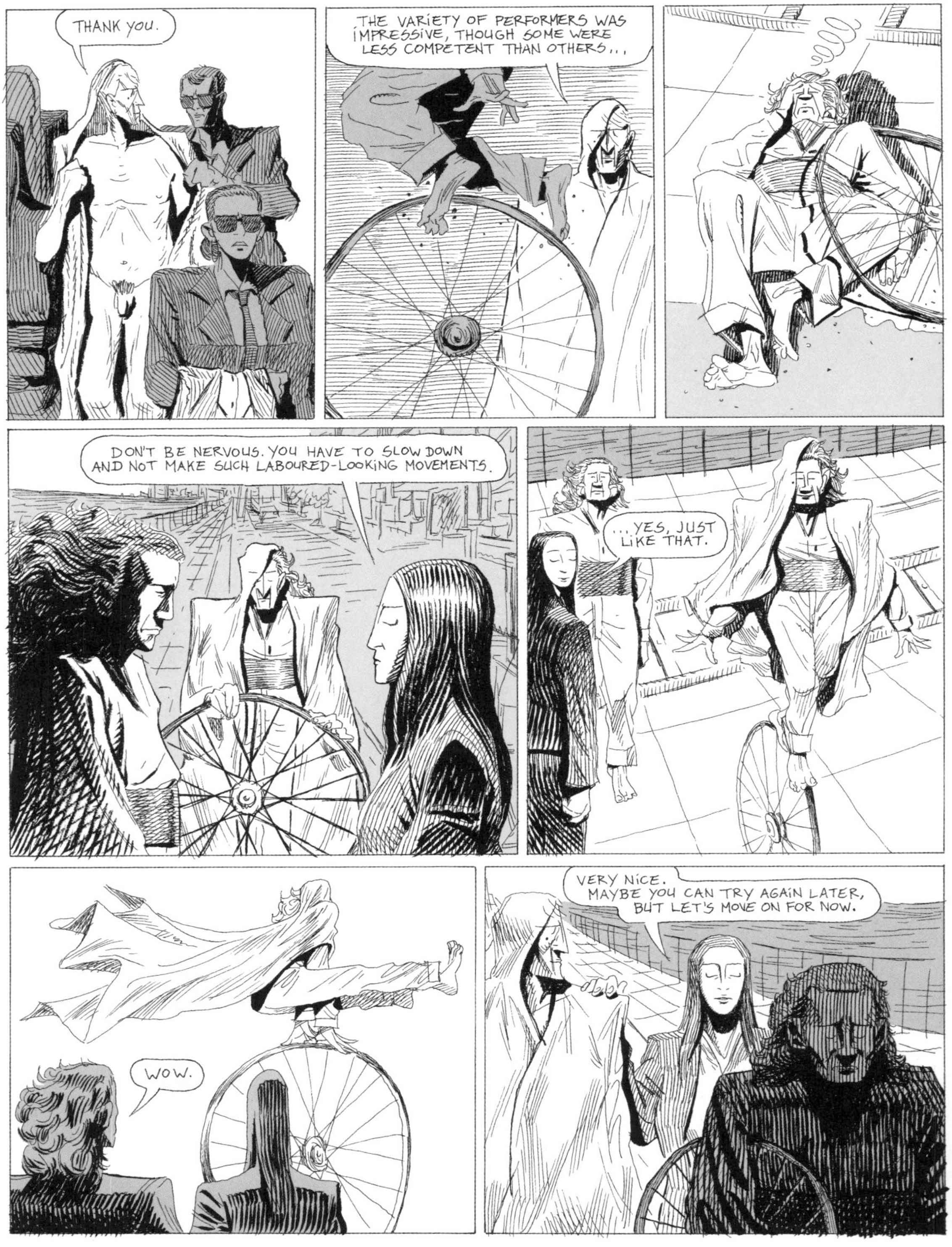
THANK YOU.
THE VARIETY OF PERFORMERS WAS IMPRESSIVE, THOUGH SOME WERE LESS COMPETENT THAN OTHERS...
DON'T BE NERVOUS. YOU HAVE TO SLOW DOWN AND NOT MAKE SUCH LABOURED-LOOKING MOVEMENTS.
...YES, JUST LIKE THAT.
WOW.
VERY NICE. MAYBE YOU CAN TRY AGAIN LATER, BUT LET'S MOVE ON FOR NOW.

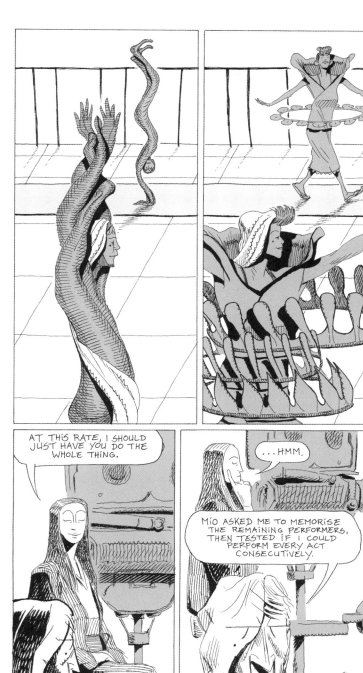

AT THIS RATE, I SHOULD JUST HAVE YOU DO THE WHOLE THING.

...HMM.

MIO ASKED ME TO MEMORISE THE REMAINING PERFORMERS, THEN TESTED IF I COULD PERFORM EVERY ACT CONSECUTIVELY.

I COULD, AND I DID.

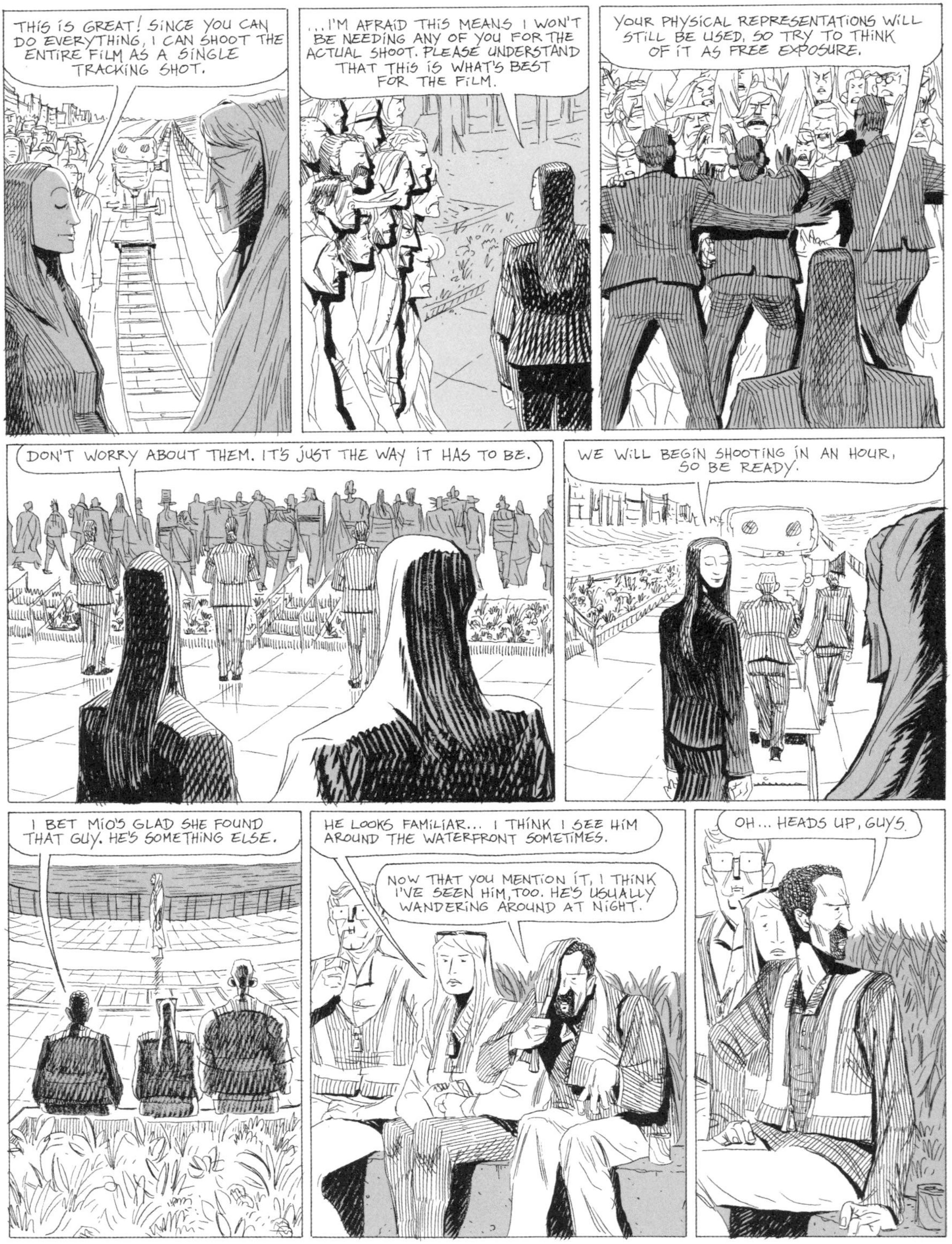

THIS IS GREAT! SINCE YOU CAN DO EVERYTHING, I CAN SHOOT THE ENTIRE FILM AS A SINGLE TRACKING SHOT.
...I'M AFRAID THIS MEANS I WON'T BE NEEDING ANY OF YOU FOR THE ACTUAL SHOOT. PLEASE UNDERSTAND THAT THIS IS WHAT'S BEST FOR THE FILM.
YOUR PHYSICAL REPRESENTATIONS WILL STILL BE USED, SO TRY TO THINK OF IT AS FREE EXPOSURE.
DON'T WORRY ABOUT THEM. IT'S JUST THE WAY IT HAS TO BE.
WE WILL BEGIN SHOOTING IN AN HOUR, SO BE READY.
I BET MIO'S GLAD SHE FOUND THAT GUY. HE'S SOMETHING ELSE.
HE LOOKS FAMILIAR... I THINK I SEE HIM AROUND THE WATERFRONT SOMETIMES.
NOW THAT YOU MENTION IT, I THINK I'VE SEEN HIM, TOO. HE'S USUALLY WANDERING AROUND AT NIGHT.
OH... HEADS UP, GUYS.

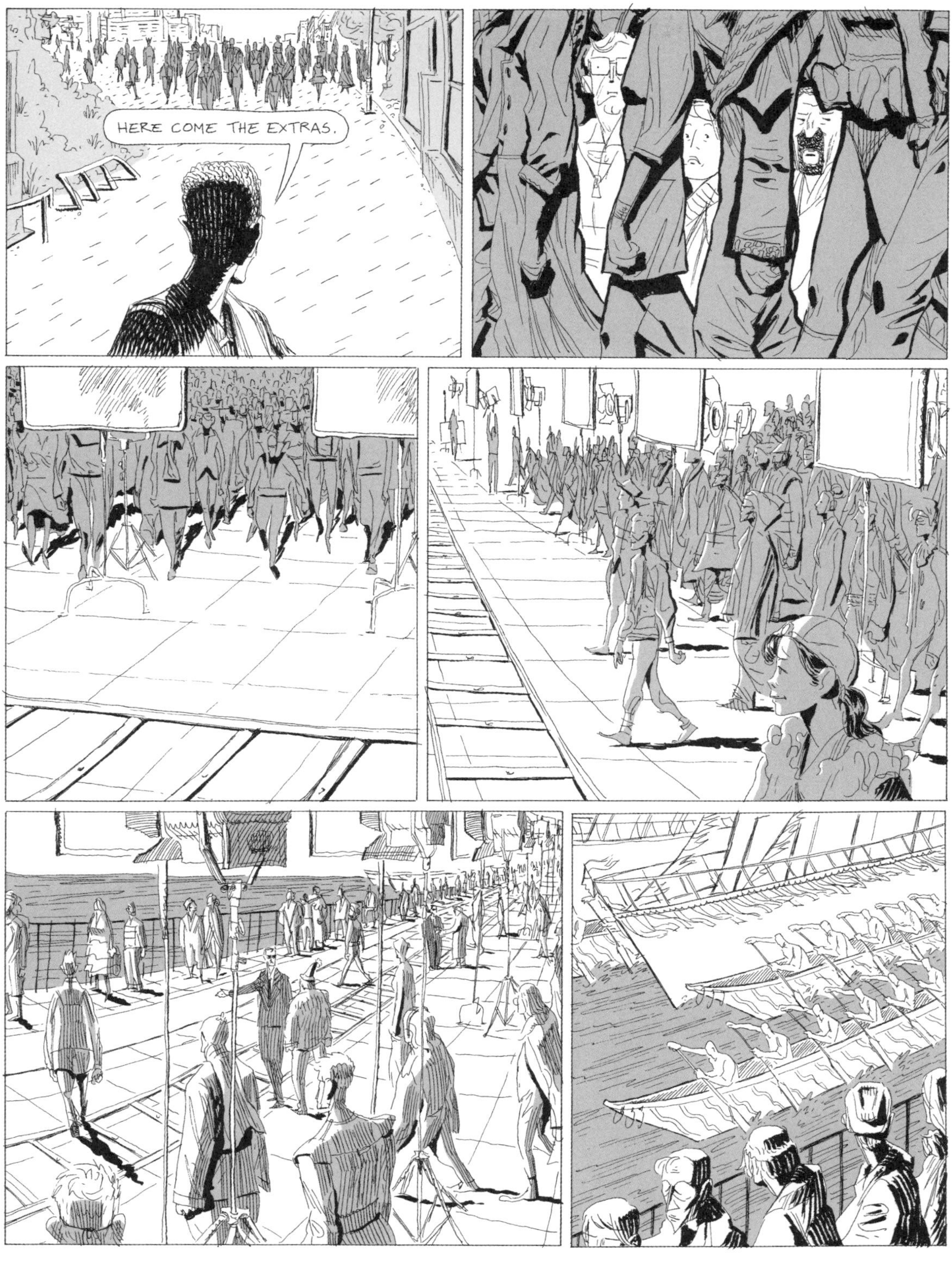
HERE COME THE EXTRAS.

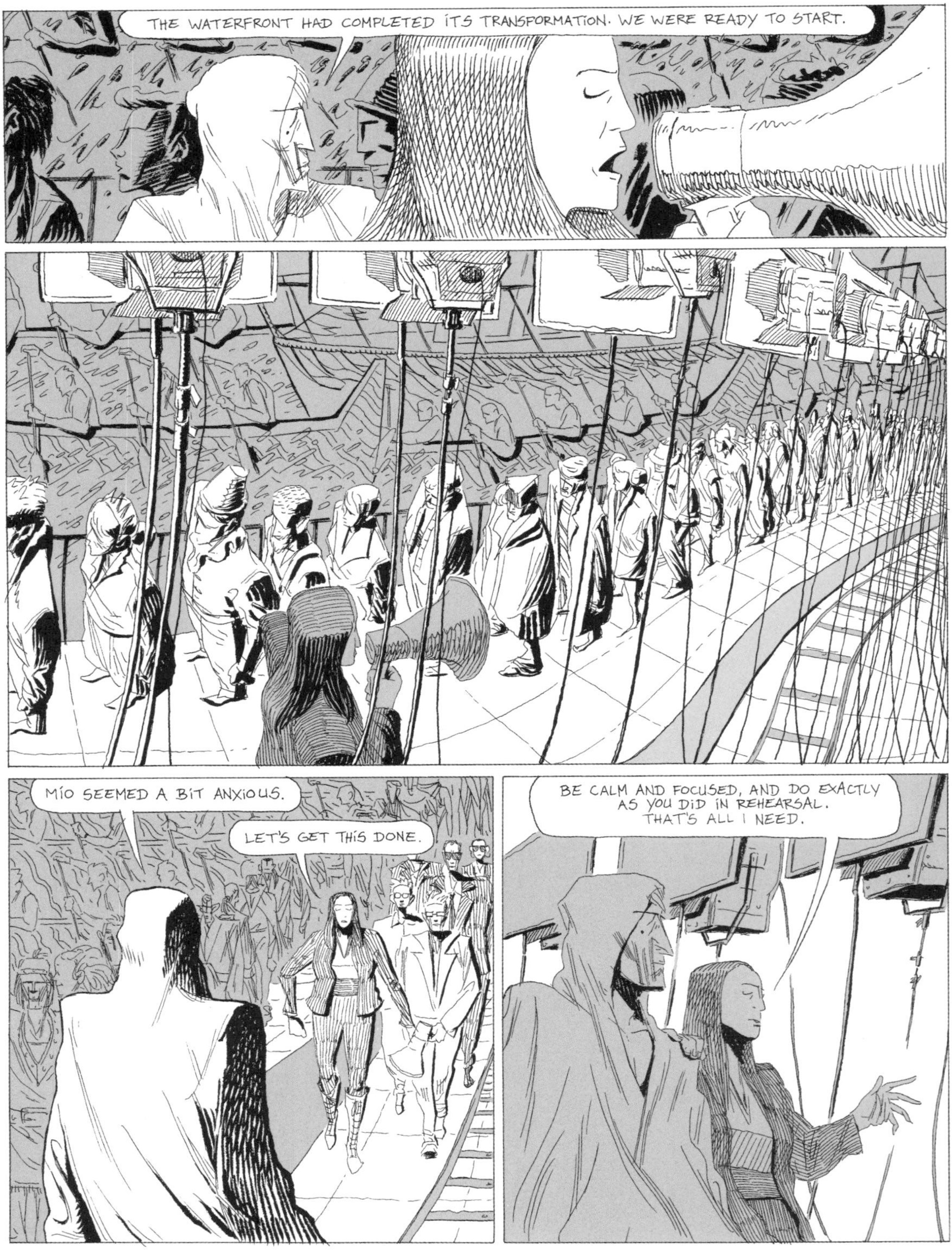
THE WATERFRONT HAD COMPLETED ITS TRANSFORMATION. WE WERE READY TO START.
MIO SEEMED A BIT ANXIOUS.
LET'S GET THIS DONE.
BE CALM AND FOCUSED, AND DO EXACTLY AS YOU DID IN REHEARSAL. THAT'S ALL I NEED.

THANK YOU.

MIO GAVE SOME LAST WORDS OF ENCOURAGEMENT,

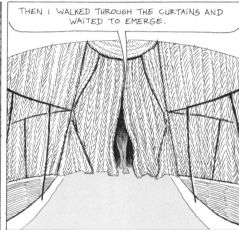

THEN I WALKED THROUGH THE CURTAINS AND WAITED TO EMERGE.

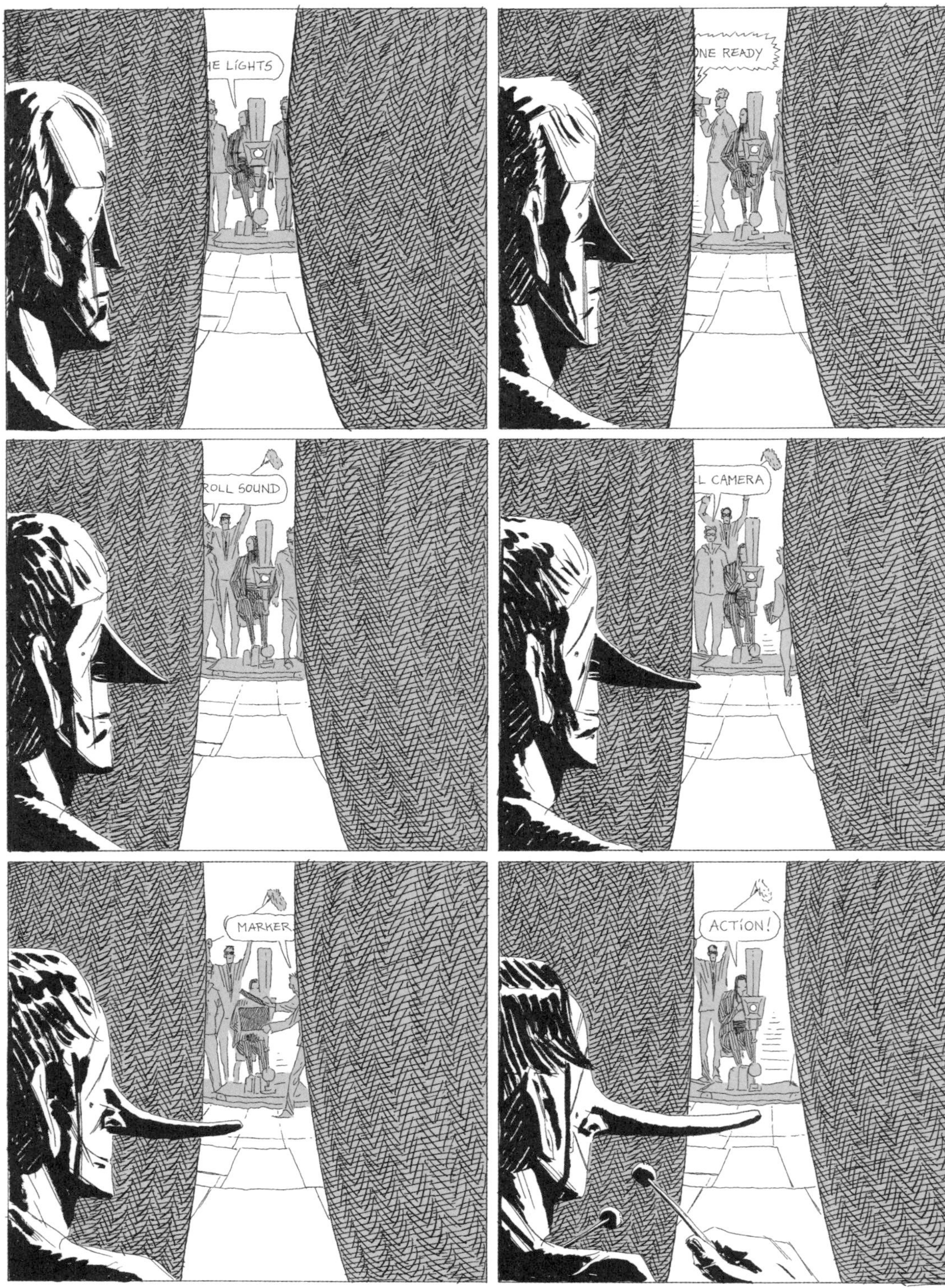
HE LIGHTS
ONE READY
ROLL SOUND
L CAMERA
MARKER
ACTION!

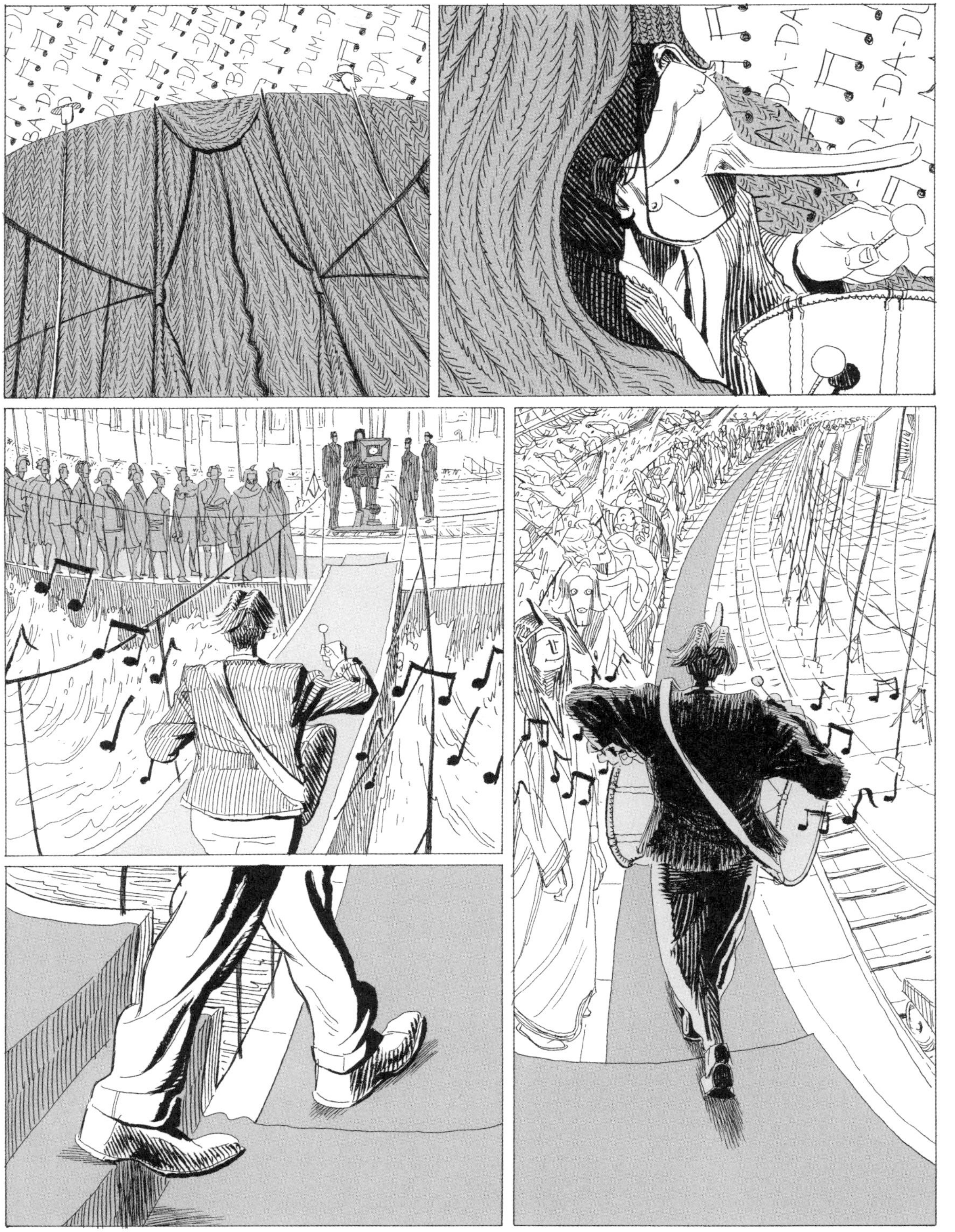
BA-DA-DUM-DA
DA-DA-DUM
DUM-DA
DA-DA-DA

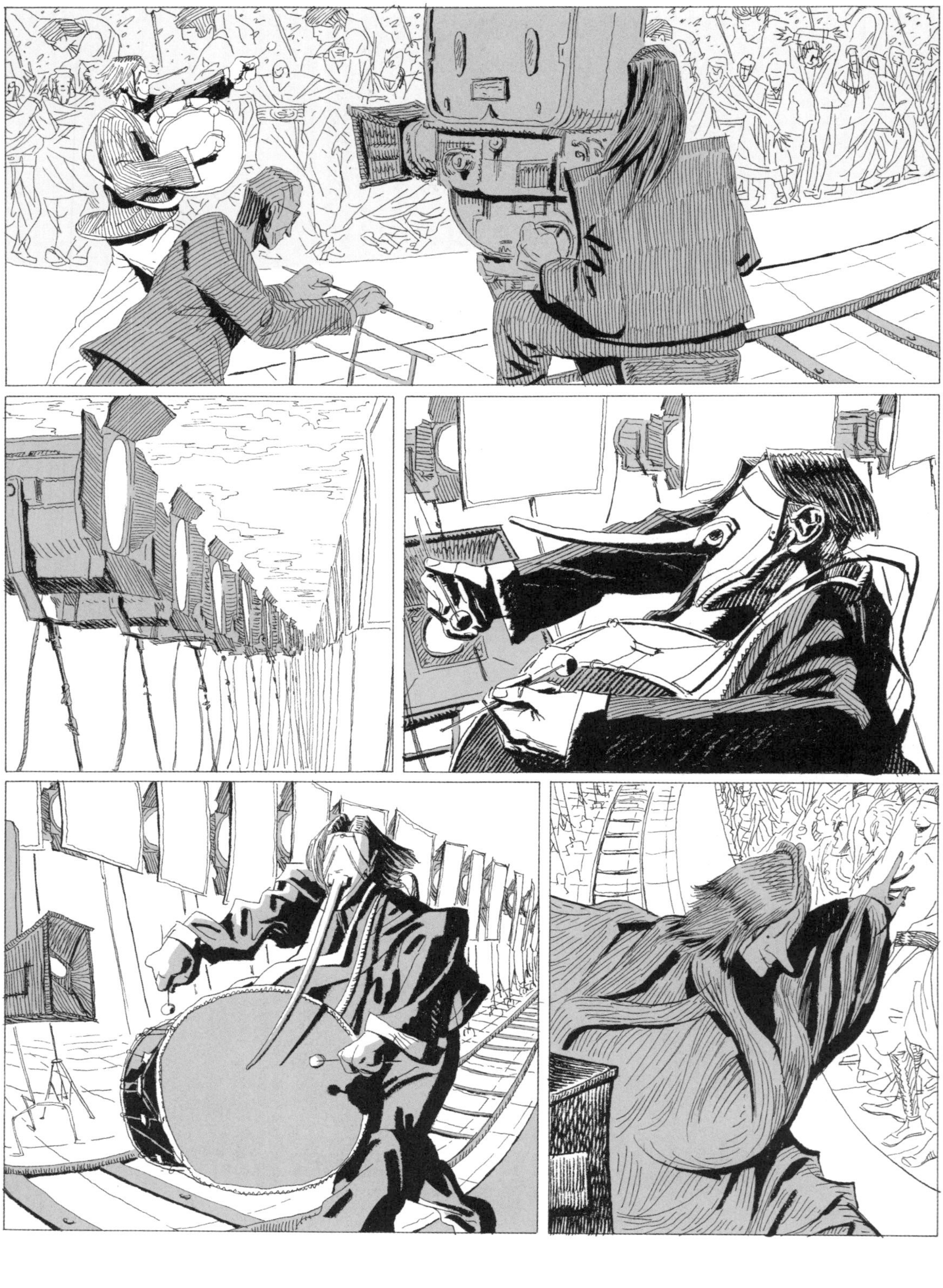

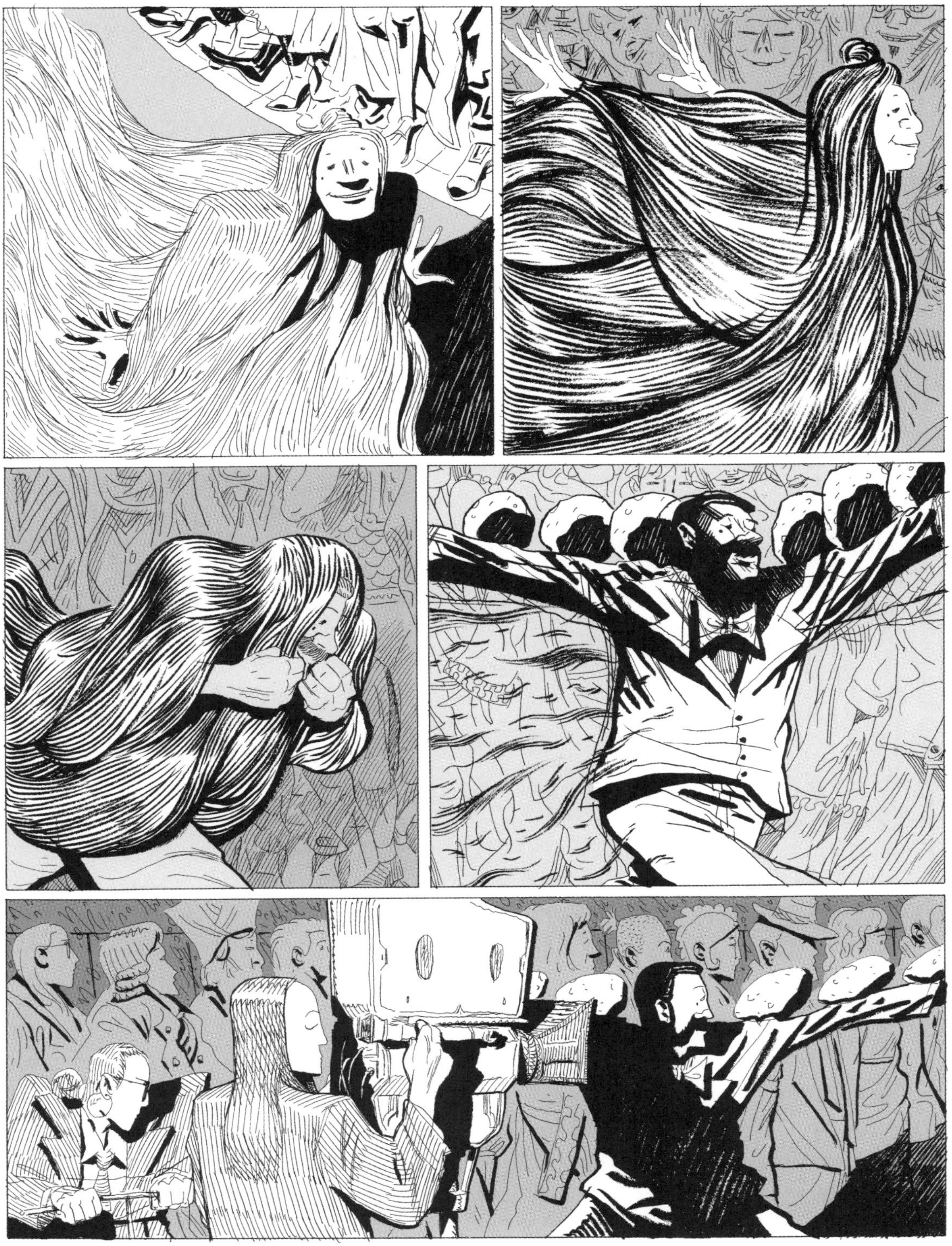

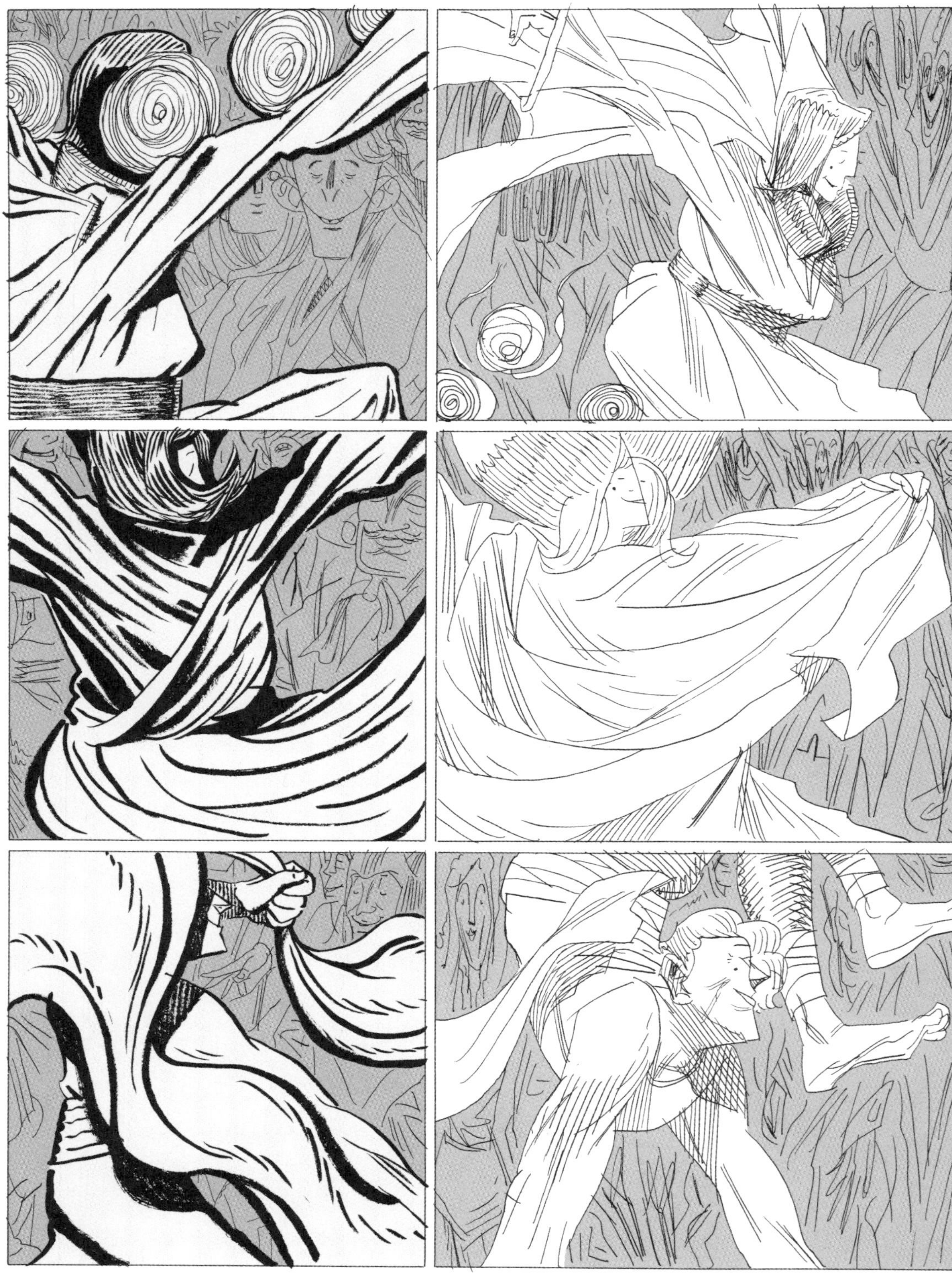

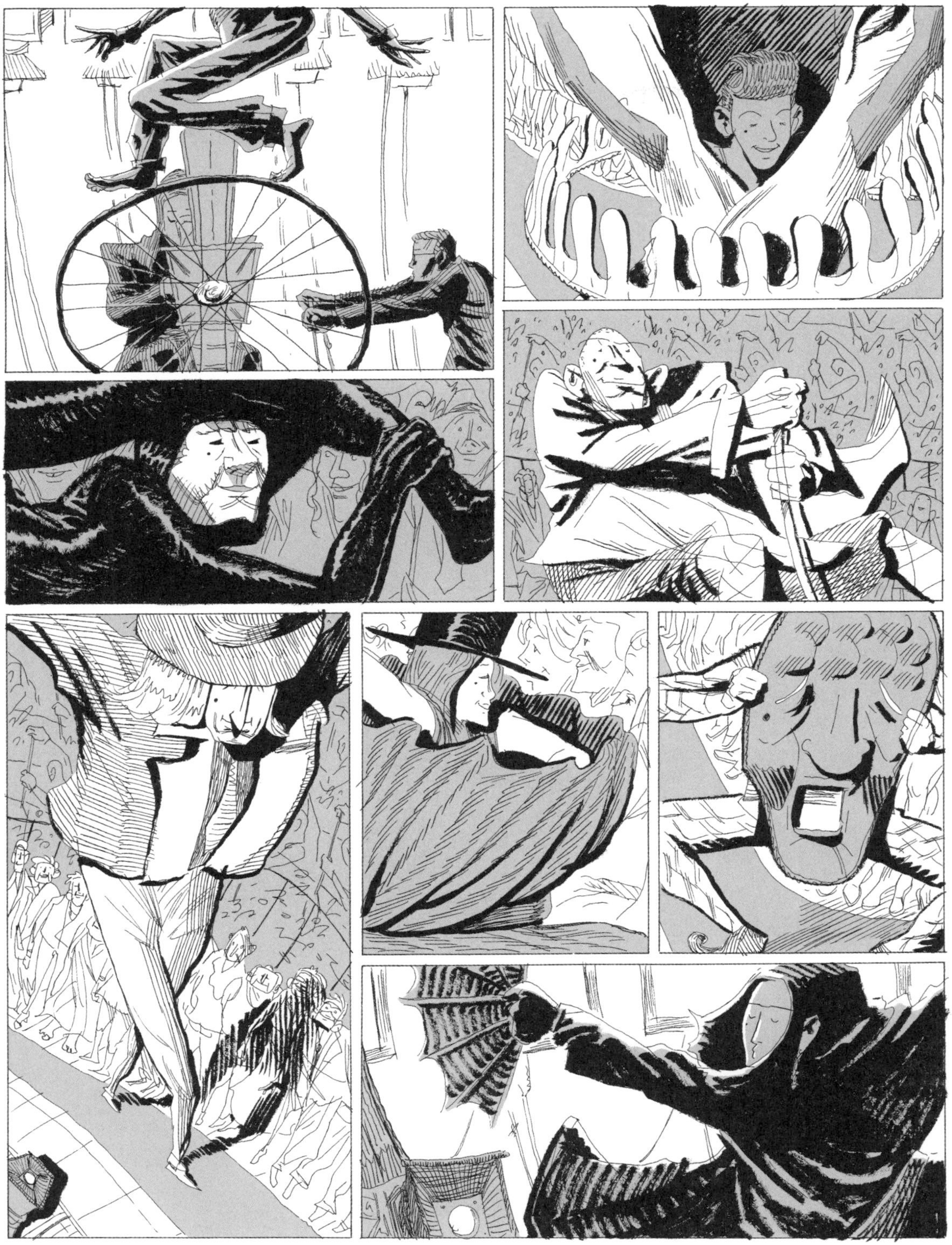

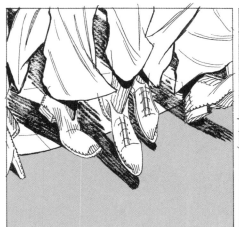

HEY! EVERYONE STAY IN LINE! YE IDIOTS!!

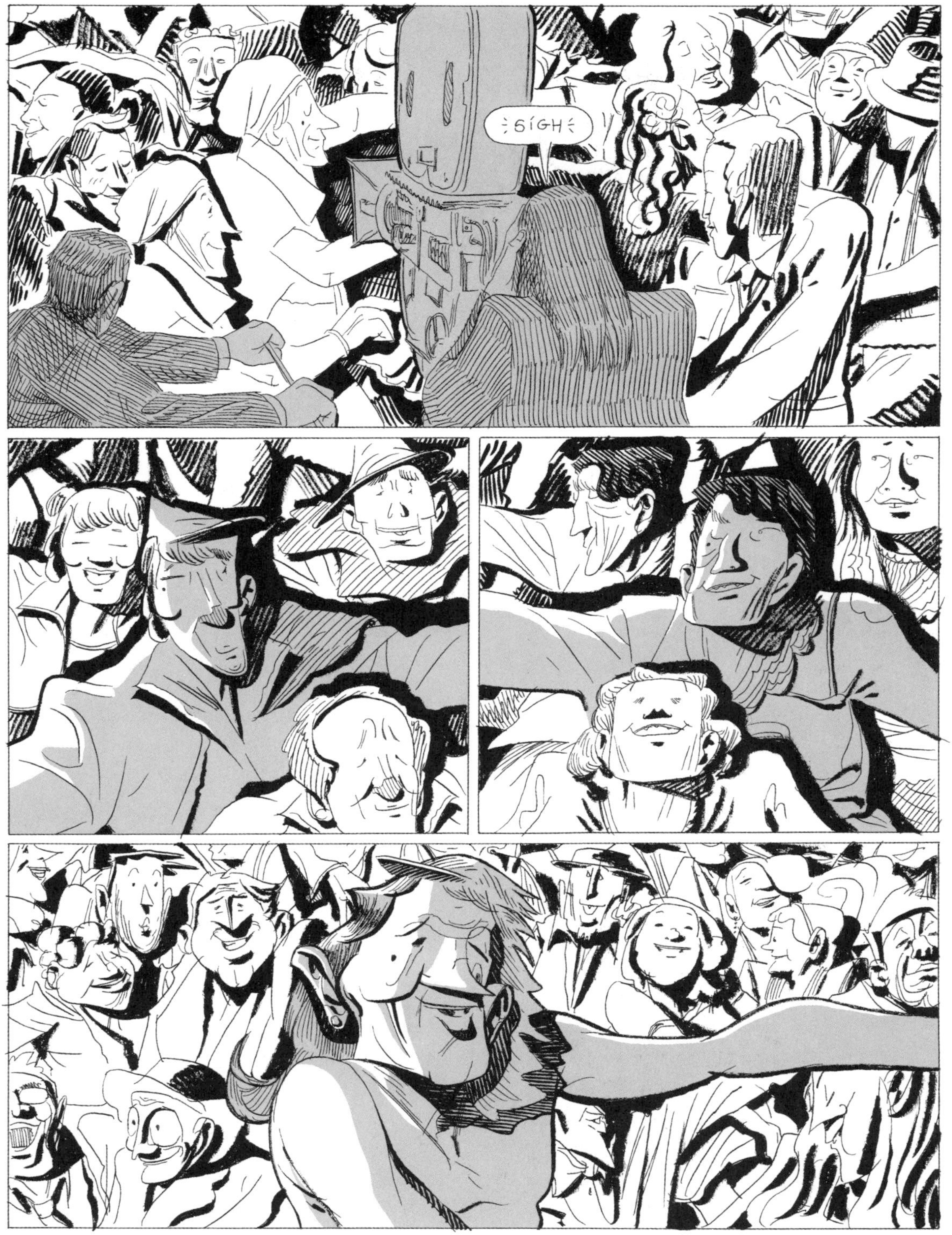
SIGH

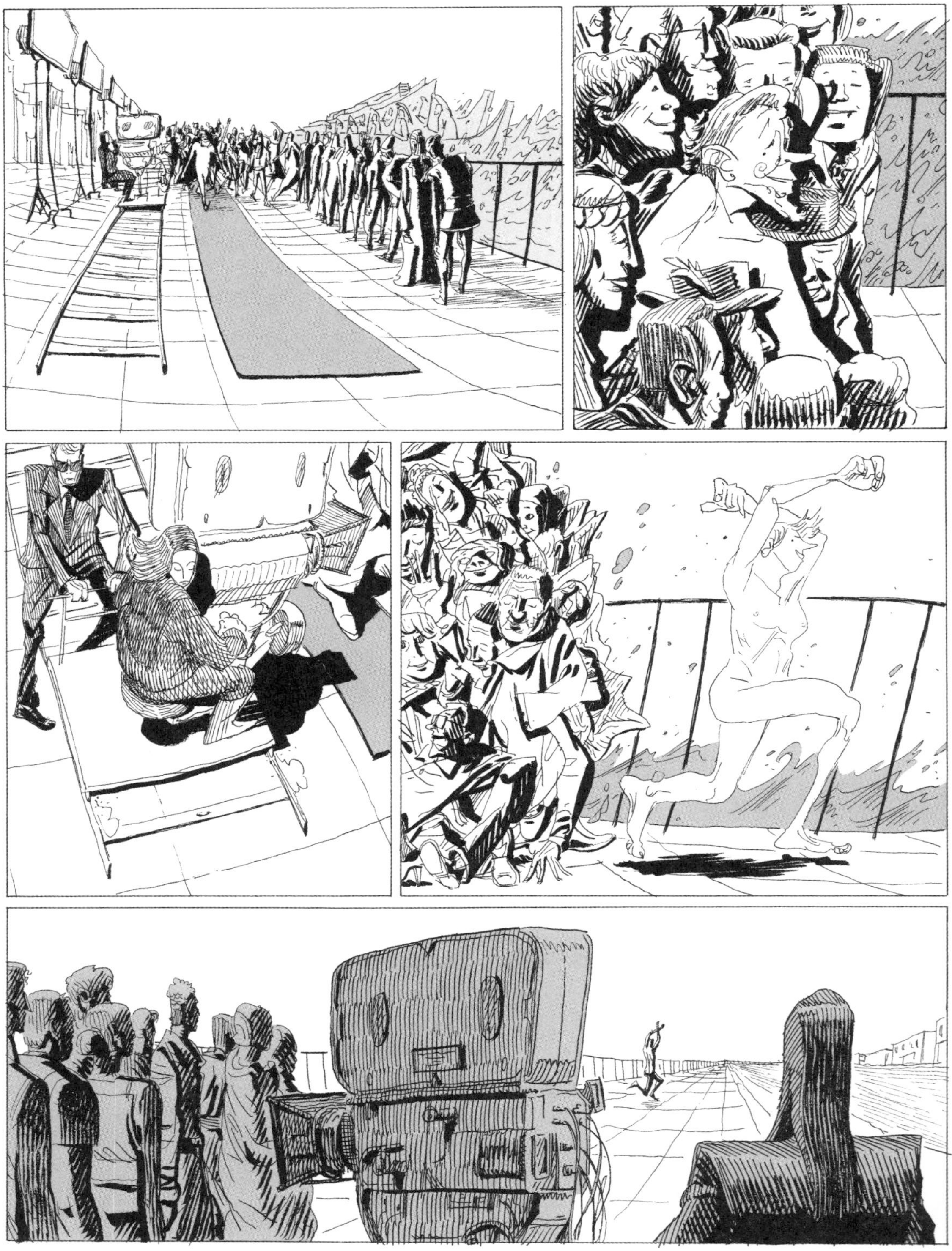

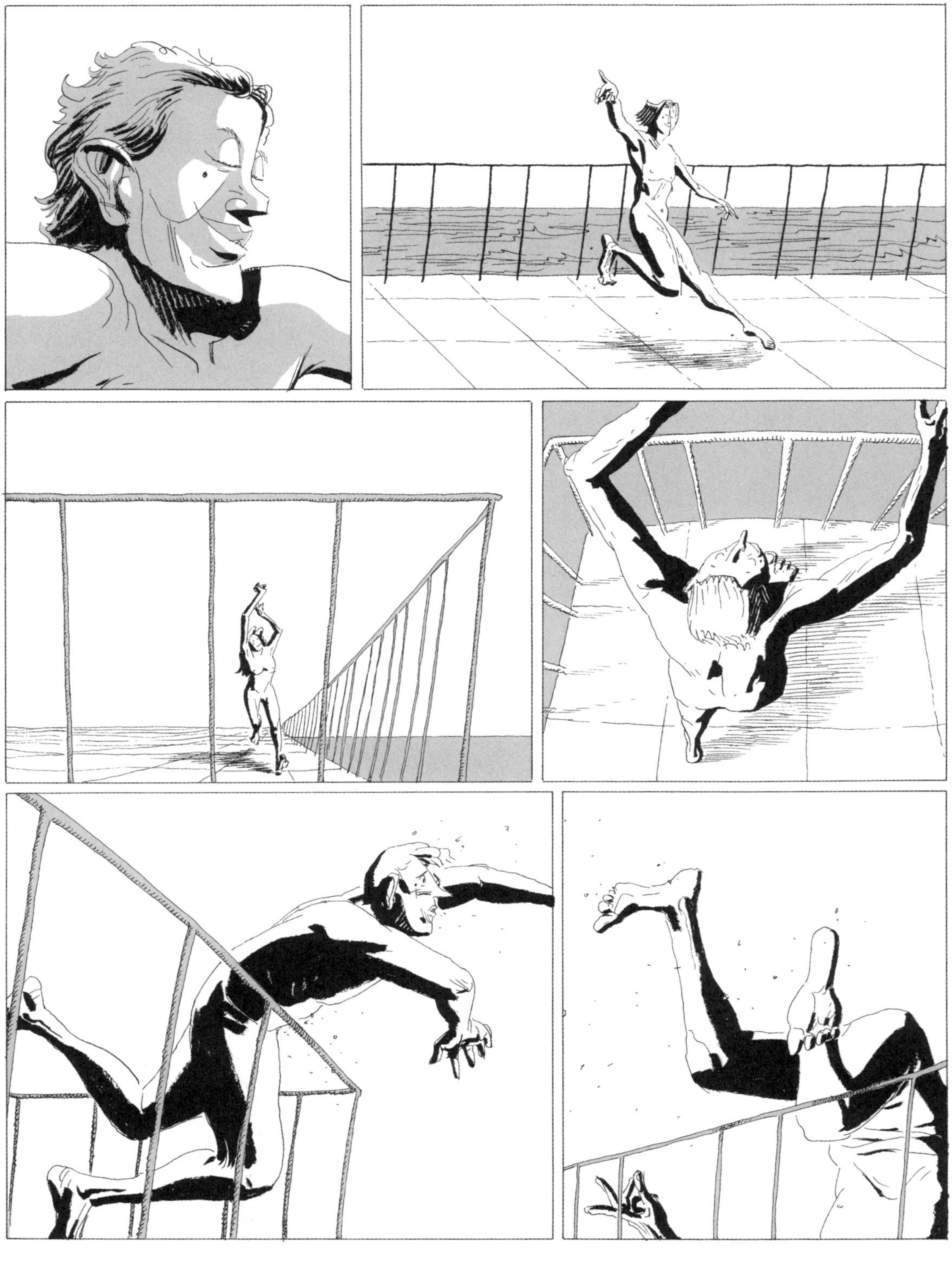

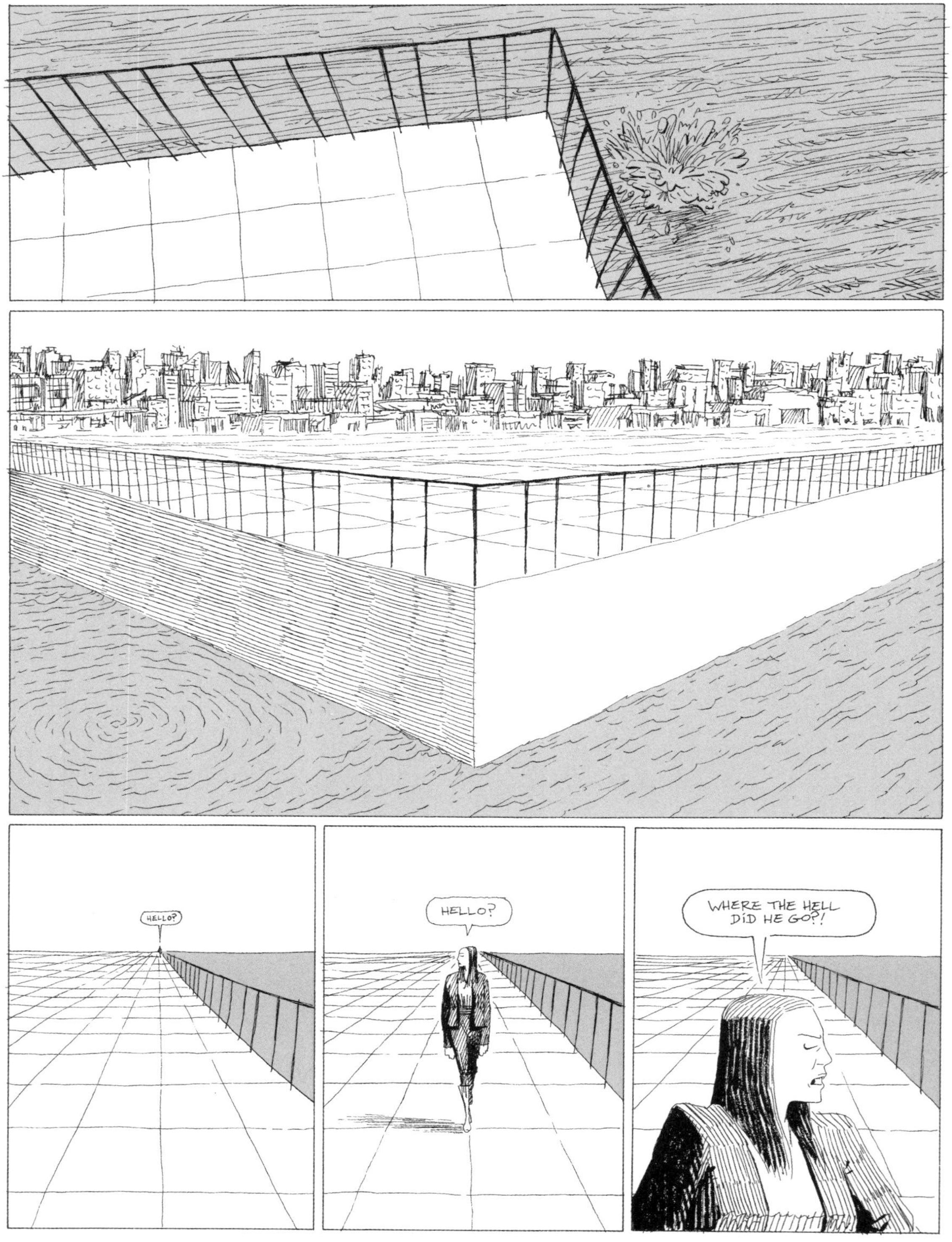
HELLO?
HELLO?
WHERE THE HELL DID HE GO?!

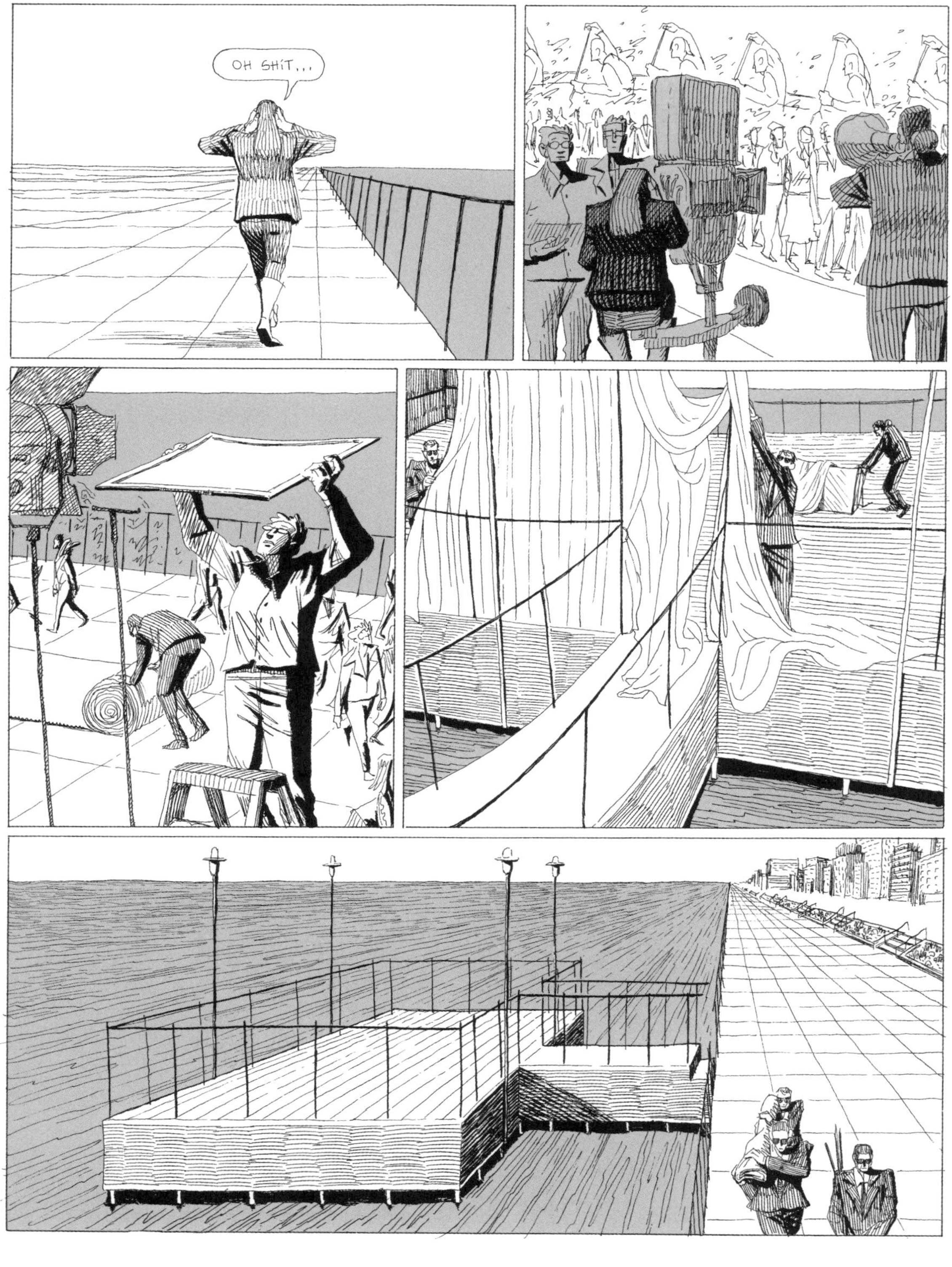
OH SHIT...

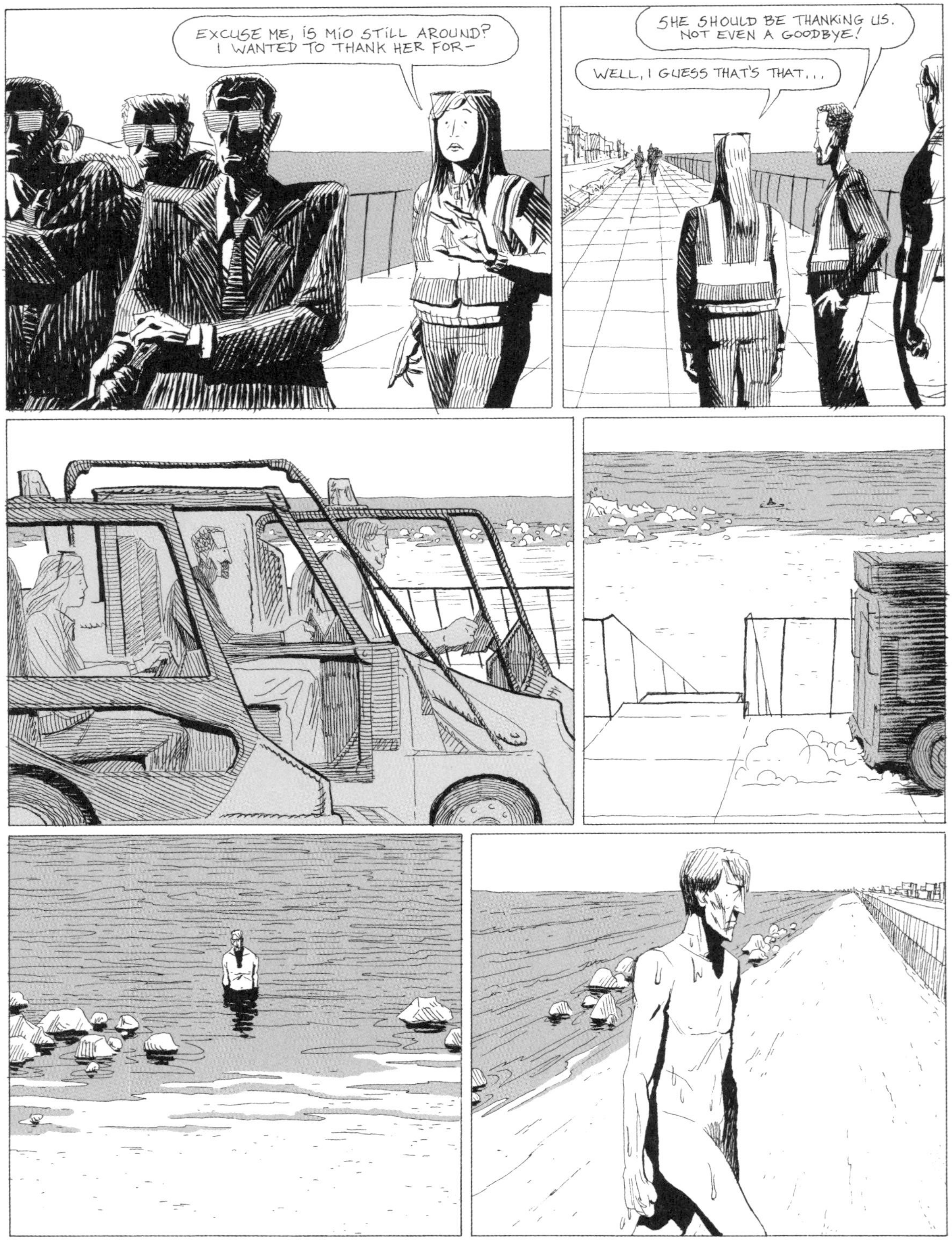
EXCUSE ME, IS MIO STILL AROUND? I WANTED TO THANK HER FOR-
WELL, I GUESS THAT'S THAT...
SHE SHOULD BE THANKING US. NOT EVEN A GOODBYE!

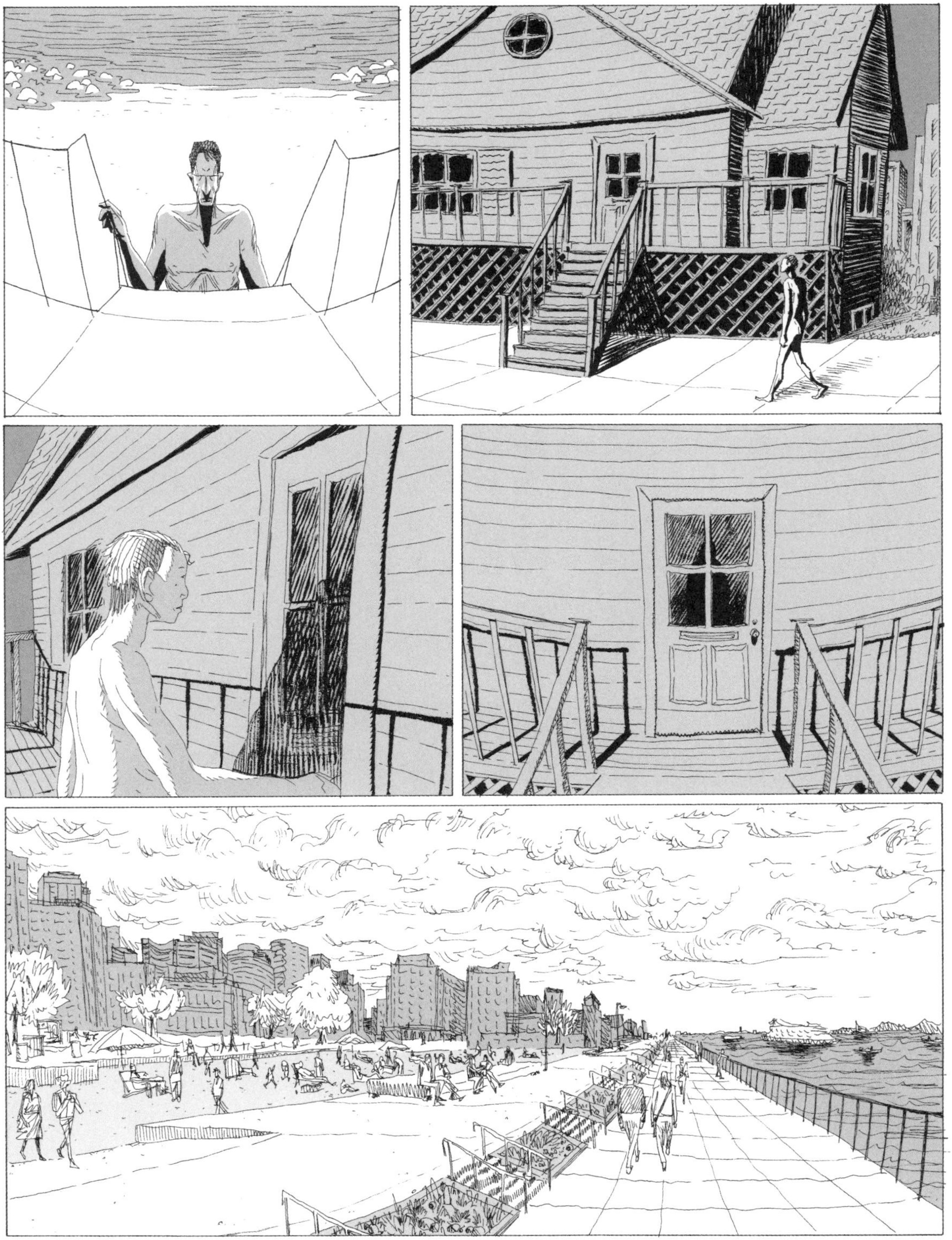

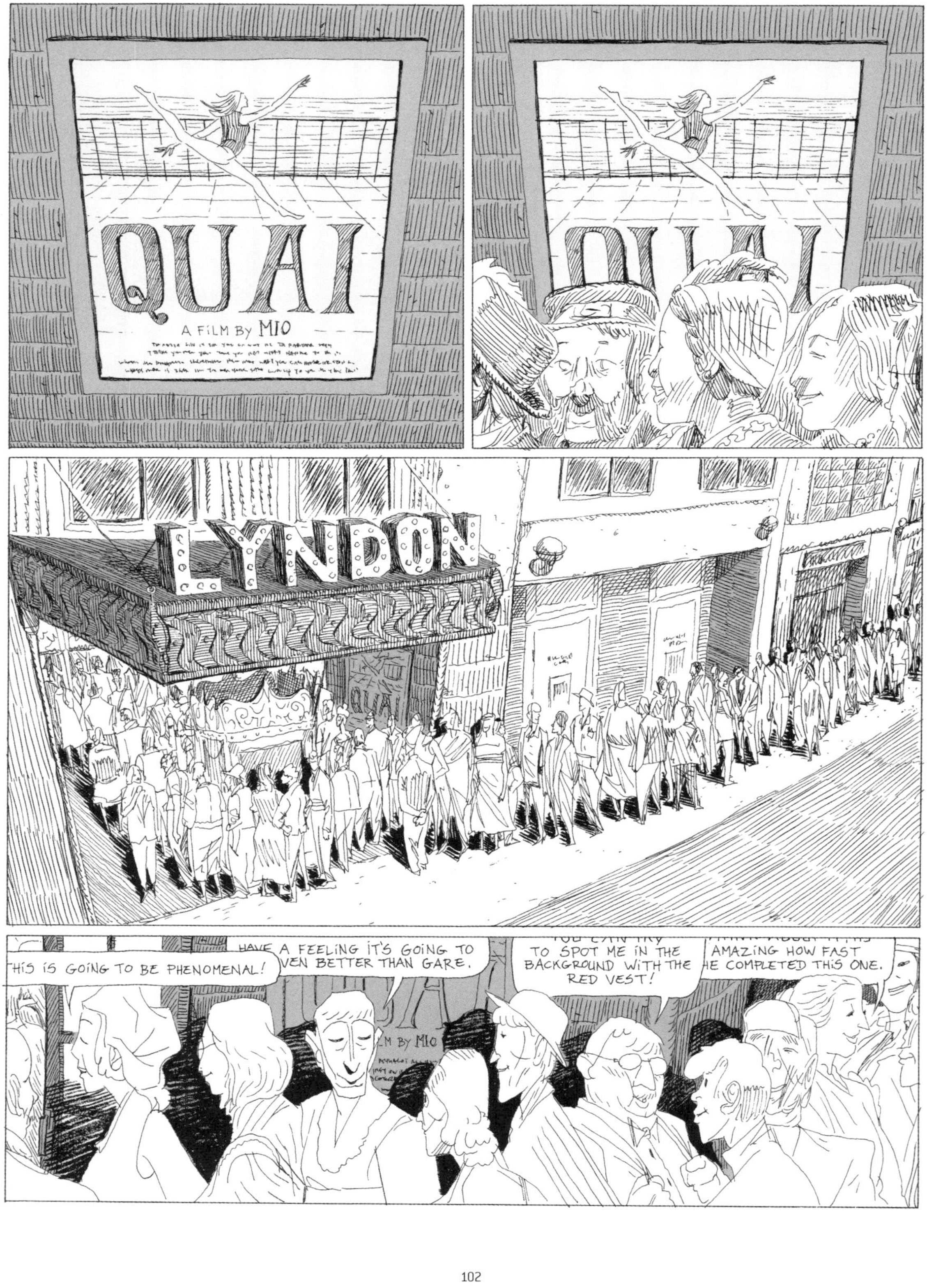
QUAI
A FILM BY MIO
LYNDON
QUAI
THIS IS GOING TO BE PHENOMENAL!
HAVE A FEELING IT'S GOING TO
VEN BETTER THAN GARE.
LM BY MIO
TO SPOT ME IN THE
BACKGROUND WITH THE
RED VEST!
AMAZING HOW FAST
HE COMPLETED THIS ONE.

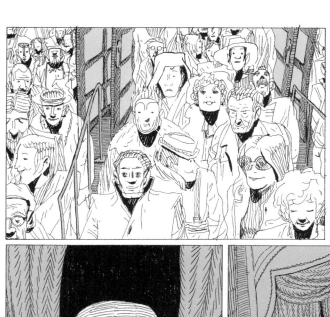

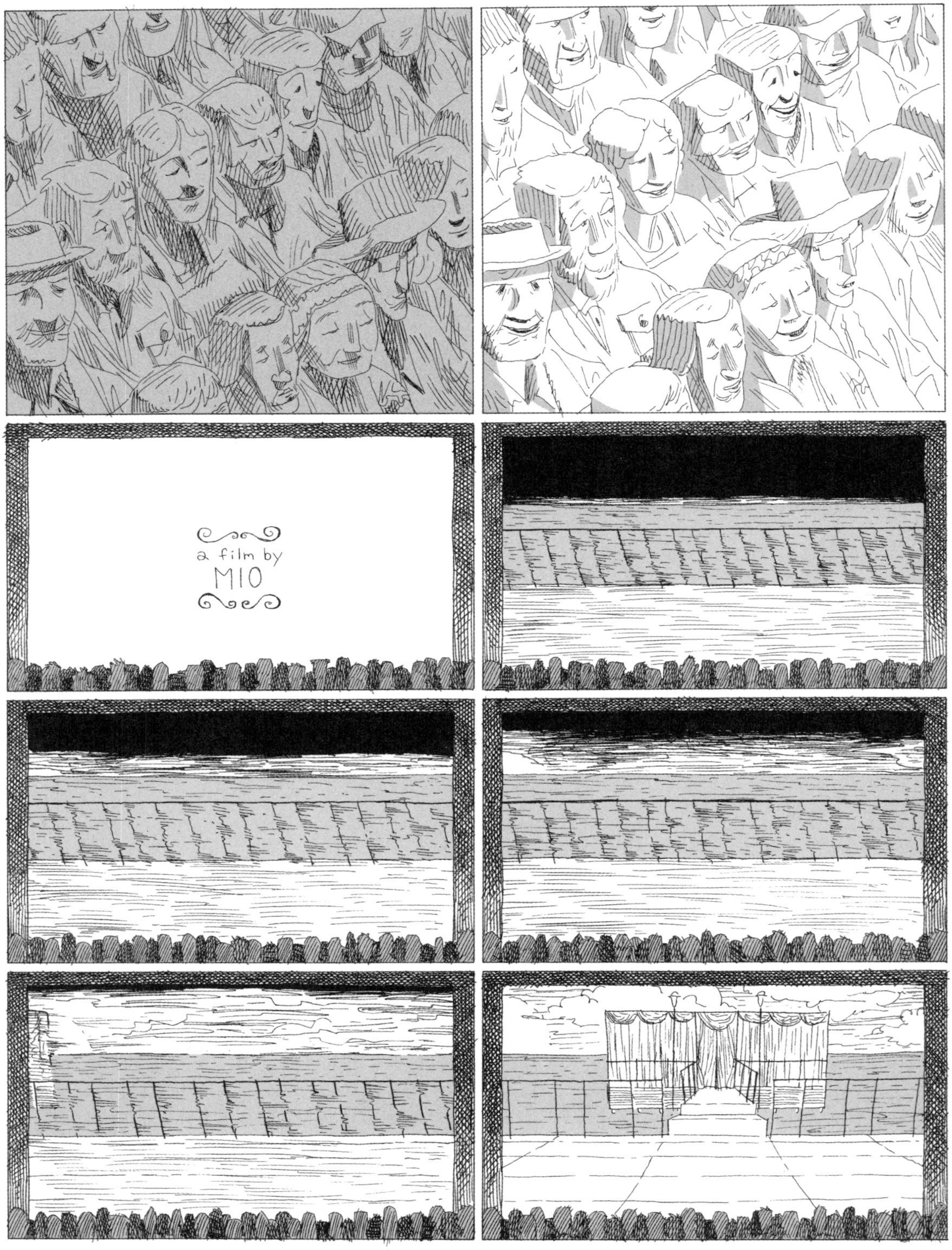
a film by
MIO

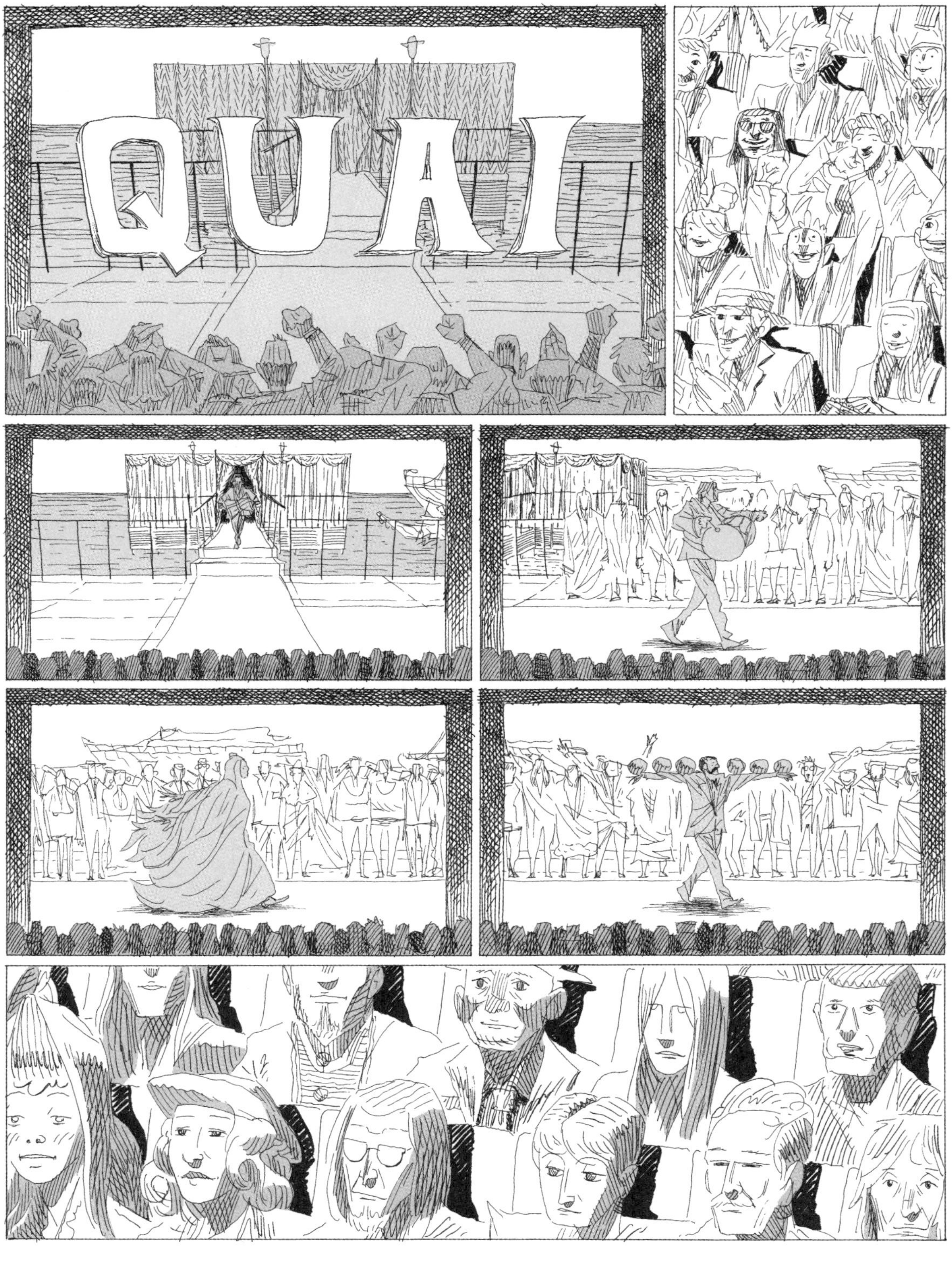
QUAI

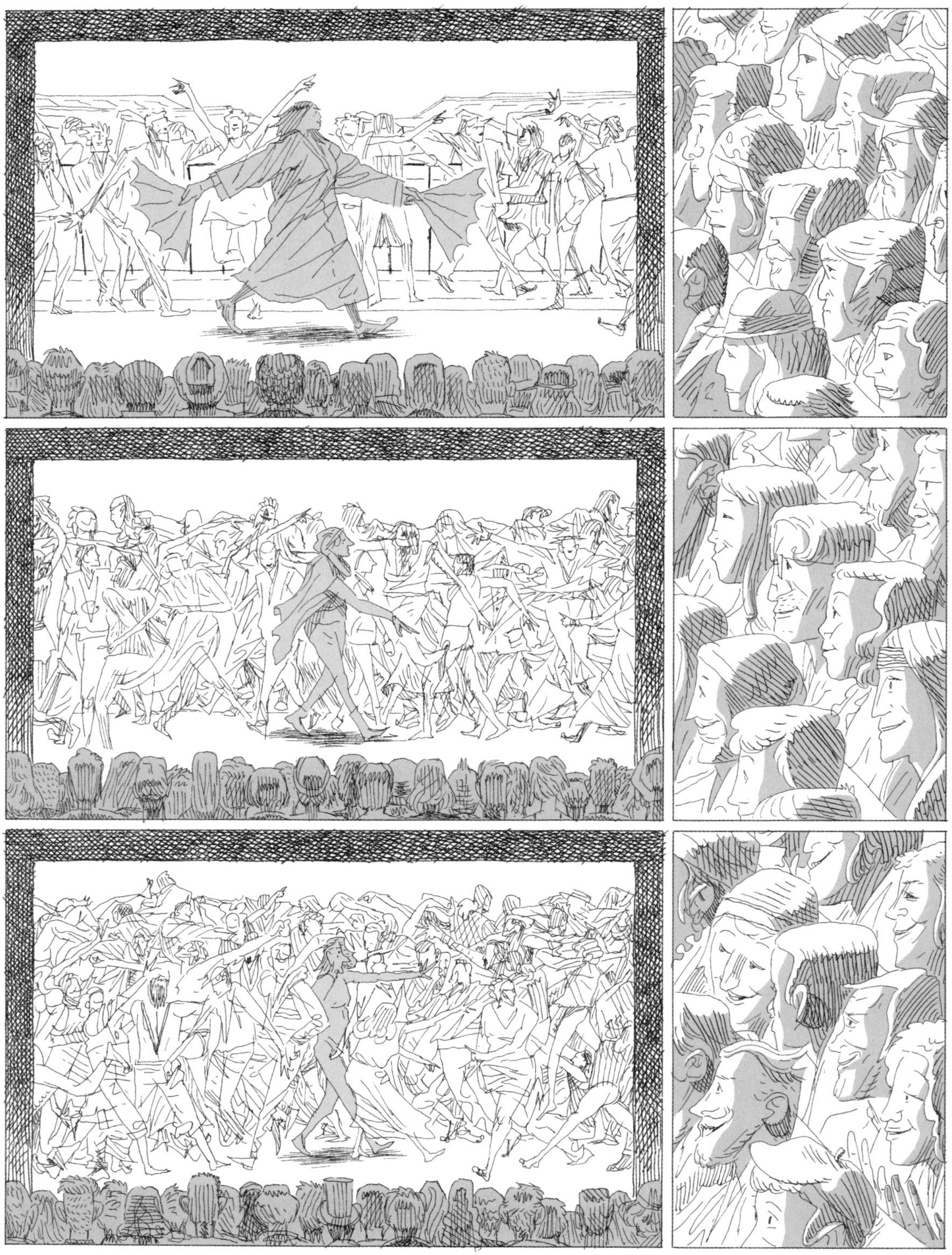

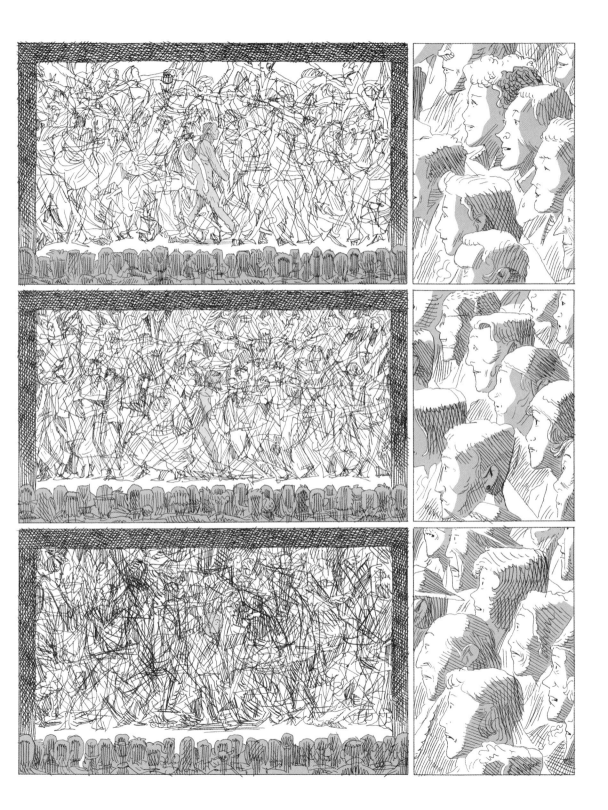

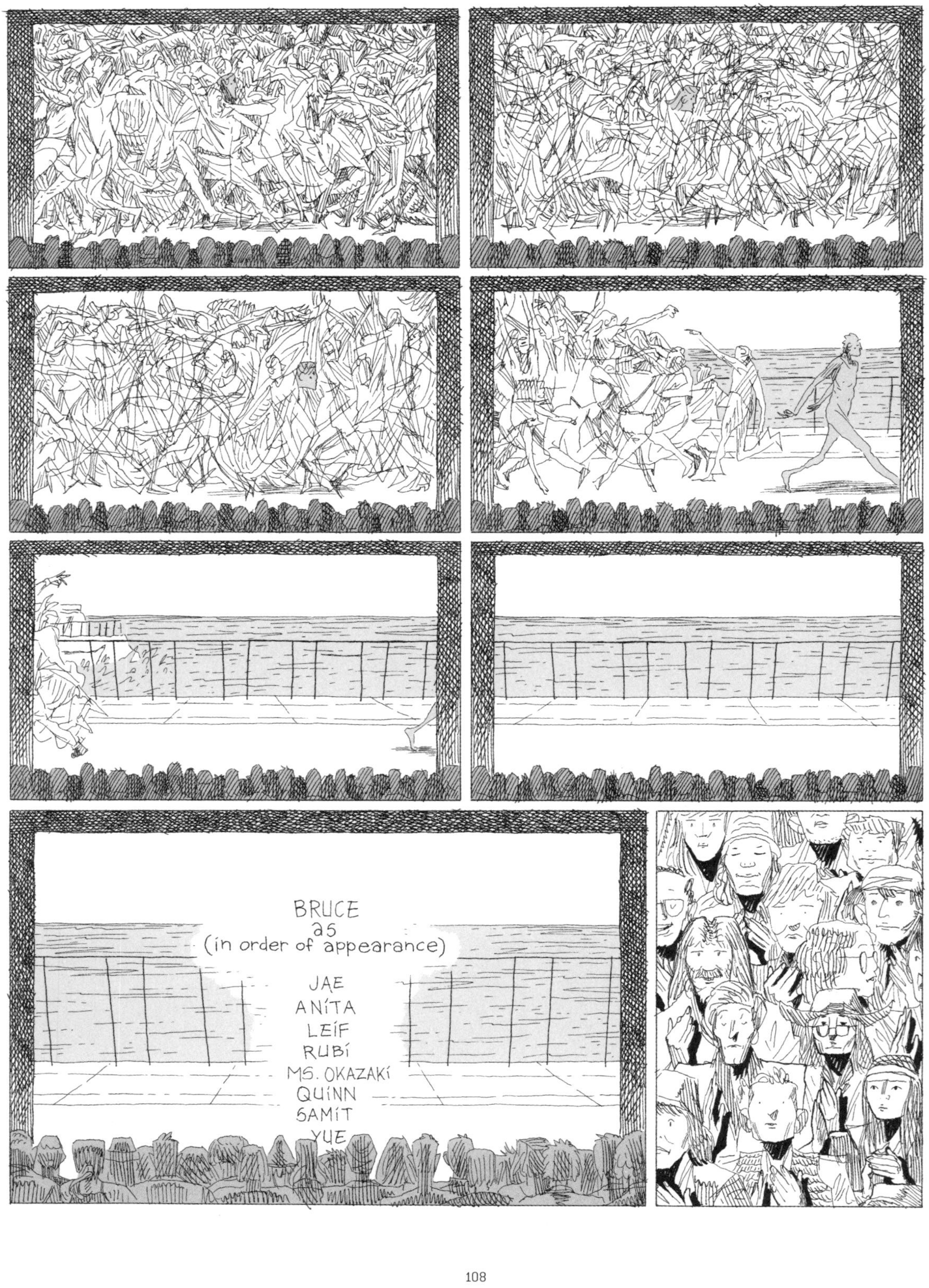
BRUCE
as
(in order of appearance)
JAE
ANITA
LEIF
RUBI
MS. OKAZAKI
QUINN
SAMIT
YUE

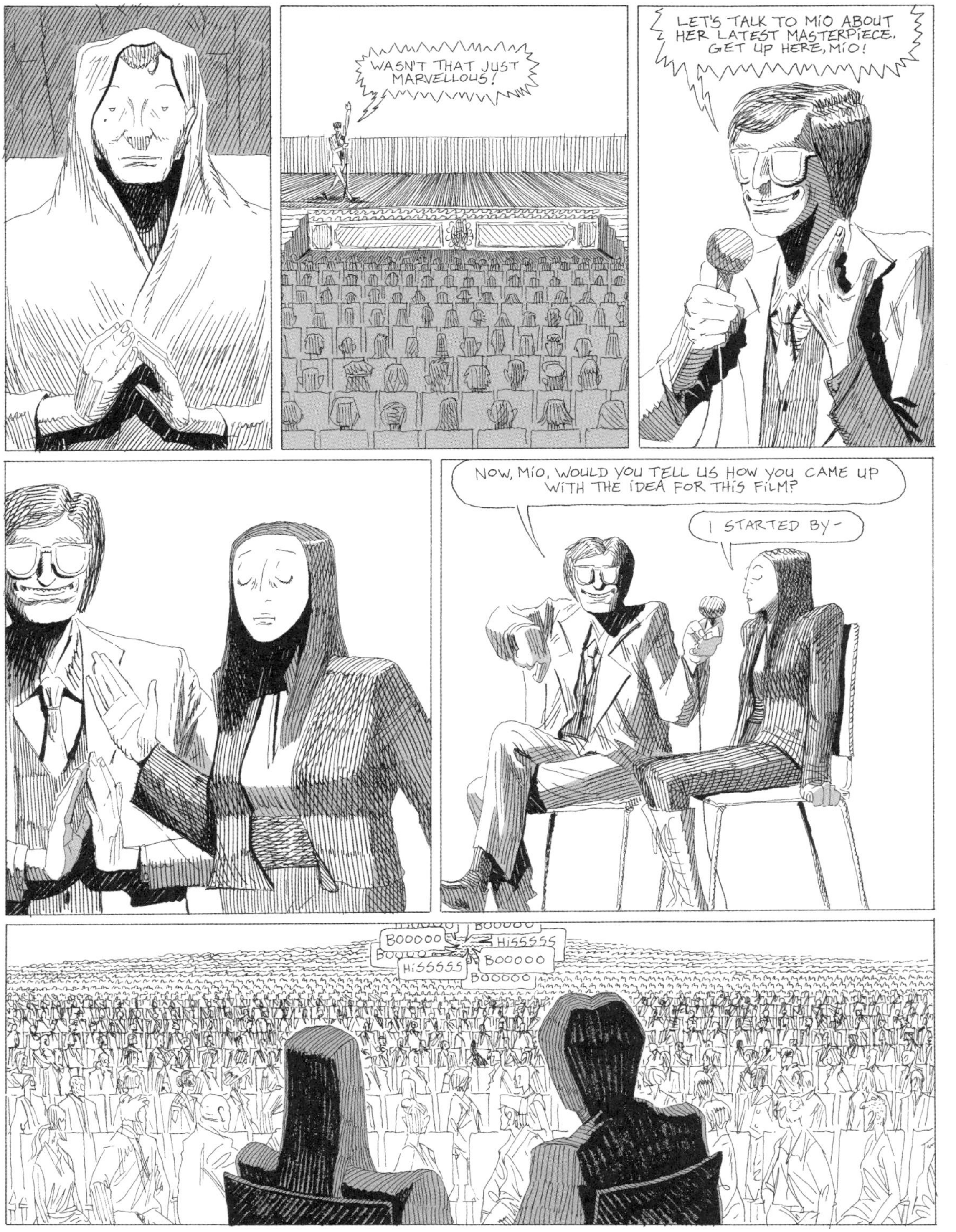
WASN'T THAT JUST MARVELLOUS!
LET'S TALK TO MIO ABOUT HER LATEST MASTERPIECE. GET UP HERE, MIO!
NOW, MIO, WOULD YOU TELL US HOW YOU CAME UP WITH THE IDEA FOR THIS FILM?
I STARTED BY-
BOOOOO
BOOOOO
HISSSSS
HISSSSS
BOOOOO
BOOOOO

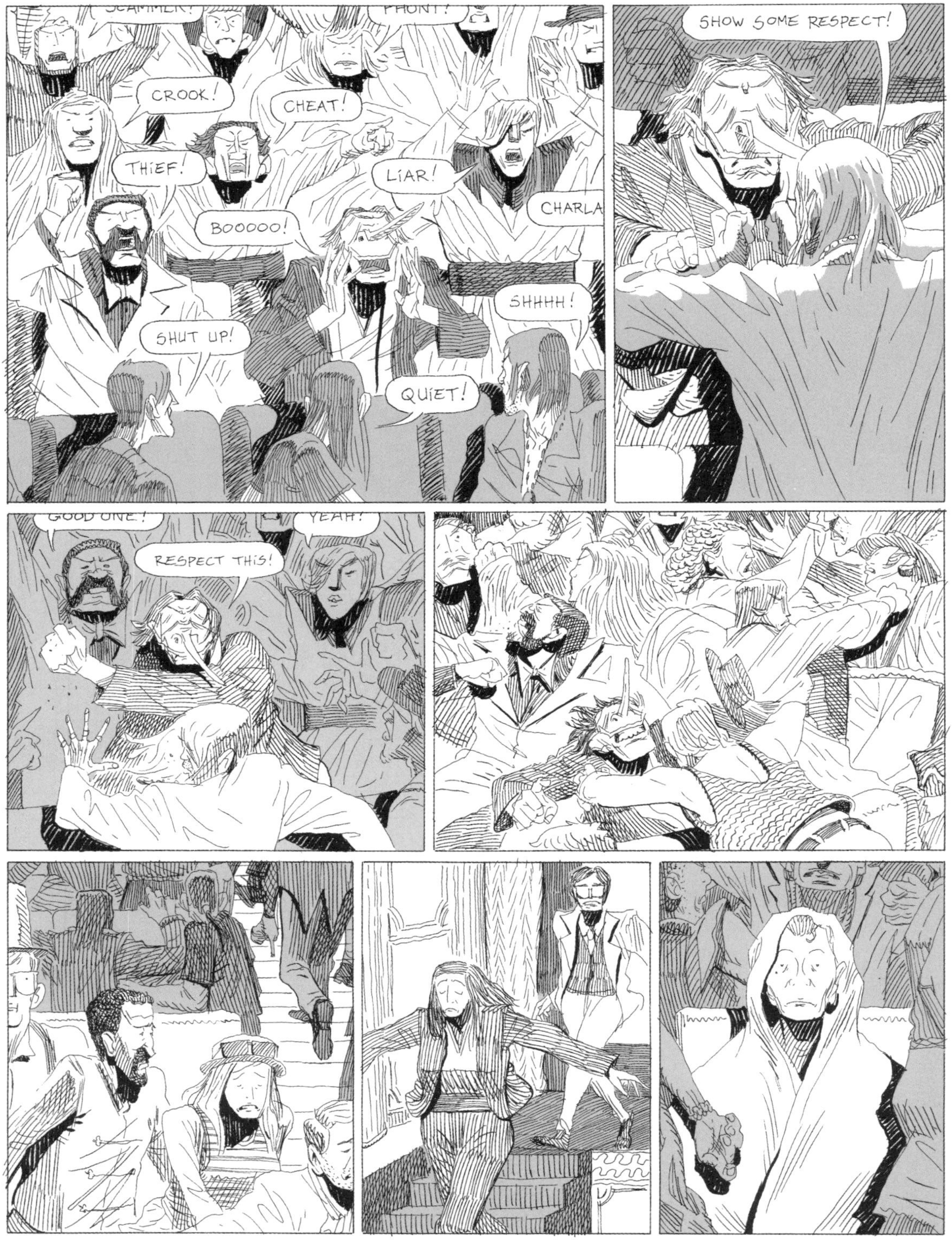
CROOK!
CHEAT!
THIEF!
LIAR!
BOOOOO!
CHARLA
SHHHH!
SHUT UP!
QUIET!
SHOW SOME RESPECT!
GOOD ONE!
YEAH!
RESPECT THIS!

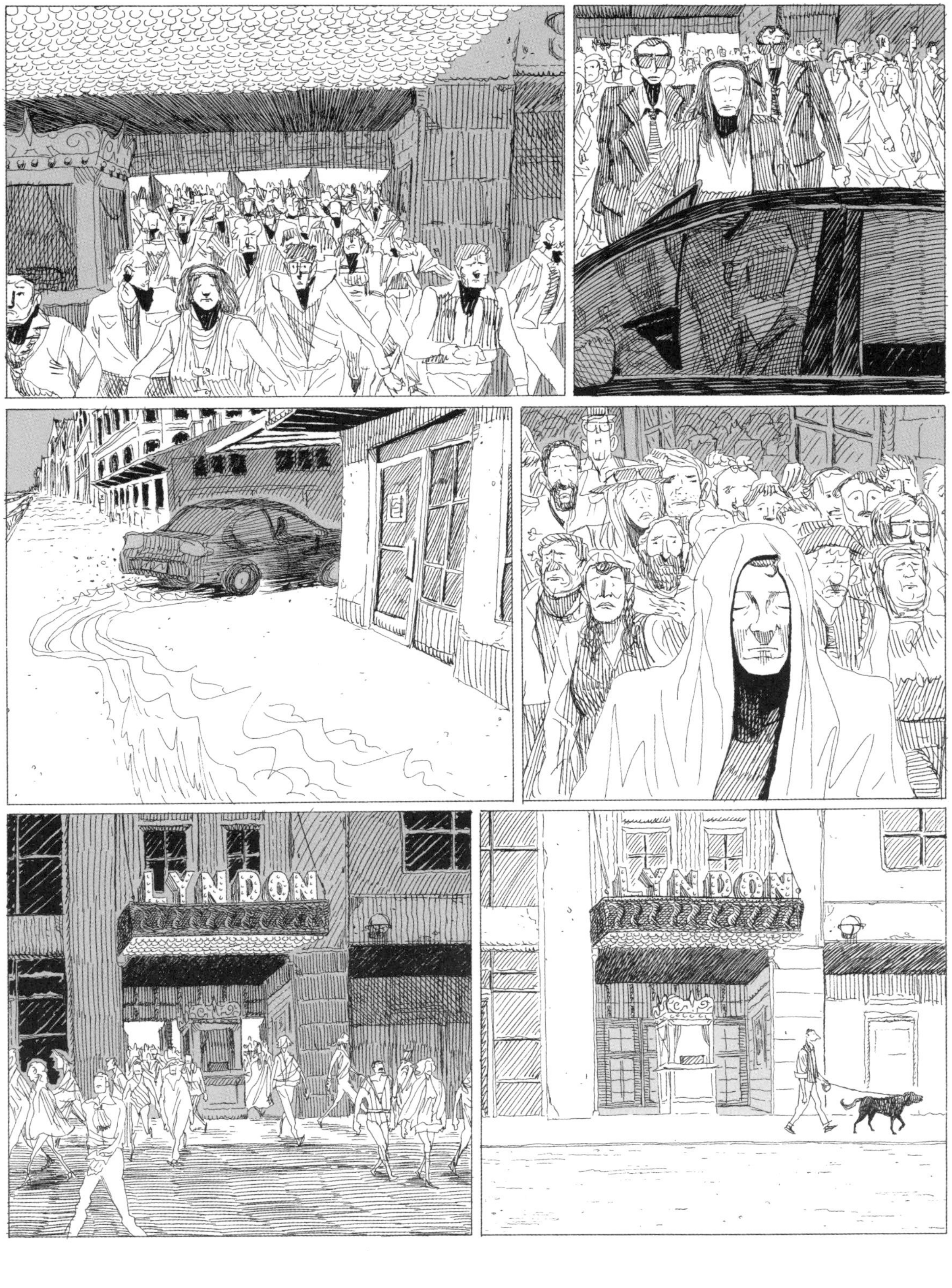

LYNDON
LYNDON

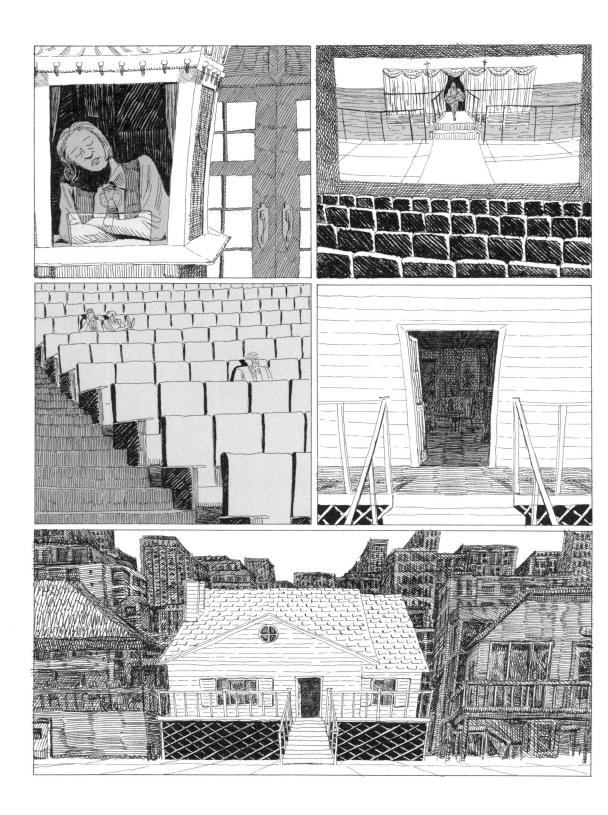

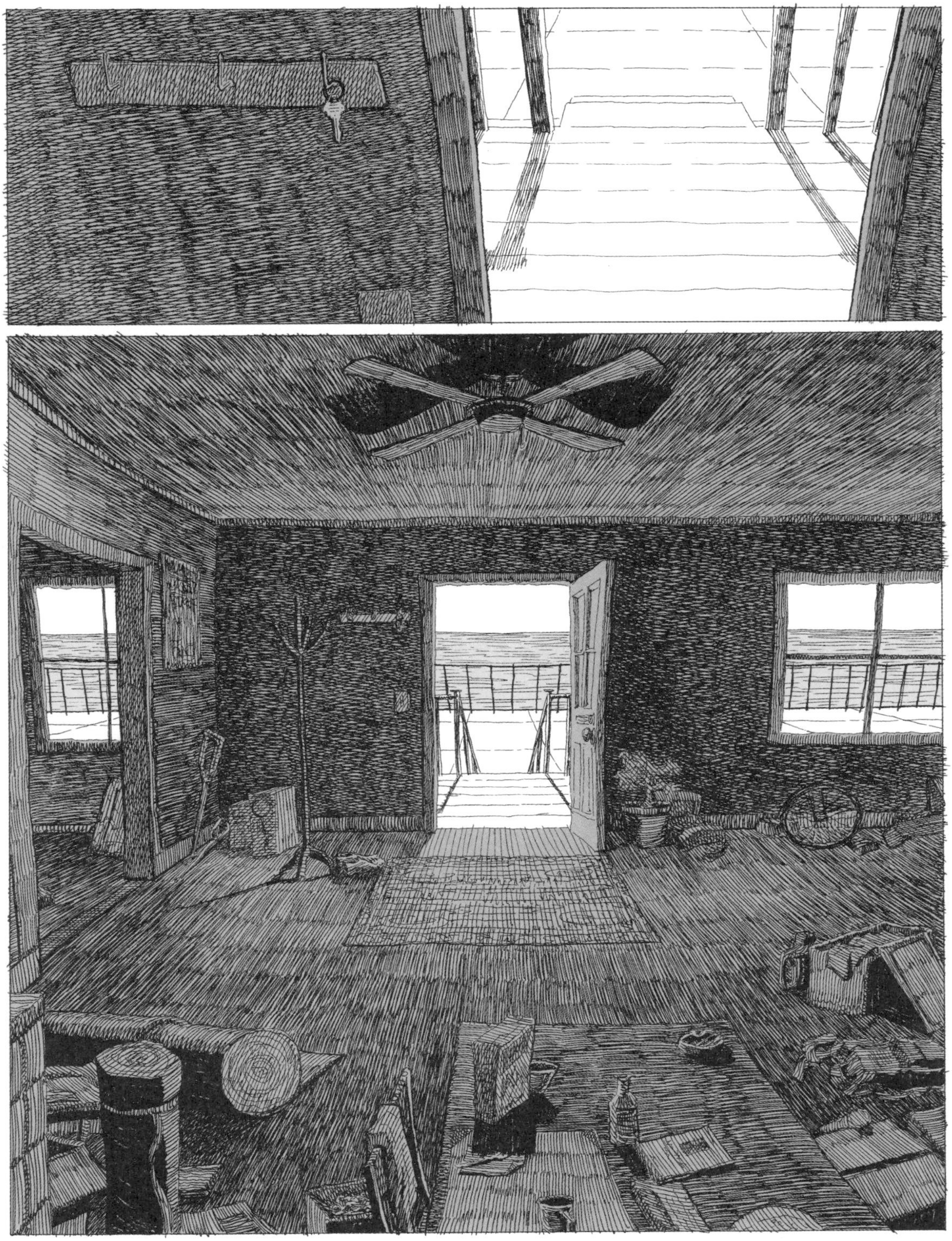

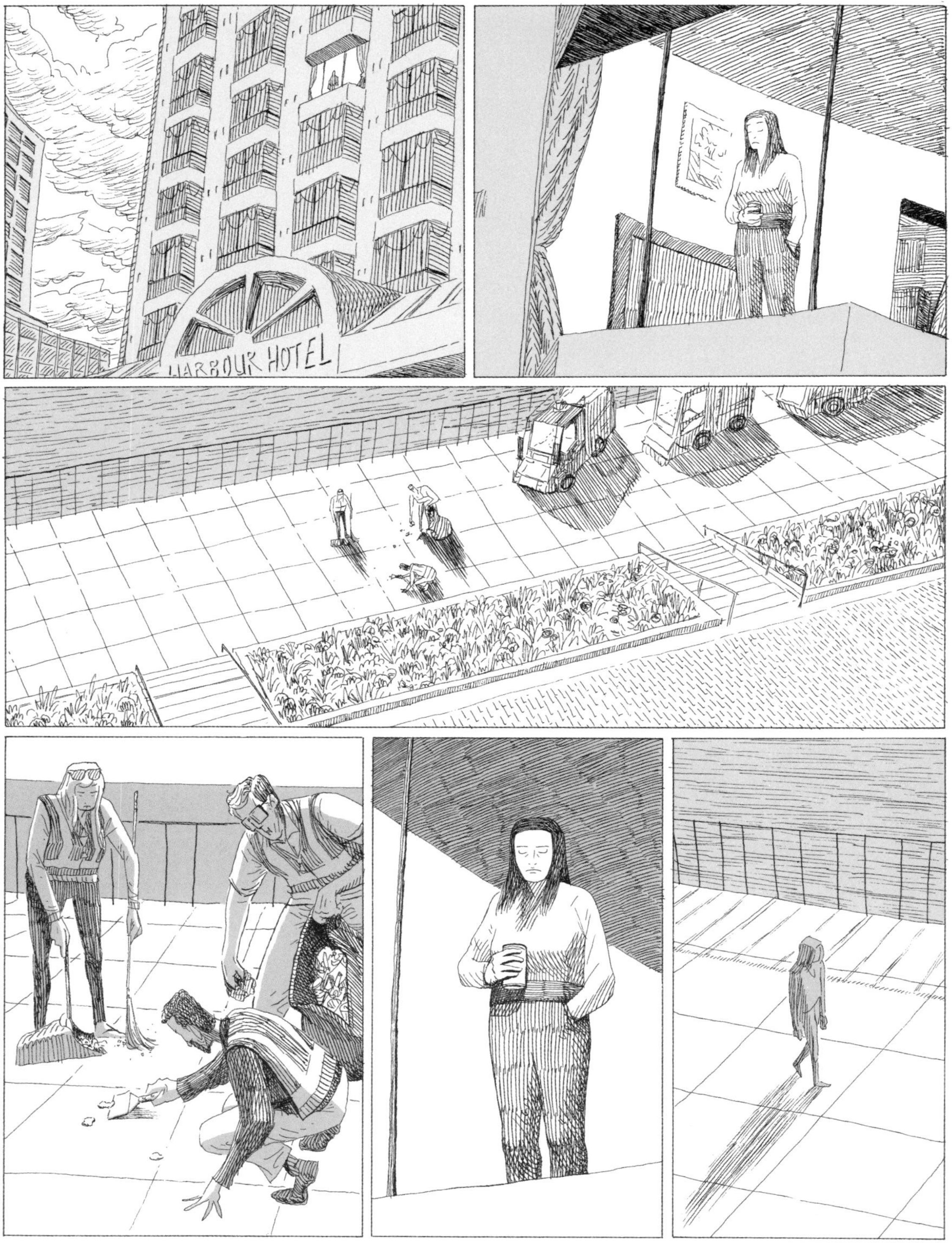
HARBOUR HOTEL

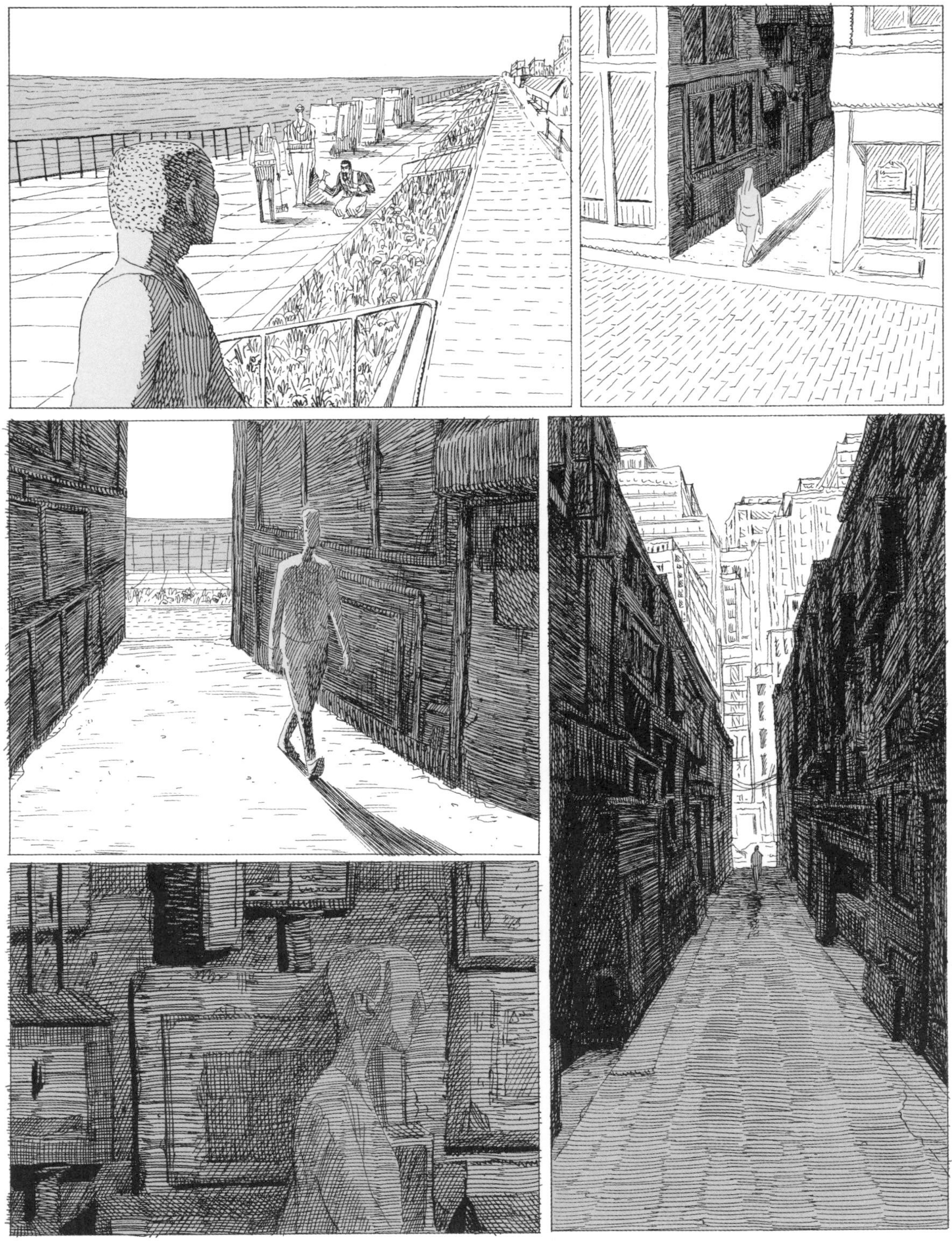

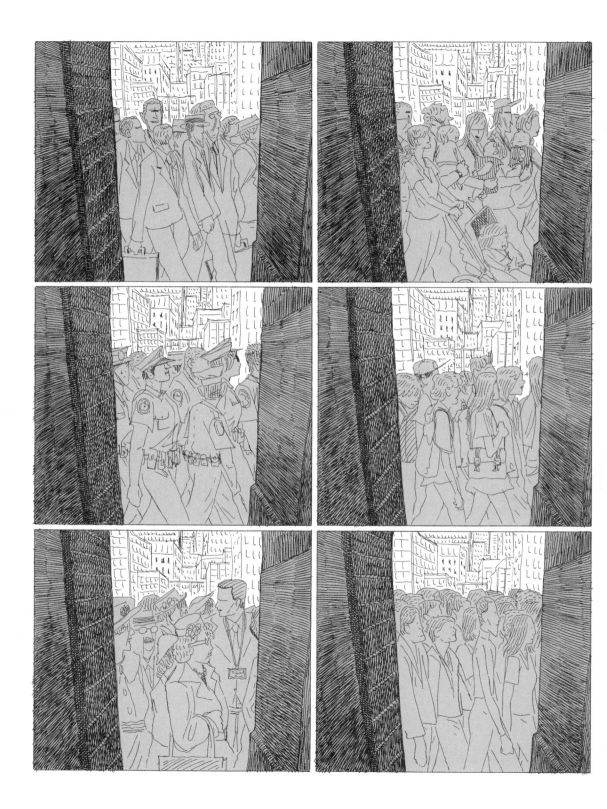

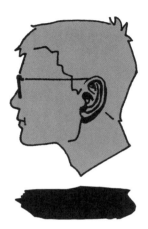

CHRIS W. KIM
is a comics artist
and illustrator.

A graduate of OCAD
University in Toronto,
his clients include
The New York Times
and *The Hollywood
Reporter*, among
others. He regularly
posts illustrations
and short stories
at chriswkim.com.

Herman by Trade is
his first graphic novel.